Teacher

James Cory Michaels

Dedication:

To my wife, Susan, my family and my friends who have
supported my efforts to write this novel. A special word
of thanks to Connie Green and Larry Collins for their
friendship and counsel.

Table of Contents

James Cory Michaels

Prologue

From the diary of Hyram Schwartz, MD – November 1985

A series of strange things have happened, and I am not sure what to make of them. I am making this entry in an attempt both to make a record for future reference and to try to gather my thoughts about the matter. These are some strange happenings, indeed.

April, last, Miriam Halevy came in complaining of bloating, weakness, general malaise and an irregularity in her menstrual cycle. I completed a pelvic exam and verified that her hymen was still intact, so I ruled out pregnancy – then ordered a full panel blood workup, told her to increase fluid intake, rest and I would call her back when I got the test results.

Imagine my surprise when her results showed her slightly anemic and very pregnant. I had my nurse schedule a follow up appointment with her the following week for a full pelvic exam and pre-natal work up, and called the patient with the test results. Miriam showed up at my office later that afternoon, completely distraught and insisting that there had been some kind of mistake because she was still a virgin.

I performed a second and more complete pelvic exam and noticed that other than the irregularity of an intact hymen, she showed all of the signs of being eight weeks pregnant. When she insisted that she had never been with a man, I explained that full penile penetration was not always necessary to facilitate pregnancy. That there were other activities which could result in pregnancy, albeit unlikely, and being engaged to be married - you know how young people get anxious for marital bliss – it made perfect sense to me even though she continued to insist that nothing of the kind had happened.

I reassured her that everything was going to be fine, dried her tears, prescribed prenatal vitamins to help with the anemia, and set a follow-up appointment to track the baby's progress.

The following week I had a visit from Joshua Stein, Miriam's fiancée, with multiple abrasions and contusions and other damage, which made it obvious that he had been in a fight. It seems as though the news of Miriam's pregnancy was not met with excitement and when she told him, Josh cancelled the wedding and broke off the engagement. There was a gang of toughs in the neighborhood who thought of themselves as purveyors of street justice - Italian boys who assumed the roll of local protection and who took exception to anyone in the neighborhood being treated badly, especially a pretty young woman. Well, they decided that they didn't think he should 'knock her up and dump her', and delivered him quite a beating.

"What else could I do, Doc?" the boy asked, "She never let me have sex with her; I never even made it to second base!" I didn't really know how to respond, and I certainly couldn't explain her condition considering what I was told.

However, the mystery seemingly solved itself a few weeks later when Miriam came in for her scheduled appointment. "Miss Halevy?" the nurse called, "Mrs. Pawlinsky?" Miriam responded.

It seems that she had married a young man she went to high school with, a Polish Catholic boy named Rudi Pawlinsky. All of the pieces came together and the picture made sense because rumor had it that the two had quite a crush on each other while classmates, but Miriam's parents would hear nothing of her going out with a non-Jewish boy, and they cut it off before anything could come of it. Now it all became clear, and Miriam wouldn't be the first girl who went against her parent's wishes. Love makes people do things they might not normally do.

Ah, l'amour!

The rest of her pregnancy was fairly unremarkable with no complications culminating in what I could only describe as a very easy labor. One very notable thing, though, an anomaly, really - the post-partum examination revealed that the hymen appeared to be still intact. Considering that she had just given birth, that would be a physical impossibility. Perhaps she really wasn't a virgin, after all.

James Cory Michaels

Chapter 1 - The Gospel According to Scott

It was my two hundred eleventh day of unemployment. The benefit checks had stopped a month previously, and the urgency of my job search had graduated from methodical to busy, busy to hectic, hectic to urgent and from urgent to frenzied.

The final overdue notice for my rent had arrived the week prior and I was boxing my things up to move out the next day, not knowing where I would go when luck would have it, as I was folding a pair of pants, I came across a long-forgotten five dollar bill. It was the first joy I felt in what seemed forever and my mind raced on all the ways I could spend it. When I thought of the national-chain coffee store who's green and white cups of frothy delight I had purchased every morning as I took my Chevy Tahoe through the drive-thru on my way to work I made that decision, quickly.

I grabbed my worn, gray hoodie and headed out the door in excitement. My studio apartment was on the third floor of an older building with an elevator, which was scary when it worked at all, and which it wasn't that day. As I headed down the stairs the smell of stale urine, cigarette smoke and despair assaulted my nose, and by the time I reached the street the idea of coffee had changed to something stronger. Instead of turning right to the coffee store, I turned left to the package store.

I remembered that the store was running a sale on a brand of vodka I found barely palatable; selling the bottle for $4.99, but the 44 cents sales tax would leave me short, so I stood on the street and panhandled for the difference.

I must have been quite a sight – a middle aged guy wearing the look of depression since I hadn't shaved or showered in three days, dressed in a hoodie and jeans and panhandling for 44 cents.

There was the usual "Get a job, ya bum" and other such comments but the most interesting reaction came from a woman who was willing to give me a dollar as long as she was assured it wasn't going to be spent on booze. When I told her that I was going to use it to pay my taxes, she stared at me for a moment, shook her head and walked off scolding me for drinking AND lying.

Eventually I found someone who wouldn't make eye contact but flipped a wrinkled dollar toward me just so he wouldn't be further bothered. I got the bottle and headed back to the apartment.

When I got there, I checked my mailbox and found a past due notice for the phone that didn't ring with a job offer, and scurried past the door of the super who called out, 'Your rent is overdue, deadbeat!' more to let the other tenants know than to remind me. Sitting down at the kitchen table with a clean glass in front of me, I opened the bottle, poured the clear liquid in, both generously and straight (I had no money for a mixer) and my mind went back to another time – another world, it seemed.

A brick house in the suburbs complete with a golden retriever, pretty wife, clean kids and the requisite SUV. I was the manager of a big box store nearby and while I was not getting rich any time soon, I was comfortable. My store was doing well under my leadership; I belonged to a service club, attended church on Sunday and had both friends and golfing buddies.

I remember the first time I met him – funny, he didn't look like Satan. He had boyish good looks, a slender build and a smile that would light up the room when he walked in. His jokes were fresh and funny and he was a real people person, calling each person by name after only initially being introduced. He was also totally business, too.

In that first meeting he publically ran down the numbers of each store, making comments and even saying some nice things about my store and some not so nice things about other stores not performing as well. He made some comments about making some changes, but I felt confident that it wouldn't significantly impact me, since my store and my management seemed to be secure.

"Yeah, I could live with a district manager like this", I remember thinking to myself, and even told Kathy about him when I got home that evening. All that changed after the holidays.

The district 'holiday' party was at the local athletic club because Mark was not only a bachelor, but also a member there. The lobby was adorned with white trees decorated with white lights and silver ribbons as we made our way back to one of the banquet rooms on the directions of the man at the front desk.

When we arrived, the room was already full, and drinks were flowing freely. Kathy was looking completely ravishing that evening, fifteen years my junior and with her hair up and the neckline of her short, gold lame cocktail dress plunging to accentuate both her long neck and ample cleavage. When I introduced her to Mark, there was almost a palatable electric current in the air, but I pretty much ignored it, thinking that the laughing and flirting between them was just them being friendly. As the evening grew it, the flirting seemed to grow with it and intensify, but I just chastised myself for being an old, jealous fool.

When we got home that night I asked Kathy if she had a good time, and she said she did. When we went to bed our goodnight kiss evolved into some unusually passionate lovemaking but I chalked it up to a combination of alcohol and an evening out. The rest of the holidays passed as they normally would and I was still completely comfortable about my marriage and my job.

I didn't even have a clue when I went to the district office the second week in January to have Mark give me my annual store review. After he gave me a glowing report, he told me I was being reassigned to one of the lower performing stores in a particularly bad part of the city. You see, Mark had just fired that store manager for what he referred to as 'unacceptable levels of inventory shrinkage' – retail speak for theft by employees or patrons – and told me he thought that a manager with a proven record of success, like myself, was needed to get the store back on track.

"This will be a great opportunity for you, Scott," he said, "I need someone like you to go in there for a few months and turn the store around. It will just be a temporary thing until we can hire a new manager, and in the meantime, I'll keep an eye on your store until you come back."

I stood there in shock – I was being reassigned from my clean, bright suburban store populated with smiling, friendly employees to a dingy, dirty inner city store with broken windows, vagrants sleeping and urinating on the property and a group of employees as discouraged as they were mean. It also meant trading my ten-minute suburban cruise for a two hour commute, each way, tangled in city traffic.

"Wait a minute," I protested, "don't I get any kind of a say in this?"

"I am disappointed, Scott," Mark told me with a scowl on his face, "I thought you were a team player…" The rest was completely unintelligible. I don't remember any of it except that it was for the good of the company and only temporary and blah, blah, blah. The rest of the day was kind of a blur and to make a long story short, the next morning Kathy was kissing me good-bye with an admonishment to do my best and keep a good attitude.

Not only did my usual ten hour days turn in to 14 hour days with the commute, the first week I was there I fired the Assistant Manager for selling drugs out of the store's loading dock, turning my five-day work week into a seven day work week, because store regulations required someone from the 'management team' at the store every day and my incompetent shift leaders, while being the best employees in the store, were still incompetent and couldn't be trusted.

Mark assured me that they would hire and assign me a new assistant manager, but it just never seemed to materialize. One week turned into two weeks, then into a month, then several months. My days became indistinguishable one from another – get up in the morning before anyone else, coffee, cereal and a two-hour commute to the store. Ten hours of complaining customers, complaining employees, fixing problems and dealing with situations of all kinds, just to get back in the car for a two-hour commute home. When I arrived, everyone had already eaten, so I warmed up leftovers, ate, showered and collapsed into bed to start over again the next morning.

The apartment in the city was Kathy's idea. She said she was afraid I was going to fall asleep on the freeway and kill myself on my commute home, and she barely saw me the way it was so she suggested that I get an apartment in the city, not far from the store. It would cut my commuting time, enable me to get more rest and then, when I did have the chance to come home I would be in a better mood and more prepared to both enjoy her and be enjoyable company, myself.

The problem was that although the new position cost me more in travel and was harder on my mind and body, the pay was the same – maybe just a little lower due to the lack of performance bonuses. Kathy said that she would find something part time to fill in the gaps and it wasn't long before she was hired on at my old store.

I tried to get home at least three times a week, but when I did get there I was still exhausted; Kathy was tired and stressed from dealing with the kids and the job, and so it wasn't any better than before. We began drinking more when we were together ("Just a cocktail to unwind") and our sex life was virtually non-existent. It seemed like our relationship got colder and more distant each time we saw one another and there was more arguing than kissing.

One of my new employees was a pretty, young Hispanic woman named Samantha with a lithe figure and large brown eyes. As I was walking through the store one day I saw two young men standing behind one of the end caps, and they kept peeking around the corner and laughing together. When I went to investigate I saw that it was Samantha who was attracting their attention while stocking shelves.

The problem wasn't what she was doing but what she had chosen to wear that day - a very short dress and a g-string - and was seemingly unaware that she was causing a major distraction every time she bent over. I called to her to stop what she was doing and see me in my office, and when she left I chewed out the two boys for their behavior - although, to be honest, I could see why they were doing what they were doing. As I said, before, she was a very attractive young woman.

When I got to my office she asked if she was in trouble and I assured her she wasn't but explained what had happened and sent her home to change into something more appropriate for the work environment. I also admonished her to dress more modestly for work in the future.

I thought that was the end of the incident until she came back to work about an hour later with her brother, Ramon, in tow. He was visibly upset with me as he approached me in the middle of the store and started referring to me as 'an old pervert' who was 'looking up his sister's skirt'. To diffuse the situation I asked him to keep his voice down and took him to my office where I explained what happened - that I didn't TRY to look up her skirt, but it was impossible not to do so.

He seemed to calm down and accept my explanation, and then explained to me that he 'might be kinda over protective' since their parents had died and he was filling the role as both brother and father and that the stress was starting to get to him. I apologized for the misunderstanding and offered a $20 gift card of in-store credit, which he refused, and we went our separate ways.

The following week I happened into the employee break room and found Samantha there alone, sitting in a chair, doubled over and crying. I asked what was wrong and she told me that it was her time of the month and that she was in a lot of pain, but was sure it would pass soon and she would be fine. I suggested to her that she might find the couch in my office more comfortable where she might be able to lie down. She smiled, thanked me, and headed to my office while I went back out to the store floor to find busy work and give her some privacy.

The next day I had an unexpected visit by Terry, Mark's assistant, and Diane Brown, head of human resources at the regional office. With little or no explanation I was curtly instructed to follow them to my office where Ms. Brown began, without ceremony, to ask questions.

"It has been alleged that you have put the company in jeopardy by violating our sexual harassment policy." she began. "You have been accused of uninvited voyeurism, making inappropriate comments about personal matters, offering female employees to 'lay down' on your office couch and attempting to pay people off for their silence using company funds."

"Huh?" – I was flabbergasted. "Really?? Could

you be more specific?"

"I think I have been as specific as I need. Do you deny the allegations?" she asked, pointedly.

"Uh…yeah." I replied. "Can you tell me who alleged these things?"

"No", she said, "because that would be a violation of the accuser's privacy."

"I suppose my Constitutional right to face my accuser means nothing?" I asked.

"Mr. Hansen, this is not a court of law, merely an internal investigation." she shot back, "At least for now." she added.

"Hold on," Terry piped in, "I am sure that there is a reasonable explanation."

I looked at him, "There might be, if I had a clue what we were discussing."

"There is no reason to get ugly, Mr. Hansen", Ms. Brown said.

"You might think differently if the shoe was on the other foot," I shot back.

Undaunted, she continued, "Did you or did you not look up one of your female employee's skirt with two other male employees?"

It was all becoming clear to me. "Oh, you're talking about Samantha? It couldn't be helped. The way she was dressed and bending over like that…"

Ms. Brown cut me off. "You admit it, then?"

"I put an end to it as soon as I realized what was going on!" I said. "I stopped it immediately, sent her home to change clothes and chastised the male employees about their behavior," and then continued to explain what happened. When I got to the part about offering her brother the gift card Ms Brown cut me off.

"So, then, you also admit to attempting to bribe Ramon Sanchez with company funds to keep quiet about the incident?"

"It wasn't like that at all," I said, "it was a good faith offer for his trouble which he refused, and there were no strings attached."

"Do you make a habit of offering company funds to strangers in order to keep yourself out of trouble?" she asked.

"I wasn't in trouble, I did my job – and no, I don't offer company funds to keep out of trouble."

She threw another barb, "Just to Mr. Sanchez, then?"

I turned to Terry, "What is going on here? I haven't done anything wrong!"

"It is just an investigation, Scott," he stated calmly, "and if you have done nothing wrong, it will come out that way."

"It seems more like an inquisition," I snorted.

"Oh," Ms. Brown continued, "I guess that leads us to the part about you inviting female employees to lay down and relax on the couch in your office…"

"Oh my God!" I exclaimed and walked out. The blood was pumping through my veins so hard that my temples were pounding with each beat. I briskly walked the aisle running along the back of the store to the drinking fountain by the restrooms and drank fully. The cold water was both refreshing and reinvigorating. I then took a deep breath and turned to head back to the office when I saw Terry coming toward me.

"What the hell are you doing?" he asked, "Trying to make yourself look more guilty than you already do?"

"Oh, please," I said. "This is obviously a witch hunt. I have seen this type of thing before and we all know how it ends. I will be temporarily suspended until the 'investigation' is completed, and then will be asked to resign even though I know I have done nothing wrong - - and you know, too, Terry!"

"One way or the other, you have to finish this…if

for no other reason than to jump through the appropriate hoops," he said.

"Jump through the hoops to make my termination less able to be challenged, you mean."

He said nothing and we walked back to the office in silence for the next round. Ms. Brown was sitting in my chair waiting for me. "So, tell me about asking Ms. Sanchez to lay down in your office and relax," she began.

"She was crying in the break room." I started, "She was sick and when I asked her if she wanted to go home, she said it would pass shortly. I then asked her if she wanted to lie down on the couch in my office and relax until she felt better and that was it. I wasn't in my office at the time and didn't go in until she had decided that it was not going to get better and she was going to go home. I think it was some kind of menstrual thing."

"Do you make a habit of monitoring your female employee's menstrual cycles?" Ms Brown inquired.

I didn't respond. I really didn't know how to respond to her ridiculous accusations. I just looked at her in silence for what seemed like an eternity. Then, one word escaped my lips.

"Really?"

"Really", she said.

"No."

"So, you only monitor Ms. Sanchez's menstrual cycle?" she quipped.

"I don't monitor hers, either."

"It seems as though it means a lot to you," she probed.

I was finally beaten. I rolled my eyes and said, "No, it does not."

She brightened up. "Well, I think we have heard enough. Would you be good enough to give me and Terry a moment?" she asked.

"Sure," I mumbled and walked out of the office.

I stood there with my back to the wall and my head in my hands. It was only a matter of a minute or two when Terry asked me to come back in.

"Well, Mr. Hansen, we appreciate you answering our questions," Ms. Brown began, "but we need to review your answers and decide if we should take action and if so, what the appropriate action should be. Until then you can consider yourself suspended without pay pending the completion of our investigation."

I shot Terry a knowing look.

"Terry will accompany you to the parking lot. You may want to take any personal items with you, and please leave your company cell phone, keys, nametag and any other company property you may have on you. Thank you very much for your cooperation," she smiled brightly.

I wanted to knock her teeth down her throat.

Instead I grabbed the picture of Kathy and another of the two kids, and walked to the front door in silence with Terry. It was definitely a 'perp walk,' and I felt like everyone in the store was staring at me as we walked together. When we got to the door Terry offered me his hand.

I just looked at him, turned on my heel and walked to the Tahoe. I started the car and then told the hands-free system, "Call Kathy."

"Hello?" she answered. I could tell by the tone in her voice that something was wrong.

"You would not believe what happened to me," I began.

Her voice was curt and laced with anger. "I have already heard."

I was surprised. "Really?"

"Yes. I can't believe that you were starting an affair with one of the girls in the store, Scott. What were you thinking?" She didn't give me a chance to respond before continuing, " I know you have been lonely, and I was really kind of expecting something like this, but with an employee where it is going to cost you your job? Don't you care about me and the kids?" She was crying.

"Kathy..." I began.

"Don't you 'Kathy' me! I don't want to hear it, I just hope you're pleased with yourself and will find happiness in your new life with your Puerto Rican whore!"

She hung up and I was in shock. I dialed back and it went straight to voice mail. Shock turned to hurt. I tried to tell my side of the story to her voicemail but the message time ran out before I finished. I called back and she answered screaming, "Don't you get it? I don't want to hear from you, asshole! Leave me alone!" then hung up.

Hurt turned to anger. I called back and it went straight to voicemail, again. I don't remember what I said, but my tone was much different this time but I did finish my side of the story. When I got to my apartment, I opened a bottle of Dewar's, grabbed some ice and proceeded to ease my pain with alcohol.

After two or three glasses I picked up the phone again, and again it went straight to voicemail. I figured she had time to listen to the messages by then, if she had taken the inclination, so I left a message telling her that I thought she was acting childish and that she should grow up and we should have an adult conversation about the situation.

There was no response.

Then, after a few more drinks I called again and left another, angrier message. A few more drinks, another call. Then a few more and another call. The drinks and the calls eventually blended together until the bottle was gone and I passed out.

The next morning I was awakened by a pounding at the door. My mouth felt and tasted like someone had taken a long walk in there wearing shit covered boots, but

I stumbled through the fog and opened it.

"Scott Hansen?" the kid asked.

"Yes"

"You've been served!" he said as he slapped a manila envelope in my hand, then turned and walked down the hall.

The envelope contained a restraining order. It said that I couldn't make any phone contact with either Kathy or the kids, and that I was not to go within 100 feet of them, the house, the kids' school or the store where Kathy worked until the order was lifted.

That was seven months ago. Kathy used the voicemails I had sent that night to not only keep the restraining order in place, but to also get full custody of the kids and keep me from even getting visitation rights.

I lost pretty much everything in the divorce. Kathy got the house. I got the Tahoe and the payments I could no longer afford. She got the savings accounts and I got the bills.

Oh, and the job ended almost exactly the same way I predicted to Terry on that fateful day. The only difference was that they didn't let me resign and fired me for cause – especially since I had conveyed a threat to another employee - - Kathy. I consulted with a couple of lawyers but they both told me that since we were in a 'will to work' state, any employer could fire any employee for any reason, or for no reason at all.

I filed for bankruptcy but had to give up the Tahoe as part of the deal. I had no job, but was told I needed to pay child support, and was almost immediately behind in my payments, which couldn't be discharged through the courts.

Sometime in the four months it took for the divorce proceedings to finish, Kathy started dating Mark, my ex-district manager – or should I say openly dating (although I have no solid evidence otherwise). The day after the divorce was final, he moved in with her. On one desperate day afterward I managed to get a ride out to the old house and watched as Mark kissed my wife goodbye (she quit working after he moved in) and was laughing with my kids as he took them to school.

I really shouldn't have done that to myself.

When I came back from my lovely little stroll down memory lane, the bottle of vodka was gone and I was still lucid. I guess I had been drinking a lot more than I used to in order to build up that kind of tolerance. It was then that it occurred to me that my life was over and everyone knew it except me – until now. I knew what I had to do.

I grabbed my hoodie and headed out the door, again. It was getting dark but was still light enough that the super caught me passing his apartment in the hall.

"You're outta here, loser!"

"I got your loser!" I shot back. There was no response.

It had just started to drizzle and the night drew close. Perfect, I thought, just the right props for the scene to end the story of my life, as I trudged along the sidewalk toward the bridge. The yellow halos of the streetlamps illuminated my path but gave no warmth.

I sensed him beside me before I saw him. He was about my height and the bulky, black leather jacket he was wearing concealed his slender build. The stranger's appearance did nothing to set him apart from the thousands of other twenty-somethings I had seen that day – t-shirt, jeans and grubby tennis shoes.

He walked beside me in silence for a few blocks, not going past me, not lagging behind me, just keeping pace in his silence. The drizzle eventually caused his boyish, brown, mop of curly hair to stick to his head and I became uncomfortable but not afraid. It might have been his appearance or maybe just the resignation that it would all be over shortly anyway, but I felt an unusual lack of concern.

Periodically the street lamps illuminated the sidewalk with yellow-lit circles and as we entered one he took my elbow in his hand.

"Scooter, you don't want to do this. Your life has so much meaning and so much potential!"

I stopped in shock and stared at him with my mouth agape. How did this stranger know my name? More so, how was it that he was calling me by the nickname my mother gave me – one that had not been used to refer to me for at least 15 years!

"Wha…who…??" I stammered.

The young man stepped in front of me, and he shook his head to keep his shaggy brown mane from falling in his eyes. He smiled, and it was as if his whole face lit up. "Hi, I'm Chris," he said, and stuck out his hand to shake mine.

I just stood there for a second and then took his hand. When I did, I felt power like an electrical current come into my body. Where once was weakness, was now strength; darkness, light; despair, conviction. The cobwebs in my head cleared and I realized that I was suddenly as sober as a judge.

He knew my name – but not only that, he knew that I was going to kill myself, although I had not said anything to anyone. Standing there holding his hand I saw for the first time in a long time that there was hope, that I could easily go on and I felt ashamed at my weakness.

I began to cry.

Then Chris wrapped his arm around my shoulders and said, "It's going to be alright. Come on; let me buy you a cup of coffee. When was the last time you ate?" He turned me around and we started walking the other direction, away from the bridge.

I couldn't say anything. I just walked with this stranger softly sobbing. He was at least ten years my junior, but I could sense such knowledge and wisdom from him – but there was no pretentiousness in him. He knew my name. I didn't know how he knew it, but he did - - and I sensed that he knew a lot more about me than just my name or my actions of the past eight hours or so.

He kept his arm around me and steered me into an all-night coffee shop/café in the neighborhood. It was warm and well lit with the smell of freshly brewed coffee and baked pies. "Hi, Ronni!" Chris called as we entered and a pretty, young waitress turned to look at us, "Could we have a couple cups of coffee and a menu?" he called and led me to a booth by the window.

A statuesque brunette, the waitress came over with two cups in one hand, a pot of coffee in the other and a menu under her arm. "Hi, Chris," she smiled as she placed a cup in front of each of us, placed the menu between and filled the cups with strong, black, steaming coffee.

"Ronni, I would like you to meet my friend, Scooter," Chris said.

"Scott," I mumbled under my breath.

Not phased at all, Chris corrected himself. "Oh, I'm sorry – Ms. Veronica Pace, I would like you to meet Mr. Scott Hansen."

I felt a bit uncomfortable and embarrassed correcting Chris, and I wasn't sure why but she smiled. "Hi, Scott, it is nice to meet you," she said as I picked up the menu.

Then she turned to Chris. "Fresh apple pie? Just came out of the oven."

"Sure," he said, "with a slice of cheese?"

"Okay."

He continued. "I think Scott will have the Swiss and mushroom burger with a side of fries."

My mind was reeling. He had just picked out what I was about to order.

Ronni flashed Chris a big smile, and then turned to put the order in. Half way across the room she looked back at him, but Chris didn't seem to notice. He was just looking at me and smiling, not saying a word.

I then reached for the dish of coffee creamer, put two in my coffee and still he hadn't said anything. He just sat there looking at me and smiling. I was confused and feeling more than a little uncomfortable.

"Has someone hired you to follow me?" I asked, and then immediately regretted asking the question.

Chris chuckled. "No, nothing of the kind."

"Then how do you know my name? Better yet, how did you know what I was going to do, and what I wanted to order off the menu?" I took a long drink of the stiff java. Even with the cream it burned my tongue as it entered my mouth.

"Scooter, in the days ahead you are going to see, hear and experience many things you are not going to understand." Then he paused and asked, "You don't mind me calling you 'Scooter,' do you?"

I shook my head as I realized that I really didn't.

He went on. "You see, I know more about you than your own mother. Perhaps more than you know, yourself. I know everything about you, and I have chosen you."

"Chosen me? For what?"

"To help me."

"Help you do what?"

"Help others," he said.

Ronni came back to the table and topped off the coffee. I grabbed another creamer as she headed back to the counter.

"I chose you," Chris continued, "as the perfect someone who can be my friend, my companion and my confidant."

"Wait a minute," I objected. "This isn't a gay thing, is it? I mean, to each his own, but I just don't swing that direction."

Chris let out a hearty laugh, "Oh, heavens no.

Nothing like that at all. I would tell you that you were cute but not my type, but honestly, Scooter, you're not that cute."

I was embarrassed. "Okay, but I noticed that you didn't respond to the waitress.... what was her name? Ronni?.....flirting with you. What was I supposed to think?"

Chris just smiled, "Yes, she is a beautiful woman, isn't she? A rare quality, indeed, to find a woman who is beautiful on both the inside and the outside - - and maybe even a little more on the inside."

"So, are the two of you a couple? I have a feeling she would like that."

"Yes, she probably would," he mused. "But I am not about that."

Puzzled, I pressed, "Okay, then what are you about?" .

Ronni brought the plate with the burger and fries, as well as the one holding Chris's pie. "Enjoy!" she said.

"I told you. I am about helping people," he said.

"Can you elaborate more?" I asked, and then took a bite of the burger. It was thick and hot, and the juice ran down my chin and onto my fries before I could wipe it off with a napkin.

"Patience," Chris said. "You'll see in time. Suffice it to say that I have a special...uh...mission I have to perform, and you are the perfect person to help me."

I almost choked on my burger. "Me? I guess you haven't read my efficiency reports, have you?" I said, sarcastically.

"I don't have to, I can see your heart." He was being serious.

"So, what is this mission? Can you expound for me?"

"Not yet, it is not time. However, I can assure you that it will be exciting and that you will help me and many others." He smiled and brushed the mop of hair from his eyes.

As we talked more, I didn't really hear his words as much as read his eyes. They were dancing, sparkling, and full of joy and excitement. Before I knew it my burger was gone – more coffee, more conversation and the next thing I knew it was midnight and Ronni was putting on her jacket, getting ready to leave.

"I need you to go with Ronni, Scooter." Chris said to me, "you'll crash at her place tonight."

"What about you?" I asked.

"The dishes aren't going to do themselves you know," he chuckled.

We both got up and I followed Ronni out the door. I never did go back to my apartment to pack my things. As a matter of fact, I never went back to my apartment, at all.

As we walked down the street I started small talk with Ronni. "So, how long has Chris worked at the diner?"

"He doesn't really work there," she said. "He just started helping out a few weeks ago."

"Just started helping out?" I said.

"Yeah, it was all pretty strange," she continued. "We were really busy that night and both the cook and dishwasher had called in sick. It was just me and Mario, the owner, and he was cooking, but the dishes were piling up. We were almost down to the point where we couldn't serve, when Chris just walked in to the kitchen and started washing dishes."

She smiled as she remembered, "He just walked in and started working like he had been there for years, but neither Mario nor I had ever seen him before. He's been back every night since and has never filled out a time card or asked for a penny. Mario has put out a standing rule that he can eat whatever he wants whenever he wants, but tonight was the first night he ever asked for anything – and that was for you."

She only lived a block or so from the diner and we were already at her door.

"Wow," I said as she opened the front door and we proceeded up the brightly lit stairwell to her apartment. "He just knew you needed help and did it?"

"Pretty much," she said with a smile as she opened the door and turned the light on in the apartment.

It was small, but clean and cozy. There was an old bookcase along one wall with some paperbacks and mementos and pictures lined up – all of it was free of dust. Beside the bookcase there was a small desk and the requisite laptop of a millennial. The couch was overstuffed and too old to have been purchased new, but in surprisingly good shape, and there was a clean and comfortable chair that didn't match, but completed the set, nicely.

The small kitchen, complete with white cabinets and an old iron and porcelain sink led to a hallway that had a bedroom on each side and a bathroom between. The bath was clean and had an old iron claw-foot tub with a suspended brass ring to hold the white plastic shower curtain.

Ronni opened the door on the left to a small bedroom, Spartan in nature, with only a double bed, a folding chair beside it and a small chest of drawers. "My roommate used to live here before she got married and moved out, and I just haven't found anyone I like to take it," she explained unnecessarily. I personally didn't care how it came to be, but was just grateful for a place to crash.

When she shut the door, I stripped off the hoodie, kicked off my tennis shoes and collapsed on the bed. Despite the strong coffee, I was out cold before I knew it.

It was the morning light streaming through the curtains that woke me. As I looked around I realized that my shoes and my sweatshirt were missing. On the chair beside the bed was a new polo shirt, jeans, belt, underwear, and under the chair were brand new tennis shoes with socks tucked inside and on top a note that read:

"Clean up and throw away your old clothes. New clothes for a new day and a new life. – Chris"

I picked up the clothes, and stepped into the hallway to find myself alone in the apartment. In the shower I found a bottle of my favorite shower gel and shampoo, and I lathered up completely. After the shower I dried off with a soft, clean towel and put on the new clothes. I found it both strange and comforting, although no longer shocking, that they fit me perfectly.

When I stepped from the bathroom I was greeted with the smell of toast and frying bacon. Breathing it in deeply, I stepped into the kitchen to find Chris cooking and Ronni sitting at the table, waiting for me. He turned when he saw me, and approached me with a hug.

"A new day, Scooter," he said. "Let's make the most of it."

James Cory Michaels

Chapter 2 - The Gospel According to Murray

It was a normal night, a Wednesday, I think. Anyway, I'm sitting at the corner diner, enjoying my pie when they come in. I am not sure who the goy was, but the other one, I recognized him, immediately. He was the grandson of Cy and Flo Halevy. Oy vey, what a scandal that was.

Miriam was a sweet girl, a good little girl, always dressed in pretty dresses and well behaved in schule. As she grew, she became quite the beauty. I remember her Bat Mitzvah, what a big party and what a good time everyone had.

Then, when she went to that public high school, there were some rumors – something about her having eyes for a goy, but her parents put the kibosh on that, and quick – or at least everyone thought. I remember her engagement party to that nice Stein boy. Good family, good stock, that one. Yes, she would never have to worry, marrying into that family. Jewelers, they are – and diamond brokers.

Anyway, then there was a huge engagement party – lots of food, and some very nice engagement gifts, especially from the Steins. Thank G_d that they didn't have the Te'naim because shortly after the party she comes up pregnant, and come to find out, it wasn't the Stein boy's baby. What shame on her family!

Then, soon afterwards, she marries that Polish boy. Good family, and nice people, but really – they don't have a pot to piss in or a window to throw it from.

Ah, but that boy – Rudi, I think was his name, G_d rest his soul, did right by her. He worked construction, that one – and also worked part time on the docks to fill in, so Miriam could stay home with the babies. Oh, and some beautiful babies they were! Blonde hair and light eyed, every one – well, except the first and oldest. Dark brown curls and brown eyes, that one – nothing like the daddy, but a real good boy.

I heard that the Rabbi performed a bris in secret, but the Poles had a huge doings when he was baptized as a Catholic! Cy tore his clothes, and Flo cried for days. They didn't speak to their daughter for years after that.

But, we saw young Christopher around the neighborhood. It seemed like he was always helping someone, you know? The shop keeper, at the news stand, cleaning up some mess, doing odd jobs for a penny or two, even watching his younger siblings for his mother.

Then one year, when the boy would have been 13, I think, he came to synagogue. It was Yom Kippur and he was dressed in a yamaka and kittle and took his place right beside Cy. He had no training, but chanted and sang the whole service just like he had known it since the cradle. I suspect that he had seen the Rabbi in private, but when I queried our Rabbi, he said it must have been another, because he was as surprised as any.

After that, it was a different story with the relationship between Cy and Flo, their daughter and her family. They went to his birthday parties and Cy watched his basketball games. Oh, how proud Cy was of young Christopher when he made the high school varsity team his sophomore year and then was named Second Team All-City the next year.

Then, it happened. It almost seems like the young man was born under a dark cloud or something. That summer his father fell from a building. They say that when you fall that far you die before you hit the ground, but who knows? I hope so for his sake.

Anyway, Cy and Flo had moved to Florida, so they were unable to help. Young Christopher wound up quitting school and started working construction to provide for his mother and family.

Then, a few years back, I heard the family moved to Florida to be closer to Cy and Flo, but Christopher stayed here. I hadn't seen or heard much from or about the boy, since, until he walked into that diner that night.

Always wondered what happened to him. Oh, well.

James Cory Michaels

Chapter 3 - The Gospel According to Veronica

The night Chris and Scooter walked into the diner was a turning point in my life. It wasn't the first, but it might very well be the last.

After showing Scooter to the spare room, I fixed myself a cup of herbal tea and changed into a t-shirt and pajama shorts. I had been hesitant when Chris first asked me to put him up in for the night, but he assured me that Scott was a good man who was down on his luck, and I had never known Chris to be wrong about such things.

When I sipped my tea it was bitter and warm and calming, as always. After drinking it, I put the cup and saucer in the sink, ran some water into it, went to my room and lay down on my bed, but I couldn't sleep. I tossed and turned for an hour or so, then decided that I might as well take a walk. I changed into jeans and a shirt, slipped on a jacket and headed down stairs. As I opened the front door to the apartment building I heard a familiar voice. It was Chris.

"Hi, Ronni, having trouble sleeping?"

Ronni – the nickname my dad gave me when I was growing up in Northwest Iowa. My family lived in a small house in a small town in an agricultural community. With my mom, dad, two brothers and sister the small house we lived in was crowded, but we made do. Mom named me Veronica after her favorite character in the Archie comic series and my dad gave me my middle name, Lake, so I would be named after a famous actress.

After I got older I looked up her bio, and still am not sure if it was a meant as a compliment or not.

Growing up in Iowa was advantageous for me because there wasn't a lot of competition. I was one of the prettiest girls in school, being both the Homecoming and Prom Queen and even coming in as second runner-up in the Miss Iowa pageant. Although I dated the popular, athletic boys, my interests were in the arts, not sports. I excelled in band, choir and theater. After high-school I went to the University of Iowa as a liberal arts major, but after a couple of years there I got bored and left the land of tall, waving corn fields for the lights, bustle and opportunity of the city.

From there my story takes a less than desired, but not wholly unexpected turn. Not only did the city have more opportunity, there was also a lot more competition for that opportunity, and the second-runner up for Miss Iowa suddenly didn't mean I was the most attractive girl in the room, none the less the surrounding neighborhood.

I took some singing and dancing classes, and supported myself waiting tables while looking for work in my chosen career field, acting, but found the opportunities for work were few and far between. After two years the best I had done were parts like 'extras in a crowd', or a cameo in a commercial. The longer I was there the more desperate I became.

After a several months and many rejections, my agent approached me with the idea that I might want to go the 'extra mile' for a part. What he meant was a 'quid pro quo' arrangement where I would trade sex for a part. At first I resisted, but eventually reality slapped me in the face and I started letting it be known I might be acceptable to such an arrangement. My first time on the 'casting couch' made me feel dirty, but it landed me a role where I actually spoke two lines and gave me some thirty seconds on camera.

After that, the 'casting couch' offers started coming with more and more frequency as the word got out, but unfortunately the job offers lacked the same numbers, or interest. It all came to a head when I walked in to an audition and the casting director told me to close the door, drop to my knees and blow him – using those exact terms. I was shocked at the crassness and directness, and I did close the door, but it was behind me as I walked out.

Next was the phone call to my agent. It went something like this:

"Hello, Maury? Fuck off and die."

"I knew you were just another bimbo from fly-over country." Click.

That was when I realized that I was making more money waiting tables at the diner than acting with or without the 'favors', and traded my dreams for a small apartment, an apron and sore feet.

On the night I met Chris I had no idea what a mess the place was until I got there. It didn't take long for me to read the panicked look on Mario's face to figure out that we were in trouble.

The cook had called in sick and the dishwasher had just not bothered to show up, and for whatever reason we had more customers and we were busier than usual. Mario was working in the kitchen, and I was serving, but there was no one to clean the dishes or the pots and pans, and we were running out of them quickly.

I thought we were going to have to close the doors because things just got too busy, then without a word this guy walks in the back door, hangs up his jacket, throws on an apron and starts washing dishes. I actually thought it was someone Mario had called until he asked me if I had.

However, Chris just started working that night with no training and doing a marvelous job. It was like he knew where everything was and where everything went like he had been doing it for years. About 11 o'clock that evening things slowed down, and Chris left the diner saying, "Well, looks like we took care of that! See you tomorrow!"

He did show up the next day. As a matter of fact, he kept showing up every day but what was really strange was that he never asked for a dime. After showing up every night for a week, Mario asked him to fill out an application, but he declined. He then tried paying Chris under the table, but again he refused and said that he didn't need the money.

Mario was confused and feeling guilty when he told him to at least allow him to repay him by feeding him, and Chris smiled – "Okay," he said, "I can do that, but more importantly – if you see someone hungry, feed him. If someone is thirsty and asks for something to drink, give it to him. If you see someone standing around outside and shivering, let them come in and warm up. If you do that, you will not only repay me, but also repay your Father in heaven for this restaurant He has given you."

Mario bristled at the last comment. "Wait a minute – this is my joint. I built this through my hard work and my sacrifice."

Chris cut him off, "I understand that, but who gave you your health? Who gave you your intelligence and your ability to work hard? Who do you think sent me to you to help you out?"

"Uh…." Mario stammered

Chris continued, "More so, who gave you your parents who gave you the seed money to start the place?"

Mario was shocked. "How did you know…how could you know…"

"It doesn't matter," Chris injected. "But it is said that all good things come from God, and this diner is a good thing, is it not? You are a good man, Mario, but even the best man is nothing in comparison with the goodness of God."

Mario thought about what Chris had said for a moment, and then hung his head. However, he has been true to his promise to Chris. Where he used to throw derelicts out on the street, he now feeds them, gives them coffee and lets them stay as long as they need. The interesting thing is that not long after he started this policy, and has been doing as Chris said that not only has the diner been busier than ever, we are also making more money, and that people are spending more per ticket. He used to throw these guys out because he thought they made the other patrons nervous, but that obviously he was wrong.

Going back to that first night he showed up at the café, I took a few moments and checked him out pretty well. There was never anything unusual or what would be considered attractive about him – he was pretty much medium height, medium build and a shock of curly brown hair that kept falling into his face - but there is this quality about him that is hard to explain.

He never flirted or made a pass at me, but the way he smiled and the way he looked at me made me feel like I was not just the only person in the room, but in the whole world. He would ask questions about the real me –the inner me, was always interested and never judgmental, regardless of what I told him.

I fell in love pretty much immediately. Then, I tried to seduce him.

I invited him over for dinner one evening. I got rid of my roommate, made lasagna, and then took a shower, being careful to thoroughly wash and shave everything. I dried and curled my hair, put on a sexy, low cut black dress, then opened a bottle of Chianti, lit candles, dimmed the lights and put some romantic, soft jazz on the iPod.

At two minutes after the appointed time there was a knock on the door. I opened the door and was a little disappointed to find him standing there in his usual t-shirt, jeans, tennis shoes and leather jacket. He came in, took in the atmosphere of the room, and then said, "Ronni, we need to talk."

He pulled a chair out from the table and moved it to one side so two chairs were together, sat down and motioned me to sit in the other. He took both of my hands in his, leaned forward, looked deeply in my eyes and started to talk.

"Look," he said, "I love you, and I really appreciate all of the effort you have put forth, but I don't want to have sex with you."

"Are you gay?" I asked, "Because I really don't get that vibe from you."

He chuckled, "No, I am not gay, and you're a very attractive woman, but you don't understand – I don't want to have sex with you, but want you for so much more."

I was confused. "You want to marry me?"

He laughed again. "Why would I marry you if I didn't want to have sex with you? No, I want much, much more from you. I want your body, your heart and your soul."

"You are the strangest man I have ever met."

He started laughing out loud, "Oh, Ronni, you don't know half of it."

With that said, we both got up, turned on the lights and he helped me in the kitchen. We had nothing less than the most delightful dinner I could imagine – no sexual tension, no pretension, just laughter and earnest conversation. We finished off the bottle of Chianti and opened up a bottle of Merlot I had stashed for a special occasion continuing to talk into the wee hours of the morning.

I did most of the talking, actually. He asked me about my life growing up, my parents, my brothers and sisters, my transition to the city, even my acting career. I told him everything…it was so easy and he just kept smiling and nodding and touching my hand.

After the merlot was done, he suggested we get some sleep. I grabbed a couple of pillows and blankets and Chris crashed on the couch while I toddled off to bed and had one of the most peaceful sleeps of my life. No dreams, just a sense of belonging, being loved, being protected and that someone really cared about me, just because I am me.

I woke the next morning feeling great. No hangover, no feeling of exhaustion which usually accompanies a night of drinking, just a combination of a sense of calm and having a great amount of energy. I got out of bed and stretched and took a deep breath of the best smelling air laced with the scents of fresh coffee, bacon, eggs and toast. Chris was in the kitchen and had been a very busy guy.

His timing was perfect. As I entered the kitchen Chris was putting my plate on the table, in front of a fresh cup of coffee and glass of freshly squeezed orange juice. The bacon was perfect, the eggs exactly how I like them and my coffee was splendid. Again, I felt like a princess with him just making me breakfast.

After eating I put my dishes in the sink and poured myself a second cup of coffee while Chris started eating his own breakfast. Somehow the coffee didn't taste quite as good as that which he poured. I sat down at the table.

"So, where do we go from here?" I queried.

"What do you mean?" he said.

"You said you wanted my heart, my body and my soul – so here it is," I continued, "now, what are you going to do with it?"

He chuckled, "Nothing for now…just be your friend, but I will hold you to your offer."

"So, just keep things between us as if nothing happened?" I asked.

"Nothing did happen, except two friends sharing a

meal and getting to know one another better."

"You told me you love me."

He smiled, "Yes, I do."

I felt as though I should be frustrated and the physical manifestation of that frustration should be coursing through me, but all I felt was a peaceful calm.

"You hardly know me. How can you say you love me, especially after the things I told you about myself and what I have done?"

He took a sip of his coffee, "Would it shock you if I told you that I already knew?"

I leaned forward, "Concern me, possibly, but I am not sure anything I found out about you could shock me, any more."

He smiled, "I wouldn't be so sure."

I was becoming a bit concerned, "What do you mean?"

"You'll know when it is time for you to know, but now the time isn't right. I promise you, though, that it isn't anything bad."

"Okay, as long as you're not an axe murderer or a child molester."

He looked taken aback, and then burst into laughter, "You can rest assured that I am neither of those!" and continued to laugh out loud.

After that day, things went back to normal – I worked at the diner and Chris washed the dishes. My roommate moved out, and I asked Chris if he wanted to move in to help with the rent. He declined and told me not to worry, everything would work out.

Even though my roommate moved out and I was short her contribution to the rent, I never really had a problem with money. My tips were better, my expenses less, it even seemed like I had more discretionary income than I did when she lived there.

Yes, everything was pretty much back to normal –

until the night he brought Scott into the diner. Scott looked like someone had put him through the wringer multiple times. He was dirty, smelled of booze and reeked with body odor, but Chris didn't seem to notice, so I took his lead and tried to ignore it as well. I am ashamed to admit it, but I wretched into my mouth a bit when Chris asked me to take him home with me and give him a place to sleep.

I was up earlier than Scott was that morning, and was having a cup of coffee when Chris came in with two bags, one from a local retailer and one from a local grocer. He handed me the groceries – bacon, eggs, orange juice, English muffins, some fruit and canned goods; then went in to Scott's room with the other bag.

I started making breakfast, but Chris wouldn't hear of it. We had both finished eating when I heard the shower running in the bathroom and Chris got up, cleared the table and started to cook again. Just as he was finishing up, Scott emerged, clean, shaven and looking like a completely different man.

Chris went over to him, hugged him and said "A new day, Scooter, let's make the most of it."

Then he looked at me and said, "You need to get dressed. It's almost 9:00, and you have to be at work at four, so we don't have much time."

I got up and got dressed. While dressing I thought to myself that it was amazing that I had not even thought to question where we were going and what we didn't have much time to do. I pulled on a sweater, some jeans and some sturdy shoes for walking since Chris seemed to walk just about everywhere. I brushed my hair and checked myself out in the mirror.

"Gorgeous," I said to no one, being alone in my room, "I don't get why he doesn't want this!"

When I emerged, Scott was finished eating and Chris was just finishing the dishes. He dried off his hands, grabbed his jacket and we headed out with Chris taking the lead, Scott and I following close behind.

Following Chris and watching him was amazing. I have never seen someone talk to so many people on the street. He seemed to know each and every one of them and called many by name. He shook so many hands he would have put a politician to shame, and it seemed as though everyone either knew him or wanted to know him. I said something to him about this, but he just shrugged and casually dismissed it saying, "I grew up in this neighborhood, you know."

But, it kept up. We walked for miles, through many different neighborhoods and still such congeniality I have never seen. The neighborhoods changed, but not for the better. The farther we went, the more minority populated it became and progressively became poorer and meaner with fewer people on the sidewalk, and less people who were willing to make eye contact.

Two young men approached us, one black and the other Hispanic, and demanded our money. Chris said, "Sorry, sir, but we don't have any money."

"Sir?" the Hispanic one said. "Fuck your 'sir,' and take your 'sorry' and stick it up your ass. Give us what we want, or we will give you something you don't want." and produced a previously unseen knife, apparently for military use, and with a blade about five inches long.

Chris immediately took action. He moved faster than anyone I have ever seen outside the movies when he pushed the knife from his assailant's hand, and then like some kind of Kung-Fu master spun him around, pulled the hem of his t-shirt over his head and pulled him to the ground, completely disabled but unharmed. The second man took off like a shot.

Chris ignored the runner even though he wasn't breathing hard and said to the man on the ground, "I told you, I don't have any money. If I did, I would give it to you without the knife but now you made me do this." He continued with genuine concern in his voice, "Are you okay?"

He knelt in front of the man, helped him compose himself, then took him by his forearms, looked at the needle marks there and said, "I don't have money, but I can give you something better. Are you ready to kick the shit you have been shooting? Meth, right?"

The man looked dumbfounded and then started to weep.

They were both crying when Chris embraced him on the sidewalk, put the man's head on his shoulders and kissed him on the head. When they separated, the man had a look of peace on his face, and I saw that the track marks on his forearms were healed with no scarring.

"Just like that?" he asked Chris.

"Go home to your wife and son. Tell her you have kicked and you're ready to turn your life around. She loves you and will take you back," Chris instructed.

Then he produced a 3x5 card from his pocket and handed it to the man. "Tomorrow morning at six, be at this address and tell this man that you need a job and that Chris sent you. You have a background in construction and he needs you, desperately. It will be a good fit, and stay well – no more poison, okay?"

The man looked up, healed and with a grateful look in his eyes he took Chris's hand and began to weep, again. "Thank you, sir. Thank you so very much! No more poison, I swear."

"You don't have to swear, I believe you." He smiled mischievously and added, "and I won't tell you what to do with your 'sir'… my name is Chris."

With that, one more hug and the two went their separate ways.

After a few more blocks a scantily clad young woman approached Chris.

"Hey, baby, twenty bucks for a quickie or a blowjob, ten for a hand job." she advertised.

We all three stopped, and then Chris turned and approached her. At first she looked smug as she thought she had a customer, then confused as he came nearer, then fearful and tried to get away but was stopped by the wall of the building behind her.

Then her voice changed to something otherworldly. "Get away from me, I know who you are and I know what you are!" she hissed.

Before she could say or do anything more Chris put his hand on her head and commanded, "Come out of her, now," he continued with more power in his voice, "All of you, come out! I claim this child!"

With that, her eyes rolled back into her head and her body began to levitate several inches off the ground before it started to convulse like a marionette attached by invisible strings to the world's worst puppeteer.

Chris turned to Scott and pointed to the side of the girl nearest him, "Go stand there and get ready to catch her," he commanded.

The convulsions lasted forty-five seconds, maybe a minute, but it seemed like hours before she fell with one last spasm that left her off balance and spent. Scott caught her easily and she looked small and frail. She was just a baby, really, maybe twelve or thirteen, and probably all of eighty-five or ninety pounds by the look of her - not the street hardened hooker she appeared to be when she approached us.

"I know just the place for her," Chris said to no one in particular, then turned to Scott. "Follow me," he instructed.

The apartment complex was about three blocks away, and Scott was really not in that of good shape, but he didn't say a word, even when struggling to climb the stairs. On the fourth floor Chris stopped at a particular door and knocked. A middle aged woman answered, and her face lit up when she saw Chris.

"Hi, Helen," he said, and gave her a hug. "I need a favor of you. Could you take this child, her name is Heather, nurse her back to health and take care of her for a few days? I will send someone around to collect her when she is ready and they will pay you for your trouble."

"For you, Chris," she said. "Anything."

Scott carried Heather into the bedroom where Helen directed him, then another embrace between Helen and Chris, and we left. Back on the street, we continued in the same direction we had been previously traveling.

I looked at Scott and he at me, and the look in his eyes told me that he was just as astonished and confused about the things we had just witnessed. I was beginning to wonder if I was hallucinating or dreaming when Chris turned to me, smiled amusedly and said "No, Ronni, you're wide awake and everything you have seen is real."

The bright afternoon sun and my watch both showed that it was just after one o'clock when we turned the corner and I saw it. Our destination was obviously a derelict building standing alone with nothing but empty lots on either side. "We're here," Chris announced, and for the first time this day I felt a little dread.

James Cory Michaels

Chapter 4 - The Gospel According to Moe

I had just gone to the kitchen to make myself a bologna sandwich with lettuce and cheese when I heard the ruckus from downstairs. I grabbed my gak and headed to the door with a "Mother fucker! Can't a man even eat around here?"

The building was pretty run down, with no electricity through most of it because the crack heads had stolen the wire to sell the copper, so even though it was the middle of the day, there was no light other than that coming in through the broken windows and holes in the wall, but I saw the strangest thing. There in the middle of the building were three well dressed white people standing in a circle as well as they could, backs together and their arms held straight out, palms up like a cop trying to stop traffic and around them were the junkies and crack heads that used the place as a flophouse yelling and hissing like a nest of snakes.

Now I had only worked for "King" Tyrone Washington for three years, but even I knew that three middle class white folks getting killed in his 'district headquarters' would bring the po po and a bunch of heat that we just didn't need. I raised my gak above my head and rapped off three rounds sending crack heads running to the corners of the building like cockroaches.

I then turned my attention to the strangers, "The fuck ya'll think you're doing? You got a death wish? You wanna die?"

The female was tight. She wasn't dressed for the club or nothin' but you could tell she was seriously smolderin'. The guy in the polo shirt looked like he was lost and didn't know how to get back to his white bread neighborhood. The both of them looked like they were about to shit their pants, but the dude in the leather jacket started walking towards me. "We're in no danger," he said. "But you might be."

I figured he was shitting me. I mean the dude wasn't even packing. "The fuck you say? Who the fuck you think you are, Mr. Diehard?"

Chris started to laugh, "No, my name is Chris, and you – Moses Malone Stockwell – you are gonna catch hell from Tyrone when I am done here."

"Done doing what?" I asked, then I leveled my gun directly at his head and said, "I am gonna ruin your day unless you back the fuck up, jack."

"What I came to do," he said, "is clean these people up and by doing so ruin a big part of your customer base, and I am going to burn down the building including the shipment you just received."

I looked this dude in the eyes and realized that there was no fear. "You the heat?" I asked.

"You have no idea. Yeah, I am the heat, but I am no cop," he said, and moved even closer.

"I said stop, mother fucker!" My voice cracked on "mother" and I knew I sounded more scared than menacing so I said it again, "stop right there!"

He didn't listen and kept coming at me like a fool, and before I could pull the trigger, he just took the gun out of my hand.

"Now, you have two choices – well, not really," he stated. "You can either help me, or you can run and deal with one pissed-off Tyrone." I knew the option would be suicide, and obviously so did he.

Then he acted like I wasn't even there when he turned his attention to the female and the male who were with him. "Go stand by the doors and if the person going past you says "Yes," touch him on the forehead. If they don't, just let them go."

Then he addressed the others in the building. "You need to leave, now. If you want to kick the junk you have been poisoning yourself with, just see one of my assistants and say yes to them. Otherwise you are free to leave. Oh, and don't take a long time to decide, because the building is on fire." He snapped his fingers and as he did so I saw a flash come from the kitchen. A few seconds later I heard a crackle and then saw the flames through the door I left open. "Don't panic, but don't wait," he continued to the crowd. "You have time to leave if you do so now, but time is wasting."

Then he turned to me and asked, "So, what are you going to do?"

"Like I have a choice? What do you want me to do?" I asked.

"Stick with me, and I will let you know when the time comes, okay?" Then he handed me back my gun, still loaded, but somehow he knew I wasn't going to use it.

While this was going on, the crack heads all scattered for the door. Some ran, some others fell, but most of them were pretty calm, considering. They just walked to the door, and a lot of them paused at either the male or the female long enough to be touched and went their way.

I just stood there like I was stupid and catching flies with my mouth. I remember I was pretty concerned about the fire and the building, but not as much as I was about the new shipment of heroin and cocaine that had just come in the night before. Chris, though, was as cool as shit and just stood there until the last junkie left. Afterwards we walked out the door with the other two like nothing, then crossed the street and watched the building burn as the fire department stood and watched.

Honestly, they really didn't seem to give a shit about

the building. Since there were no other buildings around there wasn't like the fire was going to spread far, and they seemed more concerned about not wanting to breathe in the smoke from the combination of old construction materials and junk. They just stood there and watched it burn, for the most part.

Chris turned to me and asked "So, how much do you think Tyrone lost in the fire?"

I thought a second and said, "Shit, I don't know. Twenty million, maybe, wholesale? Maybe seventy on the street?"

"Yeah, that's pretty much what I figured."

We stood there for a long time. Chris turned to me and said, "Okay, Moe, it's a little after three, now. Ronni needs a ride to work and you have nothing else to do but dodge Tyrone. Take her to work, get something to eat, and I will hook up with you later."

I didn't even ask when and where because there was too much shit running through my head, so I nodded to the girl and headed for the Escalade. She gave me directions to a diner I had seen before but never ate at, but otherwise there wasn't a lot of conversation.

She just sat in the passenger's seat staring at her hands in silence, but she couldn't hide the fact she was one gorgeous female. I figured that this guy, Chris, was hitting it so I didn't try to play with her.

I went in to the diner with her, sat at the counter and picked up a menu. I guess I must have been thinking about my momma, because I ordered the open-faced turkey sandwich with mashed potatoes and gravy and green beans, and a large glass of milk, just like she used to feed me.

After a second glass of milk to wash down my slice of chocolate silk pie, I tried to pay, but Ronni said they wouldn't take the money, so I left a $10 tip and headed out the door to the Escalade and my apartment. I had just got on the road when I realized that I was in a world of shit and that Chris hadn't even shown his face. When I got to the crib, I poured myself in the chair and got lost in a Tyler Perry sitcom before I heard someone at the window. I grabbed my gak and crouched behind the chair before I saw who it was.

It was Chris.

I opened the window and started to give him shit about coming through the fire escape when he cut me off. "I couldn't come in the front door, Tyrone is using it with two of his 'associates'." he said as he started to the door. "And I figured this was the best way to do it." Then he stood by the door, counted to five, and opened it. I heard Tyrone's voice shout something as Chris stepped into the hall, and then quiet as he closed the door behind him.

I don't know what was said, but first I heard Tyrone start to go ballistic, then it sounded like Chris said something back, and then I couldn't hear anything else. The silence went on for a long time, then the door opened and Chris walked in.

"Quickly," Chris ordered, "pack a light bag. You can't live here anymore."

Normally there would have had to be more explanation, but this had been anything but a normal day. I had seen this guy disarm me and then burn down a building and a shitload of junk by just snapping his fingers. Then he goes out to front the most dangerous man in the city and two of his crew, by himself and unarmed and comes back without a scratch. I just grabbed a few things, threw them in a bag, then grabbed the keys to the Escalade and headed out.

In the hallway I see Tyrone, Lee and Perry lying there like they was dead. Before I could say anything Chris said, "No, they're not dead. They'll be fine in the morning, but I wouldn't worry about them messing with you anymore."

Then I followed him down the stairs and into the night.

Chapter 5 - The Gospel According to Lee

I have seen 'The King' mad, but never this pissed. Ever.

"A fire? A goddamned fire?" he fumed, "Where the fuck was Moe? Where the fuck IS Moe? I bet he was screwing some crack ho! Motherfucker! I am going to break a foot off in his ass. Damn! Fuck that, I am going to cap his stupid ass! He's a dead man. Dead, I tell you!"

A soft knock came on the door.

"Get the fucking door, Lee. The fuck do I pay you for?"

I went to the door and opened it. It was one of the 'house people' as I called them - addicts hanging around the house trying anything and everything to score their next fix. The woman at the door was one of the first and worst. Back in the day she was a pretty hot female, but now she was a dirty skank with nappy hair and too many holes in her mouth where her teeth used to be.

"I got something to tell the King," she said while visually shaking and twitching. "About the fire this afternoon."

I told her to get her ass out of the hall, and then escorted her to the room where Tyrone was sitting in the huge leather recliner he called his throne, in order to have an audience with one of his serfs.

Truth is that it's hard thinking of Tyrone Washington as King, nonetheless saying it. The first time I saw him he was a punk kid getting his ass kicked on the playground. At first I thought it was funny, but then he was getting his ass kicked so bad that I felt sorry for him, so I cold-cocked one of the dudes beating him, and the others took a powder.

After that, he hung out with me and my crew every chance he got, maybe to feel like he belonged somewhere. Then, I don't know how, but Tyrone got connected with a serious source, so he put together his own crew, and then asked me and some others to hook up with him and we started running and selling drugs. Chronic, at first, then coke, crack, meth and junk. Like I said, it was a serious supply so soon we had more money than we could spend, and more pussy than we could fuck.

Maybe because he had gotten his ass kicked so much, maybe something else, but that nigga became totally ruthless. The first time I seen him cap someone – it was a dealer who came up short. Tyrone had him get on his knees in front of him, then took a .44 and made him suck the barrel like a dick before he capped him between his eyes, blowing off the back of his head. The freaky thing was the look on his face – a look of total pleasure came to his face almost like a junkie who just finished shooting up and I swear he might have cum in his pants.

That was about that time that people started referring to him as King, and those who didn't, regretted it.

Anyway, when the female went in to the room, Tyrone asked her, "What you got for me?"

She was shaking with sickness and fear and twitching. "Valuable information. Very valuable information, King," she said and then added, "very valuable."

"On your knees, bitch! Don't you know that you address your king on your knees?" Tyrone shouted, and Perry shoved her down before she had a chance to get there herself.

"I am sorry, King, I won't do that no more," she continued. "I promise."

"Damned right you won't do that no more." Tyrone

said and then he asked, "So, what you got?"

"I am hurting, King. Can I have a taste? I just need a taste." You could tell she was in some kind of bad shape.

"Depends on what you got, bitch," and then continued. "But for a taste, it better be good."

"It is, King," she said. "Good information."

"Well, then," Tyrone said, "the fuck you waitin' for?"

"I goes down to the house this afternoon looking to score. I hadn't been but a few minutes when three white people walked in like they belonged there. Them others in the house tried to attack 'em, but the three of them, two males and a female, kept them away just by holding their hands out in front of them, like this." She held her arms straight out in front of her with fingers pointed up and palms out and me and Perry laughed.

Then she went on, "Then Moe came out shooting his piece like he was in a movie or sumptin' and scared off all the regulars. That is when the one man approached him – he must have been the leader. At first I thought Moe was going to cap him, but this man took the gun away from him like a bitch and started ordering him around."

Tyrone was really pissed. "Moe just let some punk ass take away his piece? Fuck! I always knew he was a bitch-assed pussy!" He started losing control and throwing shit around the place screaming like he was losin' his mind.

When he settled down a bit, the female went on, "Then this white man told all of us to leave. He say that we could kick just for asking, but I didn't do it, King – I likes it way too much. Then he set the house on fire just like that." She snapped her fingers and then went on, "He say if we wanted to kick just tell one of them other two 'Yes' as we left the building but I swear, King, I didn't do it. Then, when everyone left, the male give Moe back his gak but he don't shoot him. The two of them walked across the street like nothin' happened and watched that sucker burn to the ground."

"Moe got his piece back and didn't shoot the fucker?" The veins on his forehead and neck were popping asTyrone stood up and pulled his gun, "That mother fucker gotta pay!"

"What about my taste?" the woman whimpered, "You promised me a taste!"

With that Tyrone unzipped his fly, "I give you a taste – a taste of my cock!" and whipped out his dick as he noted, "And you being on your knees puts you in the perfect position." Then he looked thoughtful and said "Tell you what, if you do a good job, I might get you high, bitch."

He stood in front of her and she took his cock in both hands and started sucking it. The whole scene made me kinda sick so I went in the other room, poured a drink and sparked a blunt just to mellow out a bit.

A little while later, Tyrone yelled for me to come back in. I guess the woman did a good job, because she was now laying curled up on the floor and floating inside her own head.

"Get the keys, then you and Perry bring the car around," Tyrone said, then he motioned to the junkie, "and take out the garbage wit cha."

As we left, Perry grabbed the female by her head and I grabbed her feet and we carried her out. Then when we got outside Perry just let go without saying nothin', dropped her head on the sidewalk and it cracked with a sick thunk like an over ripe melon. Blood started pooling around her head as I pulled her to the side by her feet, leaving a trail, and then let her feet down gently and turned to Perry with a look of disgust.

"Shit, man. What? I ain't no garbage man, and bitch didn't give ME head," he excused himself.

We jumped in the Hummer and drove it around to the front door just as Tyrone was walking out the door. When he got in, he said, "Word has it that Moe is at his crib. Let's start there"

On the way there I was thinking about what the junkie bitch said and I couldn't believe it. Moe and I have run together for a long time now, and there ain't nobody as smart, tough or loyal as that motherfucker – straight up OG. He was one of the original crew and I just couldn't see him not only punking out, but turning. Just wasn't anything like him.

Wasn't long before we were outside Moe's crib. We exited the vehicle, walked through the lobby, entered the mirrored elevator and pressed the button. On the way up, we got ready for business and checked out hardware to make sure we were locked and loaded. It was pretty cool that Tyrone obviously had enough respect for Moe that he wasn't taking any chances when we approached.

As we made our way down the hall, Tyrone pulled the hammer back on his pearl handled and chrome .44, and about twenty feet before we got there, the door on Moe's apartment opened – but it wasn't Moe who came out. Instead it was a white boy with a leather jacket and a mop of curly hair on his head. He looked like a punk, but he damned sure didn't act like one. When he saw us instead of running away, he walked right toward us.

Tyrone leveled his revolver and pointed it at the man's head. "Who the fuck are you?" he demanded.

"I'm Chris," the man said. "But you probably know me as the one who burned your building and cost you a ton of money," he said.

"The first dead man I get to talk to today, you mean," Tyrone shouted.

"Ya think?" the man said. "Funny, I think you're wrong about me and just who's the other dead man supposed to be?"

"That punk-ass pussy, Moe!" Tyrone said.

The man in the leather jacket started laughing – not a good move to laugh at Tyrone. "I think you're wrong about that, too," he said as he walked toward us, no sign of fear at all.

Tyrone was shaking, now. I thought it was from anger, but thinking about it, I am not sure he knew what to think. Dude didn't have a gun, but not only was he not scared, he wasn't giving Tyrone any respect, and the King didn't know what to do. His voice started shaking as he said, "You gonna keep me from it, punk? What cha gonna, do?"

The man stopped but kept smiling, "Me? Nothing," he said, and then continued as he jerked his thumb over his shoulder, "but he might."

When he said that it was like the air in the hallway parted like the door of a tent and revealed this creature like I had never seen or even heard about. It must have been at least ten feet tall with a body of intense fire and red burning eyes. It had four faces, one on each side of it's head and huge arms and hands, one holding a lightning bolt like a sword and the other a ball of red fire.

I dropped my gun and my knees buckled when heard the man in the leather jacket's voice in my head. "I would like you to meet Michael, he works for me. He commands an army of millions like him and does my bidding. You might want to know that while these creatures can kill, they can never die."

With that this creature opened his mouth and his voice sounded like a jet engine. The gun fell out of my hand and I had never been so scared of anyone or anything in my whole life.

"The next time you want to threaten Moe or any other of my friends, I want you to take a moment and think about a million Michaels, and imagine what they could do to you," I heard the man's voice say inside my head.

I looked over at Tyrone and saw that he had already dropped his gun and was on his knees in the hall like that female, earlier and the boy was sobbing like the punk kid I had rescued on the playground so many years before.

"Now who is the punk-assed pussy, bitch?" I thought as I passed out.

James Cory Michaels

Chapter 6 - The Second Gospel According to Scott

After Moe and Ronni left, Chris and I stood in silence taking in the whole scene with the burning building in the middle. Then I turned to him and asked, "Could you tell me what just happened?"

Chris smiled, "Some pretty freaky stuff, eh? What do you think just happened?"

I thought for a second, then said, "Uh, my best guess is that you cured an addict, cast demons out of a hooker, and then destroyed some building which contained a significant amount of illegal drugs, had Ronni and me heal a bunch of other addicts, and made friends with a drug-dealing gang banger."

"Yeah," Chris said, "that would pretty much cover it."

"That whole healing thing," I continued, "was more intense than anything I have ever felt. Every time I touched one of them I could feel power actually flowing out of me, but then it was restored immediately for the next person."

"This is what happens when you obey God and do as He wishes," Chris said. "He will provide everything you need."

I just stood in silence and contemplated what Chris had just said. Was I working for God? Really?

"Oh," Chris continued. "If you think today was freaky, just wait for tomorrow and the next day and the day after that. You ain't seen nothing yet."

After a few more minutes of silence Chris turned to me and asked, "Are you about ready to blow this Popsicle stand?" He turned and headed down the sidewalk in the same direction in which we came.

We had just turned the corner when we were approached by another woman who, by the look of her, was another hooker. She walked up to Chris and instead of propositioning him said, "I saw what you did for Heather. She didn't deserve this life, and I want to thank you."

"Do you think that you, a precious child of God, deserve the kind of life you are leading?" Chris inquired.

She hung her head. "Yeah, pretty much," she said. Then she continued, "Besides I have been doing it so long I really don't know what else to do. I haven't developed too many marketable skills you know, and I'm not getting any younger."

Chris nodded his head. "You are still pretty young, and you have children to support. Do you think you could put your trust in me?" he asked.

"I don't see why not," she replied. "You haven't given me any reason not to."

"Okay, so if I gave you enough money to quit this business and go back to school, would you do it?" Chris queried.

"In a heartbeat."

"Well, then," Chris instructed, "cross the street and go to the convenience store. Take $2.00 and buy one Powerball quick pick ticket. Don't buy any more tickets and don't get the "Powerplay." The drawing is tonight, and while you will not win the grand prize, you will match five numbers and win the second prize. After taxes there will be more than enough left over to go back to school, get a better apartment in a better neighborhood and take care of your children while you are studying. You have five years to complete your degree."

She looked stunned and Chris continued, "Five years is enough for you to graduate. At the end of five years take whatever money is left over and give it to local charities. Now for the rest of the rules, are you ready?"

"Uh….Sure," she stammered.

"Do not use the money to buy jewelry or property. Do not use the money to buy a fancy car but instead buy yourself an inexpensive but reliable car. Do not use the money to buy electronic toys or fancy phones. Do not spend the money on drugs."

Chris continued. "Do exactly as I tell you and trust God, and He will bless you. Do otherwise, and He will turn His back on you. Now, it's time for you to get started."

She turned and ran toward the crosswalk. Then she stopped, turned around and ran back to Chris, and when she reached him she threw her arms around his neck in a warm embrace. With tears running down her cheeks, she sobbed, "Oh, thank you, sir. Thank you very much. I won't let you down."

Chris patted her on the back and quietly said, "You can't let me down. Obey God, and don't let yourself or your children down – they are the ones who matter."

With that she headed toward the convenience store and Chris continued on his way with me trailing close behind. "Do you think she will do as you said?" I asked.

Chris shrugged. "There is a lot of temptation there. The amount she will take home will be well over half a million dollars. Her instructions were implicit, but will be difficult, especially giving all the leftovers to charity in five years." Chris added, "However, if she does obey, this will be nothing in comparison to how God will bless her in the future. If she does not, it wouldn't be the worst thing God has forgiven."

As we went on, more and more people started to gather around and to speak with us. On the way to the house we had seen quite a few, especially in 'the neighborhood', but this was no comparison. By the time we had gone five blocks, it was obvious that the word had got around about Chris because the crowd around us was six deep in every direction. I would say that they were from all walks of life, but that isn't the truth. The truth is that they were mostly hookers, drunks, junkies, and even the sick – hoping to be helped out of the circumstances in which they found themselves, much self-inflicted.

There were also the accusatory voices screaming 'blasphemy' and 'fraud' and 'charlatan' but they were drowned out by the shouts of joy when those Chris touched felt his healing power go through them.

Then we came to a city park and Chris perched on the back of a bench while the crowd sat on the lawn in front of him. He raised his hands to silence them, then began to speak.

"It is written that your bodies are temples of the Holy Spirit and yet many of you have intentionally defiled, and are in the process of destroying that temple. You poison yourselves with alcohol, drugs and junk food and by doing so are virtually tearing down the walls of your body – no less than the Romans did to the Temple in Jerusalem about two thousand years ago. Why do you insist on desecrating that which God has created and has given to you for your good? That which was formed in the image of God Himself?

"Do you think I admonish you about this because I want you to have no fun, or to not enjoy your life? Not at all! I am telling you these things so that you can enjoy the best things of life, not dull your senses through the pursuits of pleasure and excesses.

"What could feel better than the embrace of a loved one or a child? What could taste better than a healthy meal? Why alter your consciousness when it is a gift of God? If life becomes unbearable and you need to escape, change your life! Each and every one of you possesses that power deep within yourself, since you are created in the image of God Himself!

"Do not embrace evil, but flee from it! Goodness is not boring, but evil is painful and is the source of much agony of the flesh, the mind and the spirit. Who finds true happiness in drugs or drunkenness or gluttony? Those might bring temporary happiness, but in the long run cause physical ruin with pain, mental agony and emotional darkness.

"There are some of you who engage in such behavior because you suffer from low self esteem, and think you are not worthy of the best things in life. However, if God deems you worthy of his love how is it that you can think you're not worthy of his blessings and the best things in life?"

Then he stood and walked among them, bending down and touching them, comforting them with a kind word until each had been attended to. Then he turned to them and said, "Go in peace, serve the Lord and one another!"

It was getting dark as we left the park. Chris mentioned, "You haven't really said a lot. So, other than it being a full day, what did you think?"

"About?" I said.

"Oh," Chris said. "The whole thing. Something you could get used to?"

"I am still trying to get my head wrapped around it, to be honest." I said. I paused for a few minutes and ran the day's happenings through my mind then said, only half apprehensively, "Get used to? You mean we are going to do more of this?" Were the truth to be told, I couldn't remember feeling more excited and alive than I had since college.

"Why do you think I recruited you?" Chris asked. "For your quick wit and humor?"

We walked for a while in silence and then I just had to ask. "So we are going to be doing more of this?"

"Yes, Scooter, we are, and many other things," he said.

We turned the corner near the diner. "Go get something to eat," Chris told me. "I will be back, shortly."

I went in and Ronni brought me a glass of water, a cup of coffee and a menu. Tonight I had the pulled pork sandwich and was going to order a soda, but remembered what Chris had told the people in the park.

After about forty-five minutes, I saw the car belonging to the thug at the building pull up in front and park. When I saw the guy from the warehouse exit it, I started to panic, until I saw Chris calmly get out of the other side.

They came in and sat at the table with me. When Ronni brought them water, coffee and menus Chris stopped her. "Ronni, Scooter, I want you to meet Moe. He is going to be joining us," he said.

"Joining you?" Moe protested. "I never said I was going to join you."

"You never said you wouldn't," Chris said. "The way I see it, your options are pretty limited – joining up will keep you alive, and the alternative? I am guessing not so much. However, you do always have the option. So, what do you say?"

Moe chuckled. "Does the offer come with a slice of apple pie a la mode as a signing bonus?"

The mood went from jovial to subdued as each of us ordered a piece of pie, then sat in silence thinking about the things we had seen and done. Ronni returned, sat the coffee pot on the table, and joined us.

I looked around and realized that aside from our table there was no one else in the joint.

Chris looked at Ronni and said, "I know you only have a two bedroom apartment and that Scott is in the other bedroom, but Moe is going to need a place to stay. Can he crash on your couch tonight?"

She opened her mouth as if to protest when Chris cut her off. "I am already working on something else and I guarantee that it will only be tonight."

"Okay," Ronni said apprehensively.

Then Chris addressed the whole group:

"I hope you realize by now that you have been called to be part of something bigger than you can understand or will ever be able to conceive in your minds. You will be heralded and condemned; you will be called famous and infamous; blessed and cursed; faithful and heretics; healers and murderers; honorable and liars; good and evil. You will be attacked physically, mentally, spiritually and emotionally. Your enemies will come from all sides and your friends and families will disown you.

"You will see things, which you cannot even begin to comprehend and do things you, cannot imagine. Always remember, however, that whatever I ask you to do, whatever you encounter and whatever you take on, you are in service to the One Living God, the Creator of the universe and He will protect you.

"Your position is higher than the prophets of old and you now command an unseen and unnumbered legion of angels. You now have powers beyond comprehension, so be careful what you say, what you do and for what you ask because it will be done.

"Do not be afraid, because fear is a tool of the enemy. You will be tested and tried, and yes, you will fail because you are human. Do not be discouraged or dismayed because of your failures, but instead keep your eye on me, follow me and in all things trust God, He will never desert nor condemn you, but instead will bless you and protect you."

We all stood, held hands and Chris led us in prayer.

"Heavenly Father, magnificent creator of the

universe and sustainer of all things, we come before you today as unworthy servants who have sinned against you and nature in all manners of actions, by what we have done and by what we have left undone and we humbly ask your forgiveness.

"We thank You for all the blessings You have given us, including ourselves – body, mind and soul – and offer them back in servitude as living sacrifices to You and to all others we encounter. We thank You for feeding us, clothing us, and giving us all the things necessary for life.

"We ask You to bless us and those we serve, that You keep us safe from physical and spiritual harm so we may do service to others and what is pleasing to You."

Then we went back to eating our pie as the diner began filling again with hungry patrons.

Chapter 7 - The Second Gospel According to Veronica

It had been nearly a month since the day the warehouse burned. That night Scott slept in the guest room and Moe on the couch, but the next morning Chris had news. As he had told us, the brother of one of his friends had a 50-unit apartment complex which was about half full and desperately in need of management.

Chris had made a deal with him for seven of the two bedroom units in exchange for building management. Personally I had never heard of such an arrangement, but it worked for us and seemed to work for the owner and it certainly wasn't the first thing which had happened that I didn't understand, nor would it be the last.

It was a nice apartment complex, dated and not well maintained, but with 'good bones' and located in a reasonably decent neighborhood. We all went to work cleaning the place inside and out. Chris and Scott did the maintenance work – repairs, painting, etc, - while Moe and I took care of the grounds and landscaping. I was surprised that a hardened gangster like Moe actually knew his way around plants and flowers, and it was both refreshing and reassuring to see him in a nurturing mode.

The first day we visited the apartment complex, Chris assigned the manager's apartment (which was the largest and best maintained) to me. I protested because I still had a lease, but Chris told me not to worry, but to speak to my building manager and he was sure that the super would understand.

I was nervous when I approached him, but the nervousness was wasted because he had been notified that morning that the building had been sold and the new owners wanted to schedule it for demolition meaning that he had to ask the tenants to leave. I moved to the new apartment that weekend.

Since then I have been kind of the 'den mother' for the team. I do grocery shopping, cooking and wind up being the domestic director, for lack of a better term. I still work at the diner, but since I pay no rent, the money goes toward my contribution to the group to help buy groceries, pay utilities, etc. We all pitch in – Moe has his SUV so he takes care of transportation, and Chris always seems to come up with a way to get gas and to pay for maintenance and/or repairs.

Scott just does everything else needed. He takes care of the team when Chris is needed elsewhere in addition to helping him around the complex. He also performs management duties like making sure the bills get paid and handling all of the other business type issues.

I asked Chris why we needed seven units, and he said not to worry, that they wouldn't go to waste - which prompted me to ask just how large he expected the team to be. He just smiled, winked and said, "I don't know … what do you think of twelve?" After the other two heard that, there was a running joke about Scott, Moe and me that we were Chris's 'disciples.' Whenever Chris would overhear us, he wouldn't say a word but rather just smile and go back to whatever he was doing.

In the days following, the rental units filled up as soon as soon as Chris and Scott could get them ready for occupancy. The people moving in were mostly young couples with small children who wanted to take advantage of the inexpensive rent as well as getting a decent and safe place to live.

Chris continued to amaze. He was like a man in

perpetual motion, stopping only for short periods of sleep – maybe four hours at a time, tops. When he wasn't working on the building, he was going out and meeting people, teaching people, and healing people. He would usually take one or two of us with him at a time, but just trying to keep up with him was almost impossible. A lot of people have taken to calling him 'Teacher,' because of the impromptu lessons he taught.

We all got to help with Chris's mission of healing, although we were as much his students as anyone else. Some of the things I saw and some of the things I did were unbelievable to me and even though I had been witnessing his acts for month, I never failed to be amazed by him. The healing of addictions, birth defects, injuries and debilitating diseases were now a common occurrence, and the curing of diseases previously considered untreatable, including stage-four melanoma and HIV, were only slightly less common.

The effect he had on the community was nothing short of miraculous. The changes I had seen in people after just a word or just a touch from Chris were mind-boggling. Hard core junkies were becoming productive members of society, petty criminals now doing random acts of kindness, tough-as-nails hookers paying attention to their families, spending time and energy with their children as well as the children of others.

We had our detractors, as well. One time when Chris was teaching in the park, a gay rights advocate confronted him.

"Teacher," he said, "tell us once and for all that homosexuality isn't a sin!"

"Homosexuality in itself isn't a sin," Chris said, "but I wish that I could tell you the same about engaging in homosexual acts."

"But," the advocate protested. "That is how God made me! Why would God give me this nature if it were sinful?"

"You may have indeed been born that way, but that is not how God made you, it is how man made you. You see, sin entered the world through one man, Adam, and now permeates itself though all of his descendants, all human flesh and all of mankind. It was Adam who made you that way, not God."

Before the advocate could respond, Chris cut him off. "Because all men born of Adam's seed are sinful you are no better nor worse than any other, it has just manifested itself in a different way than with others. Your sins are no greater nor any less than any other man, even if others condemn you through their own insecurity."

Then Chris turned to the crowd and said, "The good news, for this gentleman and for everyone of you is that not only are you forgiven but as Paul wrote, "Therefore, there is now no condemnation for those who are in Christ Jesus, because through Christ Jesus the law of the Spirit who gives life has set you free from the law of sin and death."

Then he continued. "There are those among you who will say that in order to receive this complete grace from God, there is something else required of you. Some would have to say to this man that he must change his ways, give up living with the person he loves and deny his own nature, but to you I ask, what part of "there is no condemnation" do you not understand? If that person believes that Jesus died and was resurrected for the forgiveness of his sins, there is nothing else to be required. Any other actions thought of as necessary do nothing but detract from the completeness of grace, and the significance of Jesus' sacrifice.

"To those who might say differently, I won't ask again what part of what part of 'now there is no condemnation' you don't understand, but rather why you think that you are in a better position to judge what is fair and what is not, than God himself? If God does not condemn them, then do you think you know better? Don't you realize that the original sin wasn't the actual eating of the fruit of the tree of the knowledge of good and evil, but rather wanting to be like God or to put man on the same level?

"It is written that Satan, in the form of a serpent, tempted Eve by saying 'For God knows that when you eat from it your eyes will be opened, and you will be like God, knowing good and evil.' That is the true sin, wanting to be like God, or even in some cases thinking that you know more or can make better decisions than He. Remember, He is the one who created you, so who are we to question?

"Instead of being angry that someone might not have to pay sufficiently for his sins, or jealous that they might 'get away with something,' instead thank God that there is no condemnation for you and your sins as well as for the other and his! This is why Jesus commanded us to not judge one another, because one who judges will be judged by the same standard which they use."

During this time both our team and our community grew. The 'team' is what we call the inner circle of people who are responsible for conducting the 'mission,' while 'the community' consists of those around us who are served by us. People would come and join us for a while, living in our units and enjoying our fellowship, and then leave again.

Chris refused no one, but soon we could tell by how he interacted with them who would stay and who would leave. He told us that his time was limited, and he wanted to spend more time and effort with those who would eventually become team members than those who would not, but I never heard of anyone who complained that Chris somehow slighted him.

There was one young woman, Melissa, who came and I found it to be great fun to have some female interaction around the place. She had moved to the city from somewhere in Arkansas to escape a bad marriage where she not only married too young, but her husband, too, was too young and soon got bored with her. As young men do, he found another woman, this one worldlier, with tattoos, face piercings and a plethora of exotic sexual skills, and he left Melissa with nothing to show for her time but an STD.

Shortly after she joined our little group a young man by the name of Alejandro started to serve with us, but it didn't take long before they became more interested in each other than the mission. Chris married them in an intimate but beautiful ceremony, helped Alejandro find work and they moved into one of the apartments.

Even with everything else going on, Chris still washes the dishes at Mario's every night. He says he likes it because it gives him time to center himself and think, and he likes the clean feeling of the dishes and his hands when he finishes.

One evening as we were walking home I could tell that Chris was deep in thought and asked him about it. He sighed and said, "This country, these people; they say they believe in God and follow Jesus, but what they say and what they do are two different things. Jesus, when He was on the earth saved humanity and didn't condemn it, even though He had every right, every justification, to do so.

"However, these so-called Christians condemn others at every turn in some kind of completely unjustified act of self-righteousness; as if they are somehow better than another person, when in reality they are just as bad in the eyes of God, if not worse. They easily recognize the sins of violence, sexual immorality and lying, but completely ignore – if not celebrate – the sins of theft and coveting.

"When God commanded Moses 'You shall not covet' He meant that one should trust in the Lord for all their worldly needs, be content in what he has been given and not pursue material things because someone else might have them. When Jesus was on the earth, He taught, "Do not store up for yourselves treasures on earth, where moths and vermin destroy, and where thieves break in and steal. But store up for yourselves treasures in heaven, where moths and vermin do not destroy, and where thieves do not break in and steal. For where your treasure is, there your heart will be also."

Then he turned to me and asked, "Don't people realize that by pursuing these things and trusting in them, it is akin to idol worship? If they believe that material things will make them happy, then they are both deceiving themselves and pushing away God?"

I had no answer, and I considered the question rhetorical, so we walked the rest of the way home in silence. When we got there Chris asked me to call together the rest of the team and have them meet him in the manager's office. When I asked him why, he said he was going to unveil the next phase of our mission, so I put out the word, and made some coffee. I had a feeling it was going to be a long night.

James Cory Michaels

Chapter 8 - The Gospel According to Buzz

I was sitting in my office when the phone rang. When I answered it was the Mayor's secretary on the line to tell me I was late to a meeting about which I had no prior knowledge. I swallowed some frustration because I already knew that is pretty much how things work around here, like it or otherwise, so I grabbed my black leather bound portfolio, checked for a pen and headed down the hall.

I have been working as political consultant for the Mayor since he first ran for City Council some twelve years ago, and this year we are running for a second term, so the happenings around the city are especially important right now, as is how people are perceiving it and how it is reflecting in the polls. Me, I am the Mayor's primary political consultant complete with my own office and a placard on the door that reads, "Robert 'Buzz' Andrews – Special Consultant."

As a political consultant, I have worked on many different elections at many different levels, including inside the inner circle of two Presidential campaigns. Personally, I would never run for office, because there is no money in public service – not compared to politics, that is. I am not, for the most part, paid by the public as much as I am paid by the campaigns. The stipend I am paid by the city in the Mayor's office, for instance, would be better than a decent wage for most people, but in my case it doesn't even pay my taxes.

No, the money is in the political machine. For instance, look at the last Presidential election cycle – each of the final candidates had spent more than a billion dollars for a job which pays just $1.6 million over four years. A good political consultant makes that in six months, and I am better than good.

Not to mention that holding elected office significantly cuts back on the types of gifts, loans and other types of income that comes your way, which may or may not even show up on anyone's books. In my case I may take a golfing vacation in Scotland, and never pay a dime – not even for gifts I bring home. Maybe it will be a Mediterranean getaway or a month on an island in the Caribbean. I usually like the Cayman Islands, because I can almost always find a nice deposit in my personal account there when I arrive. Yes, I have the perfect job – a lot of money, a lot of power and a lot of influence, plus all of the sex that goes with them, and I am never in the spotlight or in some reporter's gun sights, having to answer the difficult questions.

As I said I have worked on campaigns for national office, but I prefer where I am now. There is way too much scrutiny put on the workings of the federal government, and the sharks swimming in those waters will soon dwarf someone like me. In my little 'pond', here, there is much less public oversight and bureaucracy and the city's budget is still well over fifty billion dollars, spawning a lot more opportunities for quid-pro-quo situations and a lot less chance of those situations being discovered. Yeah, keep me at city politics forever – as long as it is a large city.

When I walked in to the meeting, the office was virtually vibrating with excitement. We knew that there had been a reduction in crime over the past few weeks, but we had no idea how much until the reports came in a few days ago.

These numbers were only over a four week period which might throw them off, but to be honest, they are nothing short of amazing - especially considering that we are going into the warmer summer months when crime statistics usually go up. The numbers shook out like this: Violent crime (-82%); Assault (-86%); Homicide (-94%); Rape (-79%); Robbery (-77%); Drug related crime (-91%); Prostitution arrests (-96%). The Mayor's initial reaction was nothing short of ecstasy and we all heralded these as great news—until we got the rest of the story, that is. Only 9% of people surveyed credited the police and city officials for the reduction, while 73% named the cause was some street preacher by the name of Chris Pawlinsky. His followers also knew him as 'Teacher.'

"Buzz," the Mayor started as I entered his lavishly appointed office. Dark rich wood tones accentuated the expensive imported rugs. On those rugs was expensive imported furniture, the cabinets of which held expensive imported liquors of all brands and kinds. "What do you know about this street preacher known as 'Teacher'?"

I looked around the office and noted the presence of the Chief of Police, the Vice-Mayor, two City Councilmen, and the Mayor's personal secretary, a striking brunette stacked like the proverbial brick house and who wore her dresses just a little too tight making her the butt of many office jokes about 'dictation.'

"Not a lot," I reported. "He surfaced about a couple months or so ago down in the combat zone. I had a couple people ask some questions, but he seemed harmless enough since it seems he has no political agenda at all."

"Everyone has some kind of a political agenda," the Mayor said, cutting me off.

"Well, in this case it doesn't really seem so, although…"

The Mayor raised his eyebrows.

"…there were some rumors that he had something to do with the fire that destroyed the drug warehouse down there a few weeks ago."

"What kind of rumors?" the Mayor asked as the Police Chief leaned forward, attentively.

"Well, they are pretty unbelievable," I said. "The word on the street is that this guy started it by just snapping his fingers, or something."

The Mayor turned to the Chief with a panicked expression. "Is that possible?"

The Chief leaned back and rolled his eyes and you could tell by the expression on his face that he knew the Mayor was no Mensa candidate. "No, sir, that wouldn't be possible - a coincidence, at best," he said. "The city Fire Marshal completely investigated the incident and ruled that it was an electrical fire, started by some kind of short in the office—a coffee pot or something."

The Mayor looked relieved. I had known the man for years and knew he wasn't the sharpest knife in the drawer but I had worked with him to conceal that from the public as much as possible. I was glad that those in hearing distance were political allies.

He continued with the Chief. "So, what do you know about him?"

The Chief sat up. "Like Buzz said, sir, not a lot. He walks around town talking to people a lot. More and more it seems like a crowd of people will gather around him, then he will stop and give them some kind of instruction. 'Lessons for Life' is what I hear the people call them."

"Crowds of people..." the Mayor mused. "How big are these crowds?"

"Well, sir," the Chief said. "They started out being just a few dozen or so, but they get bigger all the time. Mostly they are usually a few hundred, but recently I have heard the numbers estimated at as many as two thousand."

"Two thousand?" one of the Councilmen said. "Doesn't he need a permit for that many?"

"Technically, yes," the Chief said. "But they have been very impromptu, short lived and, to be honest, no one has yet to complain."

The Mayor perked up. "No one has called to complain about crowds of two thousand people blocking traffic, impeding commerce or just being a nuisance?"

"Not as of now," the Chief confirmed. "We could take a closer look at his operation and start ticketing and/or arresting them for violations of city code on our own, though."

"Let's hold off on that for the time being," the Mayor said, "until we know more about this man."

The Mayor turned back to me, holding a piece of paper in each hand. "We have this really great news about the crime rates, Buzz, but I can't take advantage of it because the people give the credit to this guy 'Chris' instead of our great police force, with the support of City Hall. Now, how can we turn this around to our advantage? These are some pretty powerful numbers, but what's the use if we can't use them for our re-election campaign?"

To the benefit of a safer city? I thought.

"Well," I said. "We could run an ad campaign and make it appear as though we are taking credit, without actually doing so. You know, shout them from the rooftops so to speak and say we approve the message creating a link, but never actually say that we caused them."

"That's one strategy," the Mayor said, "but it also might backfire on us. I think it would be better if we could get some kind of statement or maybe even an endorsement from this guy, don't you think?"

"Well, sir," I said. "We really should find out more before we crawl into bed with this group or ask them to do so with us. What if it comes out that this preacher is some kind of seedy character or cult leader or mixed up with some groups with whom we don't want to be linked, later? I'll tell you what, give me twenty-four hours to check out this guy and come up with a strategy, okay? After all, that is what you pay me for."

"Fine," the Mayor said. "You have twenty-four hours. What else do you need from us? Maybe the assistance of a police investigator?"

I shook my head. "No, sir, let me try this by myself. Then, if that doesn't work out we can do so with our internal assets before we really have to go anywhere else, in order to keep it as low profile as possible. After all, police involvement might carry with it some unintended consequences."

The Chief looked like he was going to say something, and then changed his mind.

"Then we will adjourn this meeting until tomorrow at the same time," the Mayor said. "At which time Buzz will give us a full report. Until then I want everyone – except the Chief, since it just wouldn't be appropriate – to come up with possible strategies how we can capitalize on these great numbers."

With that the meeting broke up. As I walked back to my office, I thought about the best way to do this. Since most of the reports about this preacher and his group were from the combat zone, I would probably start looking for them there, and maybe I could even figure out a way to talk to the man himself. As I caught my reflection in the window I remembered that I was wearing my usual business suit and tie, and would stick out like a sore thumb just about anywhere outside of the downtown area.

I had to figure out something quick because I didn't really have the time to go home and change, especially if it was going to be difficult to locate this street preacher. Then I remembered the running suit I had put in the trunk of the car to jog with the Mayor on 'City Fitness Day', about a month ago. I had never used it, and it was still in a bag in the trunk of my car, just waiting to escape. I ran to the parking garage, grabbed the bag from the trunk and headed to the nearest men's room to quickly change and head out for my adventure.

Even though it had been in a bag in the trunk for over a month, the running suit didn't really look that bad when I put it on. The suit was made of nylon, the t-shirt had been folded and all the clothes were freshly laundered so even though I wasn't in business attire, I was every bit publically acceptable if I ran into someone I knew. I checked myself out in the mirror before heading back to the car with a nearly empty bag in one hand, and a suit, tie and shirt on a hanger in the other.

As I left the parking garage I started thinking about the last time I had ventured to the combat zone. The difference was that it had been after dark instead of the middle of the day, and I had been looking for something very much different than a street preacher. As I got closer I realized that I was driving a very expensive luxury car to a very unsavory part of town, and while I was hoping that nothing would happen to it, I was also thinking that I probably shouldn't have increased the deductible on comprehensive coverage, regardless of the advice of my financial manager.

When I turned into the area and thinking about calling my agent, just in case, I noticed quite a difference from the last time I was in the neighborhood. At first I thought maybe it was because I was there in the middle of the day and it looked different at night, but then I changed my mind. No, the streets were just as full of people the last time as well, but this time instead of being populated by mean, dirty, angry street people, the people I saw seemed happier and much healthier.

I looked to my left and was surprised to see stores with their windows unboarded and doors wide open. To my right were young mothers sitting on park benches, casually chatting with other mothers as they watching their children play in the open with other children. Then I saw a man I recognized. I used to encounter him from time to time, on the street uptown, dirty and smelly and panhandling for spare change. Today, though, he was clean, shaven, wearing decent clothes and pushing a broom in front of a local grocery.

I found the parking garage I had used before pretty easily, and when I pulled in I immediately noticed new paint and a surprising absence of graffiti and gang 'tats' where they used to be, adorning the walls. When I handed my keys to the attendant, he actually smiled and thanked me for parking with them. I felt like I had been transported to a different planet or an alternate plane of existence.

As I exited the garage, a modestly but cleanly dressed middle-aged white man approached me. He offered his hand and said, "Mr. Andrews? My name is Scott Hansen. Chris Pawlinsky told me to meet you here and bring you to him. He is expecting you." After shaking my hand he led me off down the street to meet this man who wasn't even supposed to know I was coming.

I was flabbergasted. Here I was on this clandestine mission that wasn't even thought about until about a half-hour ago, and I am met at the parking garage by a guy who not only calls me by name, but acts like we had a long standing appointment for lunch or something. It was then that a feeling of paranoia started engulfing me and I began to wonder how sophisticated this guy's organization was, how long they had been in operation, and who his mole was in the office was.

About that time this Scott Hansen fellow turns to me and says, "Either you hide it well or expected me to meet you."

"What do you mean?" I said.

"Well, when Chris asked me to come and get you, he didn't think you would be expecting me, so I am a bit surprised that you didn't respond either negatively or at least with some modicum of curiosity."

"I was surprised," I said, "but in my business you can't ever let them see you sweat, so I have a practiced non-response." I thought that I might butter the guy up a bit, so I lied. "I hadn't expected my poker face to work out so well with you, though."

Amused, Scott looked at me and said, "Hanging out with Chris lets you see and experience a lot of things you normally wouldn't expect."

He stopped at the door of a seedy-looking dive bar, opened the door, and motioned me inside. "Chris is waiting for you." He said it as if we were in an office building and this were an everyday occurrence.

I stepped inside and the door closed behind me. The place was dark and smelled of stale beer and old cigarette smoke, but it was both air conditioned and had fans turning, and the cool air on my skin made me conscious of how much I had been sweating.

As my eyes adjusted to the lack of light, I saw a figure rise from one of the tables and approach me to shake my hand. "Mr. Andrews? My name is Chris Pawlinsky. I understand that you are looking for me and have some questions."

I realized that even though I didn't know what to expect, I certainly didn't expect a street preacher from the roughest neighborhood in town to look like this. Standing before me was a clean-shaven young man with bright eyes and an unruly mop of curly hair piled on the top of his head. He was dressed in a simple white t-shirt, jeans and running shoes – clean and presentable, but otherwise completely unimpressive. Under other circumstances, I would have never given him a second glance.

"Please excuse the accommodations," he said, "but I really don't have any place to meet people. This place is quiet, safe and comfortable and we won't be disturbed. Now, how can I help you?"

As I sat down, I looked around and realized that we

were alone in the place. "I forget my manners," I said. "Please call me Buzz, my father is Mr. Andrews. May I call you Chris?"

"If you called me anything else, I might not answer," he chuckled as he took a seat. "Although I have been called a lot of other things. My father, for example, used to call me dipstick when I exasperated him."

"You, too?" I said. We both laughed.

"Before we get started, I want you to rest assured that there is no one else hiding here, and that our conversation is not being recorded or monitored by anyone except us. Now, you're a golfing man, right?"

"Yes," I said.

"Good, I don't have a lot of jokes, but I like this one pretty well," he said. "The Father, the Son and the Holy Ghost were playing a round of golf one day. When they got to the tee box on this particular par three, the Holy Ghost had the honors, so He hit his tee shot and it landed about a foot from the flag.

"Then, when it was the Son's turn, he hit His tee shot six inches from the cup.

"When it was the Father's turn, He shanked his shot and the ball headed out of bounds and into the woods. Just before it reached the markers, this rabbit shot out from the underbrush, caught the ball in his teeth and started running for the green. At that point an eagle dropped out of the sky, grabbed the rabbit in his talons, lifted him up, over the green and just when they were over the cup, the rabbit opened its mouth, releasing the ball and it fell right in for a hole-in-one.

"Then Jesus then turned to God the Father and said, 'Come on, Dad, it's only a game.'"

I didn't know what to do. Was this a test? If so, what kind of test was it? My mind was running a hundred miles an hour and I felt anxious and paranoid.

Was he trying to trick me into showing that I was

someone who didn't show proper reverence to God? But, if that was the case, hadn't he been the one who had told the joke, so wouldn't that mean he didn't show proper reverence?

I wondered if I should act offended, but that wouldn't be in character. After all, I hadn't even been to church in probably ten years, and that was some kind of special Christmas service in which my niece had a part. I should probably do something, but what?

As all this was going on in my head Chris just watched me. After a while I think he took pity on me so he said, "Buzz, it was a joke. You can laugh. I already told you that this is a meeting with just the two of us. What is said here is between us and stays between us."

I laughed, not knowing what else to do, but I really didn't like this, much. I had spent my entire adult life playing in the political arena where every move was anticipated and a response planned, but this guy was two steps ahead of me and it made me very uncomfortable. He was direct and honest, nothing you ever encounter in politics, and I just was completely out of my element. The laughter died and an uncomfortable silence settled over the bar.

Then Chris broke the silence. "Yes, I was expecting you and I know why you're here, but there is no mole in your office staff. If you look for one, not only will you waste your time, you will also be wasting their good will. The crime numbers are great, but for once the public got it right. If your boss tries to spin them, or take credit for them, it will go against him. If I try to give him credit, then my credibility will be as bad as his, and so I really can't help you. Sorry."

I took in what he had said and quickly figured out an angle. "So, you are saying that you are taking full credit for cleaning up the streets of this great city all on your own? That public officials like our great police officers and upstanding Mayor had absolutely nothing to do with it?"

Chris chuckled. "I heard you were a master at the spin, but watching you in action is really something else. In case you missed it, I have not taken credit for anything. Have you heard me make a public statement, seen me hold a press conference, or even read a letter I wrote to the editor?"

I shrugged. "But by not giving credit to others aren't you actually taking all the credit, yourself, by omission?"

Chris laughed again, "So by doing nothing, you are saying that I am doing something? You are good."

Having an opening, I was going to work it. "You are a smart man, so you have to realize that the police of this city put their lives on the line every day to fight crime and protect the public. They do this for little pay and virtually no respect, and you want to take even this little bit of recognition away from them? How can you say that you represent the little people of this city and not even consider those who serve them daily?"

Chris had an astonished look on his face. "Wow! I don't remember saying that I represented any person, large or small. I know many of your police officers, personally – probably more than you do – and I can attest that they, for the most part, get the respect that they deserve.

"In addition, the police of this city are well paid in comparison to most cities. Their 'off the books' incomes are in the process of being cut significantly, though, considering that the ones paying it are soon not going to be able to afford it or need the police to look the other way if these trends continue."

"Are you accusing the police of taking bribes?"

"Are you saying that there are no police officers on the take?" he shot back. "Because if so, and it is on the record, I would love to quote you on that, just before I introduce you to three who are and currently are within a two block radius from this very location!"

He had deflected my verbal thrust and immediately went on the counter attack. Nice. I decided to try a different strategy.

"Okay," I said. "Then what about working together? Maybe you could attend a press conference where the Mayor thanks you for your work, and in return you let it be known that those numbers are not all your doing and thank him and the police for their efforts?"

Chris just looked at me and after several seconds of uncomfortable silence (which seemed like hours), I decided I might try to sweeten the pot. "We might be able to add a cash award or find a cushy, well paid position for you on the Mayor's personal staff."

He shook his head. "First you twist my words, then you accuse me of not supporting the police, and now you are offering me a bribe? Is this, by any chance, what is commonly referred to as a race to the bottom?"

"I wouldn't offer a bribe," I said. "I would consider it more of a quid pro quo offer."

Chris looked at me with a combination of sadness and exasperation, like he was speaking to a first grader. "Buzz," he said. "You have absolutely nothing I want. Money, power, pleasures of the flesh are not what I am about, regardless of what you call them."

"The bottom line is that your poll numbers are rapidly going up as well as your public recognition," I said, resigned. "If nothing else, could you at least endorse the Mayor's candidacy in the upcoming election?"

Chris gave me a serious look and said, "I won't endorse him or anyone else. I have no political plans or agenda, nor do I foresee any changes anytime in the future. Understand this, I am not about power or money and am really no political threat to the Mayor or anyone else. You know as well as anyone that polls and opinions are as fickle as the weather. By election day, the Mayor might see an endorsement from me as something to avoid, not seek out."

I flashed back to telling the Mayor almost those exact words.

He stood, and the meeting was over. "Now if you will excuse me, I think we both have better things to do. Please extend my apologies to His Honor, and God bless you."

I stood up, shook his hand and left the bar. It took a moment or two for my eyes to adjust to the bright daylight but when they did, I saw the man who introduced himself as Scott leaning against the wall, waiting for me. Without a word he righted himself, fell in step and escorted me the distance back to the garage in silence. When we got there, Scott offered his hand and said, "It was nice meeting you, Mr. Andrews."

I flashed my best smile as I took his hand. "Please call me Buzz. And you are, Scott, right?"

He smiled back at me like most people do when they feel like they are deemed important enough to have their name remembered, "Yes, that is correct. Scott Hansen."

I saw another opening. "Do you have just a quick moment?"

"Sure," he said. "It isn't like I punch a clock around here."

"I'm curious," I said. "How exactly is your group organized, and what is your position within the organization?"

"Organization?" He chuckled. "It is more like a dis-organization, and I really don't have a position per se. Chris calls us his friends and we refer to ourselves as a team."

I decided to bait him. "Oh?" I said. "So you must be pretty close to the bottom of the totem pole to have to play babysitter to someone like me."

"We don't have a top or a bottom, sir," he gently

explained. "We just are. Chris is the leader, obviously, but that just is. He is fantastic and most of the time can handle everything himself. The rest of us just do what he asks and pitch in to help him out the best we can."

I knew this guy; he had the look. He was upper middle class, well spoken, decently educated so probably well read and the type who is always looking for a bigger, better deal.

"That doesn't really lend itself to an opportunity for advancement, does it?" I said. "Must be hard on an obviously intelligent and talented man such as yourself. You have your degree in what … business management?"

He lit up. "An MBA from Columbia, actually."

"Really?" I realized that I had a live one on the line. Now, to make up a name, "Did you know Jack Thompson?"

Jack Thompson was a name I used when I needed one. It was common enough, and sounded sufficiently WASPish that could be from any walk of life, including an MBA.

Scott thought for a moment. "No," he said. "I can't say that I did, but that isn't unusual."

I knew this was a great opportunity. Even if Chris didn't have a mole in my organization, that didn't mean I couldn't have one in his.

"Well, his was a pretty sad story, to be honest." I was making this up as I was going along, "He got involved with this group of young people and wound up losing everything. House, cars, money, boat, wife, kids, the whole nine yards. I understand that it was some kind of midlife crisis, or something."

"That happens." Scott said with little or no emotion in his voice.

Now was the time to probe a little more. "Now, how did you get mixed up with this new-age hippy, Jesus freak group?" I asked.

"Chris approached me, actually," he said. "But I wouldn't really describe our group as new-age, hippies, or Jesus freaks. While it includes people from all walks of life, including those you describe, it really transcends all of them and winds up being something completely different."

"Okay, then," I said. "How would you describe it?"

"I've given that some thought, actually, and am not sure how. So, instead, I choose not to stick a label on it. It really isn't necessary for it to have a label, is it?"

He had just thrown up a small roadblock. "No," I said, "I suppose not." Now it was time to retake the offensive, "So, what causes an MBA to join an organization with no structure, no opportunity for advancement, and limited or no future? I'll bet the pay is minimum wage, at best."

"No, there is no pay, but I am fine with it."

"What is it, then? It's got to be something. Maybe some good access to young trim?" I said, mockingly. "It has to be something for a top drawer gentleman like you to waste his life with something like this. Tell you what: I know some people and could help you out, secure a good job with a good paycheck and introduce you to the right people … if you think you might find it possible to help me out with a small problem."

"What I like the best about our little group is the honesty we practice," he said. "There is no pretension, no politics and no games. You see, Buzz, you don't need to have a midlife crisis to lose it all. I played the game, worked hard, kept clean, did things the right way, and then one morning I woke up to find that not only had the rules changed, the whole game had changed and everything I did, everything I had accomplished meant nothing."

Here I thought I had this guy, and not only did he wiggle off the hook, he wasn't done with me by a long shot.

"I don't know what you want, and I care less,

Buzzy," he said loudly. "But the answer is no. It ain't happening, regardless of what incentive you might offer. You chose the wrong guy, this time."

I was caught and I wanted to run. Then his demeanor changed one hundred and eighty degrees.

"Have a good drive back to the office." He smiled at me and added, "God bless."

I reached in my pocket, "Let me at least give you a card if you change your mind..."

"No need," Scott said, with his palm held up like a cop stopping traffic. "If I need you, I know where to find you" and then added with a sly grin, "until November, anyway."

With that he turned on his heel and walked back in the direction of the bar.

When I turned around, the car was already there so I paid my bill and left a good tip. On the way back to the office I was reflecting on my little adventure and realized that the only thing I had accomplished while down here was to get a clearer picture of what we were dealing with. Now the challenge was to figure out a strategy, prepare a proposal and present it to the Mayor the next day.

The next morning I found myself back in the Mayor's office. Everyone had arrived on time as instructed and all the same players were there except the Chief. It was what could be best described as a totally political meeting.

"Okay, Buzz," the Mayor began. "Tell us what you found out about this street preacher and his cult of minions."

"Honestly, your Honor?" I said. "I don't really think that is an appropriate way to describe them. Although I am not sure what is the best way to describe them. The leader is not much more than a kid, 25 or 30, and he pretty much looks like any other twenty something. He has no criminal record, has no known criminal associates or aliases, and has never been in the system. He is well spoken, polite, very savvy, and comes across as someone with a lot of integrity."

The Mayor laughed. "That sounds like how you are supposed to make the public think of me, Buzz. Maybe we are seeing some kind of political threat on the horizon."

"While I would consider him a potential threat, he assured me that he has no political aspirations, sir."

"Everyone," he corrected me, "has some kind of political aspiration. Did you approach him with the idea of teaming up together?"

"Yes, sir," I said. "He shut me down completely."

"Okay, then," the Mayor said. "What do you think we should do from here?"

"Ignore him for the time being and run the ad I suggested. A feel good ad, with the great things about the city, and use the crime numbers as just one more great thing. Let's keep a close eye on him though, and see what happens in the next few weeks."

"Okay," the Mayor said, "let's do that, but I want everyone in the room to find out what you can about this kid and this group. The more we know, the more information we have, the better it will be for everyone."

The Mayor looked at me. "You better be sure of this, Buzz. We are going to do this your way, but if things start going badly, remember that you are the one with his neck on the line."

My collar suddenly felt a little tight.

Chapter 9 - The Gospel According to Linda

It had been one hell of a day and retail therapy was definitely in order. The summer was coming on strong and the heat of the day had contributed to the day being less than enjoyable, despite having spent eight hours in an air conditioned office. The boss was making everyone's life miserable, the customers were extra demanding, and it just seemed like everything was less than optimal and more difficult and complicated than it needed to be.

After a day like that, just the act of turning off the highway and into the mall parking lot made me feel better. I seemed to breathe easier just being there. Then, just as I got to the best parking space in the lot, it opened up and I pulled right in and even better, the car next to mine was a compact and not some oversized SUV or pickup. The heat from the sidewalk was intense but only momentary, and in no time the mall's air conditioning units were wafting cool air over my bare legs and under my skirt, chasing away cares brought on by a miserable day at the office.

The mall, to me, was nothing less than a wonderland. Entering through my favorite door, I was greeted by the smell of cinnamon and vanilla from the candle store. The passageways were airy and bright with different shades of white, silver and gold trim and lined on both sides by stores full of beautiful things just waiting to be viewed, held and dreamed about.

I knew that if I spent enough time there and looked long enough, I would find that one treasure I needed, even if I didn't know I needed it before, at the price I couldn't pass by and the successful treasure hunt would make my bad day dissolve into the ether. I picked my favorite shoe store as my first stop and my heart jumped when I walked in. Right there, on the display table in front were the cutest pair of platform sandals I have ever seen – and on sale, too! It was my lucky day!

Then I heard a voice in my head. It was the voice of the young man at the fountain near work. He was sitting on a bench talking to a group who had gathered there. He was talking about buying things we didn't need to make ourselves feel better, and he was against it.

I frowned and looked back down at the shoes. He said that by spending money on things we didn't need that we were trying to substitute those things for God...."trying to fill a God sized hole" were the words he used. He said that no matter what we bought or how much we had, it would never be enough, and that by doing so we were not only wasting what God has given us, but also not trusting in God to provide for us.

He said that we should, instead, fill our lives helping people less fortunate - helping God by helping others. He quoted Jesus from the Bible – "Whatever you have done for the least of these, you have done it for me."

I put the shoes back, and decided to try another store, and then another one after that, but no matter where I went I heard the words of that street preacher as if he was speaking directly to me. I went to the food court to have a large iced drink, but I still could not get his voice out of my head – not accusing me, but instead gently encouraging me to do something I really didn't want to do.

Finally, I got up from the table in the food court, walked to the ATM and withdrew the $100 I had budgeted for my shopping, got back in my car and drove to a homeless shelter I had passed every day on my way to work. I found a place to park and walked inside to make a donation and to see if I could make the young man's voice go away so I could shop in peace.

When I walked in I expected to see a seedy, dim and dirty place. While it was not well appointed and had no fancy furnishings, it was clean, tidy and well lit. The floors were worn linoleum tiles, but swept and mopped and were full of long, folding tables and chairs. At one end was a steam line used for serving, with plates and flatware on one end, and beverages on the other – but there was no one to be seen in the place at all.

Wanting to drop off my donation and leave I called out, but no one answered. Then I heard the unmistakable sound of pans falling to the floor and I headed toward the sound, through to the doors behind the steam line. When I entered the kitchen there was a woman on the floor trying to clean up the mess resulting from the dropped pans I had heard.

She looked at me and asked, "May I help you?"

I said without thinking, "It looks like you are the one who needs the help."

Without missing a beat, she said, "Great! I need you to grab those two cans of beans on the counter and heat them in one of the pots hanging, there." She motioned toward a stainless steel rack hanging from the wall full of large pots and pans. I grabbed a large one and headed to the counter where the industrial type gallon cans of green beans were sitting. I opened them, dumped them in the pan, put them on the stove and turned the burner just higher than the medium setting.

As soon as I was done I turned to the woman who was just finishing her cleaning chore. "Thank God it was only barbeque sauce," she said. "I hadn't put the meat in yet. Could you grab that bottle of sauce for me?"

I retrieved the bottle and took it to her as she was loading a large, square pan with pieces of meat, which could have been pork, or beef of some kind. "Mystery meat," she said, as if she were reading my mind. "Not sure what it is, but according to the USDA, it is nutritionally sound and it seems to be reasonably tasty."

The meat was already cooked so she put the loaded pan in an oven to warm and turned her attention to a boiling pot of water. Armed with a white, plastic bag labeled "Potatoes, dehydrated and reconstituted," she turned the hot water into a thick, off-white paste which ended up resembling mashed potatoes more than anything else.

"I don't know what I would have done without you," she said. "All my help tonight, bailed."

I heard the door open and an older black man walked in the kitchen. "I got the dishes, Miss Claire," he said. "Just make sure you save me a plate."

"Will do, Teddy," she said. "Thank you so very much!"

With that she pulled the beans off the burner and dumped them into another pan, very much like the one with the meat and barbeque sauce. "Would you be a dear," she said, "and grab the salad from the fridge?"

I opened the door and took the large round bowl filled with lettuce, a few cucumbers and a couple of sliced radishes and then turned to Miss Claire. "Got it, now," I said. "What do you want me to do with it?"

"Put it on the left end of the steam table by the plates and flatware."

When I stepped out, again I saw something I was not expecting. I thought I had heard people in the hall and I expected it to be filled with old men who had abused themselves with drugs and alcohol and who were about half crazy as a result. What I saw, instead, were some men, but a lot of women and children; too many children.

Some of the men were young and were obviously with their wives and children and of those most were trying not to make eye contact, obviously ashamed to be there. When I walked back in to the kitchen the look on my face must have said a lot because Claire took one look and said, "You weren't expecting that many children, were you?"

"No," I replied. "It certainly wasn't what I was expecting."

"The vast majority of the people in this country who go to bed hungry each night are under the age of twelve," she said.

We worked quickly and soon the food was on the steam table and ready to be served. Claire asked one of the older men if he would say grace before dinner, and he obliged with a practiced, smooth baritone voice. "Brother Sam used to be a minister before the gin got in the way," she explained later.

As we began serving, more young families with more children arrived. I remembered when I was a child that mom always had some kind of desert for us, even if it was just a cookie or a piece of candy, and then I remembered the money in my pocket.

"I need to run to the store real quick," I said. "Could you get someone else to help for a few minutes?"

"Sure," Claire said. "The hard work is done, now."

I ran to my car and went to a nearby grocery store, where I bought two cans of lemonade mix and as many packs of cookies as my $100 would buy. When I got back and opened the cookies, the laughter and happy squeals of children drowned out any other noise.

After dinner had been served, some of the people sat with coffee and lemonade while the children played and chased each other around the hallway. Teddy and a couple other men were cleaning up the dishes, taking out the trash and sweeping and mopping the floor.

Claire and I sat down across one of the tables from each other with Styrofoam cups of coffee. We were both tired and emotionally drained but we were smiling.

"I am so glad that God sent you to help me," she said. "You were literally the answer to a prayer....and the cookies were the highlight of the meal. Some of these children only get one meal a day, and this is it. It was a good thing you did by providing this treat."

I thought about my shopping trip, the shoes, the preacher's words, about everything and tears came to my eyes. The feeling I had from helping these people was so much better than I would have experienced if had I bought a hundred pair of shoes. I couldn't believe how much happiness something I considered so little had brought to so many.

"Yes, God sent me," I said. I told her about everything that happened to me that day, including what the street preacher had said.

Later. as I got ready to leave, Claire said, "Everyone here has a story, child, and yours is one of the best I have heard."

I was exhausted when I got home, but felt more alive than I had in years. A warm bath caressed my body and soothed my sore muscles, and that night I slept like a baby.

The next day at work I was still excited, and could speak about nothing else. The reaction from my co-workers was mixed – some excited, some skeptical. Others thought I had completely lost whatever mind I might have had left. Regardless of what anyone else thought, when I left work that evening, I drove my car immediately to the shelter—with a detour on the way for more cookies.

From that day forward, I was hooked. I volunteered both my time and money to the shelter, serving almost every day. Helping others made me feel so good about myself, that on the days when I couldn't make it and missed helping at the shelter, I felt like a big part of my day was missing and I couldn't wait until I was able to be there, again. Eventually I found myself spending more time at the shelter than I did at work.

Then, one day I heard that another shelter in the area

needed a director and I was asked to apply. I quit my job and never looked back. Today I make my living by every day knowing the joy of helping others.

I first moved from volunteer to center director, from center director to regional director and now I am working in Africa, helping to feed millions of hungry people and I love every moment of it.

There was another perk that came with changing jobs. I found the man of my dreams, a man who loves me unconditionally; who shares my heart to help others and who joins me in my passion. We married some years ago and have two beautiful children.

The other day I was thinking of those shoes I never bought, and reflected on all the ways my life is so much different, so much better than it was then. Shoes? Today I might not even wear shoes and I might not for days at a time but I have never been happier. When I think of the street preacher and his words I heard on that fateful day – heard not just with my ears but with my soul, I thank God from the bottom of my heart.

James Cory Michaels

Chapter 10 - The Second Gospel According to Moe

The phone buzzed in my pocket. I took it out and looked at the screen: it was Lee.

Remembering the night at my apartment, I just stared at the screen until it went to voicemail. I let out a sigh of relief and started to put it out of my mind, but then it rang again. It was Lee; again, and again, I let it go to voicemail. When it rang for the third time in as many minutes I figured that it must be pretty important so I took a deep breath and answered.

"Bout time, motherfucker," Lee said. "You ducking me?"

"Just finishing up with your mother," I shot back. "What's up?"

"Dude, we need to talk." He sounded distressed.

"You crazy?" I said. "Last time you and Tyrone wanted to meet, you came to bust a cap in my ass."

"Fuck Tyrone," he said. "Nigga don't get paid, nigga don't play."

"The fuck you say?"

He hesitated. "Be at Tony's at seven."

"Should I notify my next of kin?" I said.

"You're shitting me, right?"

I was curious, but didn't ask. "Tony's at seven," I said, and hung up.

As the appointed time grew near, my mind manufactured all different kinds of scenarios and I was dead at the end of all of them. I asked Chris about what I should do, and he smiled and said, "Go ahead and meet him. It'll be okay."

I wanted to get there early and scope it out, so, at a quarter to seven, I turned the corner onto the block where Tony's was located. The sign over the door read, The Relax Inn, but everyone called it Tony's, even though Tony died years ago. I think it is now owned by some Arab dude by the name of Harish, or something.

Anyway, it really ain't much to look at. Neon beer signs over black painted windows and a heavy door someone thought would look cool covered with naugahide and button upholstery. We used to joke about how many naugas had to give their life for that door, back when.

On the inside there is a full bar, but most of the patrons can't afford the hard stuff, so the beer flows like water. There's a pool table there that slants to one side and has a tear in the felt, but that's okay because it matches the warped shuffleboard table.

I spotted Lee sitting at the bar, watching the ancient TV on the wall – one so old that the colors no longer resemble anything in real life, no matter how you might adjust it. When I approached he nodded toward an empty table in the corner and rose from his stool to follow me. On the way he yelled over his shoulder, "Hey, Ali Baba, two cold ones over here, would ya?"

The bartender said, "The name is Mike, and they'll be on the bar. You can get them yourself. The fuck I look like, a waitress?"

He sat down in the corner and I sat next to him with my back against the wall. It made it easier to talk quietly, and I damned sure didn't want anyone sneaking up on me from behind.

"S'up?" I said.

"Shit," Lee said. "Nothin'. Not a goddamned thing since you left. Nothin' good, anyway."

"What you talking about?" I said.

"After the shit went down in the warehouse," he said, "Tyrone lost his fucking mind. Business is way down, and the Pissant Prince is hiding in his crib like a little girl because of your boy and those fuckers he got watchin' your back."

"Chris? The white boy with the mop on his head?"

"No, them others he has working for him. Don't act like you don't know what I'm talking about."

He was either getting angry or frustrated; it was hard to tell. I could only think of Scott and Veronica, and couldn't imagine either of them frightening a five year old, much less hardened criminals like Tyrone and Lee.

"Dude," I said. "I been planting flowers, mowing lawns and just hanging out. I don't have a clue what the fuck you're talking about."

He told me about the night at my apartment. When he finished, I got up from the table to get our beers from the bar just so I could pull myself together. At first, I thought maybe he was high or sumptin, but the fear in his eyes told me he wasn't shittin' me.

I looked him straight in the eye when I got back to the table. "Ten foot tall dudes with their bodies on fire and lightning bolts?" I said. "Really?"

I didn't know what to make of it so I started laughing. "Are you high? You been doing some good drugs and not sharing?"

"Don't fuck with me, man." Lee was being dead serious, "These dudes ain't nothing to fuck with. After that night, Tyrone put out a contract on you. These two picked it up, real OG's, but nobody seen or heard from them since.

"Then Ty sent out Perry and two boys from the crew – the baddest niggas we had. He wanted me to go and I told him to go fuck himself. When Perry and them didn't come back we went looking for them. Found the two laying on the alley behind the crib in bad shape, but no

Perry nowhere.

"When them niggas came to, they done lost their minds. Kept babbling about Perry being burned up by a ball of fire so quick his flesh and bones melted into a puddle and ran down the cracks in the asphalt and nothing left.

"When Tyrone caught wind he got so pissed he grabbed his gak and headed out but as soon as he opened the door the boy stopped dead, turned white as a ghost, dropped his piece, fell to his knees and pissed himself like a little pussy bitch, right there on his white fur carpet."

"You're shitting me," I said.

"Motherfucker been hiding in his room ever since. Won't even haul his sorry ass out of bed. The organization is in shambles, nobody is earning, not even the hos. The Italians keep calling, wanting to know what the fuck."

I gave a sly smile. "Sounds to me like the bones is there for someone with the right skills to put it back together, clean house, get a new crew and take advantage."

"Ah, hell no," he said. "Crew broke off, soldiers scattering like roaches. Word is out on the streets about those fire monsters, and no one will even talk about joining up. That's why I called you here, man. Can you call your dogs off?"

I looked him square in the eye, and holding both hands up by my shoulders said, "Dude, I have not seen, heard or smelled nothin like you saying. I just been driving folks around. Regular folks, and doin bitch work, like planting flowers, mowing lawns and spreading mulch."

Lee stood up. The veins on his neck were bulging. "You callin' me a liar, motherfucker?" He reached for the back of his belt like he was goin for a gun.

I motioned him to sit back down, "Just chill, baby. Ain't nobody callin nobody nothin'," I said. "I just ain't got a clue."

"So, what is the deal with this new crew of yours?" he said.

"Shit, man, it ain't a crew. Nothin like that," I said. "More somethin like a cross between a church and a ice cream social. A lot of hard work, decent food, a place to live but ain't no pay – not that I mind much. I kinda like it, actually."

"No pay? How's a nigga goin' get his? At least tell me you gettin' some trim? Saw that white girl and she be lookin good, baby!"

"Naw, man, nothin like that," I said. "Can't you get it through your skull, Lee? These folks ain't like that. Ain't no runnin, no sellin, no cappin. No one gives a fuck about gettin' respect, because that's just the way it is. It's nice, man…safe and quiet, peaceful. But, I do have to admit, a brother could use some companionship, ya hear?"

"Shit, Moe…that was never a problem when you were with our crew, now was it? Just ain't the same with you gone, brother. Perry done got himself turned to koolaid and Ty is just shittin himself."

Lee smiled at me. "There is room, if you want to make a move, you know. Said it yourself. No one gonna mess with you after them fire monsters been hangin around. The Italians are probably lookin for someone they can back in a takeover."

I thought about it for a second, and then said, "But, dude. I got something I can't get from the crew, the business, even a stack of dead presidents. I got peace, man. I'm happy. When was the last time you had that? When was the last time you were really happy, my brother?"

I had just gotten the words out of my mouth when the door opened, and these three big white gorillas wearing expensive suits and ties walked in and looked around. When they saw me and Lee, they shouted, "Bar's closed, everyone out," then pointed to us and said, "except you two."

Mike started to say something, then thought better. "Everyone out," he said. "You heard the man!"

One of the men walked over to the bar and handed Mike an envelope. "With Mr. Giannetta's compliments," he said. "We take care of those who take care of us. Now, be a good boy, and wait for us outside by the car."

The bartender looked like he was going to protest. The name 'Giannetta' was held in awe in this city, so, instead, he took the envelope and left quietly.

But, it always happens. There always has to be somebody who gets ignorant and this time was no different. One of the guys sitting at the bar, an old black man, decided that he was not going to leave and said so, really loud.

The two gorillas walked over to him, and one said to the other, "Hey, Carmine, this one must be hard of hearing, because I know we asked nicely."

Carmine said, "Maybe we should just ask a little nicer, ya think?"

The old man said, "I hear just fine. I came in here to have my beer, but you can't leave an old man in peace, can you?" Turning back to his beer he started to say, "Fuckin' wops", but before he could get it out one of the Italians grabbed the back of his head and slammed it into bar, smashing the glass, cutting his face and breaking his nose at the same time.

Then the two of them picked him up while a third opened the door. They threw him out on the sidewalk, and then took up positions on each side of the door, while the one who had been doing the talking walked outside.

In a few minutes the door opened again, and a smaller, balding man with an obviously expensive silver suit and a red rose on his lapel entered. I had never seen Mr. Giannetta before, but there was no doubt that this was the man himself. One of his bodyguards gave us a look, and we knew that we best stand up, show the man some respect, or suffer the consequences.

He walked directly to our table and sat opposite us, looking us up and down. Like a parent dressing down two naughty boys, he said, "Who the fuck are you two, and where the fuck is Tyrone?"

"My name is Lee, Mr. Gianetta, and this here is Moe."

He was not amused. "You boys only have one name? You folks in the hood too poor for two names?"

Lee was doing the talking, which was just fine by me. "Sorry, sir," he said trying to put some respect in his voice. "I am Henry Lee, and this here is Moses Stockwell."

Giannetta motioned for us to sit. "Mr. Lee. Mr. Stockwell. Nice to meet you. Now, where the fuck is that piece of shit, Tyrone? He won't answer his phone, won't return my calls, and makes me come down here getting dirty to find out what the hell is going on and where my money is."

"I think he is at his crib…I mean house, Mr. Giannetta," Lee was doing his best to answer without saying too much. "He's been really sick, lately."

"Then get the boy some chicken soup and tell him to get his ass down here," Giannetta said. "I wanna talk to his black ass."

"I am sorry, sir," Lee said, "but he isn't answering my calls, either. I think he must be pretty sick, 'cause no one has seen him in over a week."

Mr. Giannetta clenched his jaw but didn't raise his voice – he didn't need to. "I guess I didn't make myself clear. That wasn't a request."

Lee pulled his cell phone from his pocket. "I'll call him right now, Mr. Giannetta," he said, and then walked a few feet away while the mob boss and I just sat looking at each other. When Lee finally spoke, it was obvious that Tyrone had not answered and he was leaving a message.

Giannetta motioned for Lee to sit back down, then turned his attention to him. "Well, Mr. Lee, I have a problem, you see. Mr. Washington owes me a lot of money. It seems like he lost a significant amount of product which belonged not to him, but to me. Seventy or eighty million dollars, street value. But now we have no money, no product, and Mr. Washington is not to be found." Then he leaned forward and said, "What do you think I should do, Mr. Lee? What would you do if you were me?"

Lee was still avoiding giving a straight answer. "What do you mean, Mr. Giannetta? I guess you can do just about anything you want to, a man like you, sir."

"I wasn't asking what I can do, but rather what I should do," he said. "You see, this is a lot of money we are talking about, Mr. Lee. I suppose I could walk away from the situation and just forget about it - - it isn't like I don't have plenty of money. But I think that would send a bad message to my other business associates, don't you think Mr. Lee? It might make them think that I was weak and that they could steal from me, too."

Lee came to Tyrone's defense. "But, Mr. Giannetta. The product was lost in a fire, and Tyrone had nothing to do with that. He wasn't even there!"

"Mr. Lee," the boss said. "Regardless of what happened to it, I trusted Mr. Washington. I gave him my property to hold, to protect, and he failed to do so. Because of this, I have to do something, wouldn't you say?"

Mr. Giannetta leaned back in his chair and paused before speaking. "I have known Mr. Washington for quite some time and we have been business associates longer than most. In addition, I personally like Tyrone, I really do. But this kind of thing? I can't just let this slide, because if I did so it would make me look weak – and in our business weakness is a detriment, don't you agree?"

"Yes, sir," Lee said.

"Now, normally I would take care of such business myself. However, in this case, in cases like this, it just wouldn't be appropriate, considering the political delicacies of dealing within a minority community, such as this. In addition, I have found that if someone like a successor takes care of the deed, then it solidifies his position in the neighborhood as well as in the organization itself."

He looked at Lee and said, "So, Mr. Lee. Do you have any idea where I might find a successor to Mr. Washington? You know, someone who would make a suitable replacement?"

Lee looked at me, and then back to Mr. Giannetta. "Since the product was destroyed and Tyrone has taken sick, the organization has fallen apart. There isn't much there to put back together, Mr. Giannetta. Whoever takes over is going to need some additional support in order to get things going, again."

"What kind of support were you thinking, Mr. Lee?" Giannetta asked.

Lee was starting to smile. "I don't know. Maybe some cash, some guns, and some muscle until the or-gan-i-za-tion can be put back together and then some product to fill the sales pipeline."

Giannetta raised one eyebrow. "Money, guns, manpower and product? That sounds like a lot, Mr. Lee. What, then, would the successor bring to the table?"

Lee relaxed a little. "Neighborhood connections and business knowhow."

Giannetta nodded. "And, could I count on this successor to do the things necessary to handle my little problem and clean up this mess left behind by Mr. Washington?"

"Yes, sir," Lee said, barely able to contain his excitement. "If you got the right guy, that is…and, Mr. Giannetta, you could count on me."

You could almost see what Lee was thinking. The idea of all that money and that power was intoxicating and he was grinning from ear to ear like an alcoholic in a liquor store.

Giannetta scratched his chin and then nodded. "Okay, Mr. Lee, you have a deal. You know what to do. We can work out the particulars of what you need and when you need it, but before we get our business arrangement solidified, I think we have one more piece of business, here."

Giannetta turned toward the door. "Carmine," he called, "do you remember the name of the warehouse guard who failed to safeguard my property?"

"Yes, Mr. Giannetta," the large man answered. "By the reports, we got the name of the guard was Moe."

Giannetta turned to me and my heart sank. "Mr. Stockwell," he said. "Didn't Mr. Lee introduce to you to me as Moe? You wouldn't happen to have been the man guarding my product when it was destroyed, would you?"

Lee started to say something, but I cut him off with a wave of my hand. "Yes, sir. I was in the warehouse that day when the fire started." I couldn't believe how calm I was, having just confessed to a crime that carried a life sentence – but I remembered that Chris told me it would be okay, and I had to trust him. At this point there wasn't another way.

"Did you try to put the fire out before it destroyed my product?"

"No, sir," I admitted. "I didn't."

Giannetta looked down. "I heard that it was not an accident. That the fire was started on purpose by some intruder. Is that correct as well?"

I stiffened my resolve to be honest above all else.

After all, hadn't I heard Chris say that there is strength in truth? "Yes, sir, you would be right about that as well."

Giannetta looked up with fire in his eyes, "Were you not armed? Were you outmanned and outgunned?"

"No, sir," I admitted. "They were not armed, but I was."

Giannetta was really getting angry, "So you were armed, and they were not, and you still failed to stop them?"

"Yes, sir."

"Did you even try to stop them?"

I was afraid to look up from the floor. "No, sir, not really."

The veins on his temple were bulging. "Did you kill them afterward? Did you make them pay for what they did to me?"

"No, sir."

The mob king was beside himself. I had heard stories about him in his younger days, and I knew that he was capable of doing all kinds of evil things, but he was trying his best to keep his anger under control. I watched as he wrestled with the turmoil inside him, and eventually he calmed down enough to speak.

He looked up, and as calmly and quietly as he could, said, "Then you understand that someone must pay, don't you? You understand that someone must be punished?"

"Yes, sir."

Giannetta turned toward the door, again. "Carmine, bring me your gun." Then he turned to me, "I am going to do this personally. You should really take it as a compliment."

A better compliment would be not killing me at all, I thought. All I could do was sit there, and prepare myself for the worst.

When Mr. Giannetta stood, I stood also. Then he leveled the pistol to my chest as Lee moved away, out of the line of fire.

At that moment it was if a shimmer went through the room and, like a ripple across a lake, the air parted, and for the first time I saw the beings Lee had been telling me about. This time there were five of them, with bodies of fire. They all had a face on each side of their head, and they were armed with balls of fire and bolts of lightning. The fear I felt was so intense that my knees buckled and I saw Lee dropping as well, along with Giannetta's henchmen. I had never experienced such a thing in my whole life and I thought I was going to pass out until I heard a voice inside my head, reassuring me.

"Don't be afraid," I heard one of the beings say. "I am here to protect you."

Then I looked a Giannetta, but his legs didn't give out and he didn't drop. Instead his eyes turned red, and his shadow rose behind him like a giant black bat. In a deep voice that sounded like a freight train he hissed at one of the beings, "I know you, I know who you are, and I know why you are here." He continued as he pointed the gun directly at me. "So, then, this must be the one and I must kill him, now."

It was as if my eyes were telescopes or something, because I saw the muscles in his hand and fingers tighten to squeeze the trigger. Before he could, three of the beings threw the balls of fire they held in their hands and they hit him simultaneously from all different directions.

His body ignited with an explosion of blue and red flame. The gun melted, instantly running down his hand to form a pool of liquid metal at his feet. His eyes bulged as the flesh melted off his bones, then exploded and his bones fell into an ash pile where he stood – but the shadow remained behind and screamed with a bloody red mouth before it opened it's yellow-green eyes.

The three who had thrown their fireballs then raced to the shadow, tackling and wrestling it to the ground and completely subduing it. When they had it bound and tied, they took it through another hole they had opened in the air and the entire group disappeared as they closed the curtain behind them. Then I heard a voice and I knew it was the one who had spoken to me before.

"Sir," he said. "Is there anything else you require?"

"Uh, no....I guess not," I stammered.

He then bowed. "Then, with your leave, may I be dismissed?"

I saw Lee out of the corner of my eye, laying on the floor and looking at me like he couldn't believe his eyes. "I guess," I said.

With that, the two remaining beings departed and closed the air behind them.

It was dead quiet in the bar when I looked around and saw that the it pretty much looked the same as it had when we came in, except for the glass and blood on the bar, the three guards passed out on the floor, and the pile of ashes where Giannetta once was.

Lee tried to stand up but couldn't on his own so I went over to help. He looked at me with a mixture of disbelief and new found respect and said, "Tell me the story again, about how you don't know those...things....and how you never saw them before."

"This is the first time, I swear. You really weren't shittin me about them, were you?" I asked as we headed toward the exit. Then I remembered the driver, and Mike standing outside the front door.

"Dude...we better leave out the back," I said. "I don't want to try to explain what happened in here to anybody."

We turned around and headed for the kitchen door, where we ducked out the back, got to my car and headed back to the apartment complex.

James Cory Michaels

Chapter 11 - The Gospel According to Abby

It was a beautiful spring day, and I hated the fact that I was working. I have been in the business for about six years now and my story is pretty usual for a woman in my line of work. I was a girl from a broken family; I was sexually abused by my stepfather; and the first chance I had I ran away from home and was on the run when I met Lenny. I fell completely in love with him even though we had only known each other for a couple of months, probably because I was seventeen and he was eighteen and we were both from an eerily similar set of circumstances. We were small people with big dreams and nothing holding us back, so we decided to head to the city together in search of a new and fulfilling life.

I thought Lenny was the love of my life and that we would live happily ever after. Not long after we got to the city, he found a job and we started the life we had been dreaming about. Well, we hadn't been together even six months when he found the love of his life, and left me pregnant and alone with nowhere to live and no way of supporting myself.

I asked around at the local government assistance office and they directed me to an organization which helped unwed mothers, and they were nothing short of a godsend. They had a foster home where I stayed until the baby was born, and then they helped me find work, albeit menial labor, at a bottling plant, but it was enough to support me and Samantha, even though we weren't going to be getting rich any time soon.

It was at work I met Kathy, and she turned me on to a whole new and exciting life of bars, men, dancing and drugs. We found a small house with a yard where we could afford the rent in an older, decent part of town. We worked every day, but we partied every night, usually going to one of three clubs in the area where they had music and dancing five nights a week, and never checked IDs if you were female and cute.

Yes, we were both young and attractive, and had no problem finding men who were willing to pick up the bar tab, buy us dinner and even supply us with some pot and occasionally some cocaine. Kathy's brother was a year or two younger and couldn't go out with us, so he would babysit for us in trade for some pot from time to time and some other intangible benefits. Usually we would bring the guys we met at the club home with us, and he would take off for their parent's house when we got there.

However, he wasn't that much younger than me, was kinda cute, so if I didn't bring someone home with me on a particular night, and he wasn't in a big hurry to get home, we would fool around a bit. I figured it was the least I could do in exchange for his taking care of Samantha.

At first it was a lot of fun and really exciting, but it didn't take long before the whole scene got a little old. The neighbors, not appreciating the different cars coming and going all hours of the day and night, and always seeing different men coming and going almost every day, eventually made a statement and exchanged the bulb in our front porch light with a red one. I was a bit embarrassed and upset at first, but Kathy got angry and came up with the idea of leaving it on all day and all night, every night to make their little practical joke backfire on them.

It was about that same time that I met Tony, a tall handsome black man in a business suit who was scented with premium cologne and adorned with tasteful and expensive jewelry. He came over to our table, introduced himself and asked me to dance. He was a gentleman in every sense of the word, but when we danced I could feel his powerful body and his even more so powerful sexual prowess. He gave me a ride home in his late model Mercedes, asked if he could see me the next day, and gently kissed me goodnight on the cheek.

He arrived at my doorstep the next day three minutes early and bearing red and white roses. We went to dinner at one of the best restaurants in the city on one of the top floors of a skyscraper, where we could overlook the lights of the city from the comfort of our table. We had dinner, dessert and conversation while sipping Dom Perignon and taking in the fabulous views. After dinner, he drove me to a park by the river where the night air was fresh and was sweetly scented by honeysuckle. We held hands and strolled under the moonlight.

He was smart, educated, articulate and funny and was seemingly completely into me. I, too, was captivated by him, the night, the champagne and the whole scenario. When he stopped, took me in his arms and kissed me, it was like I had never been kissed before. I felt that kiss from my lips to my toes and everywhere in between. My heart was pounding as our tongues danced together and even our breathing seemed to be in sync. Between kisses, he would look deeply into my eyes with a look of longing and his brown eyes were so gentle and caring that when he suggested we go to his place, how could I have refused?

His apartment was exquisite, tasteful and well appointed. It was decorated in shades of gray and lavender and obviously professionally done.

He was the best lover I have ever experienced, any time before or since. He brought me to the heights of passion time and time again until the sun came up. He was more adept with his hands, his fingers and his tongue than

I could have ever imagined. I slept soundly in his strong arms, and woke to the smell of espresso and the sound of a shower – where I playfully joined him for more of our joint passion.

As he dressed he explained that he was already late for work, and asked if it was okay that he gave me cab fare instead of a ride home. He kissed me as I left his apartment and said he would call me. On the ride home, I kept thinking about our romantic night of lovemaking and allowed myself to fantasize what life would be like with Tony and his amazing abilities, but was concerned because with everything we spoke about and all we had shared, I had never told him about Samantha.

I didn't go out that night with Kathy, hoping that Tony would call, but the phone didn't ring. I didn't go out the next night or the night after that or even the night after that. Finally, Kathy talked me into going out with her, saying it just wasn't the same without me, but all I could do at the club was drink and think of him. Oh, a lot of guys tried to pick me up, but I found myself comparing them to Tony, and every one of them came up short in every respect, so I just went home alone.

I tried calling him several times but when I got his voice mail the mechanical voice on the other end said that I had reached a voice mailbox, which had not yet been set up, and didn't give me the chance to even leave a message.

It seemed like eons, but after two weeks the phone rang and it was Tony. He apologized for not calling sooner, said he had been busy and had to go out of town for work but also said he would love to see me and asked if I could meet him at a bistro not far from his apartment. My body buzzed with excitement as I got ready for our rendezvous, and I could barely contain myself when I saw him sitting at a table.

I kissed him as I sat down beside him, but he didn't seem the same. He was a little quieter, a bit more serious and a lot more aloof. He said that he had thought about us and about our future a lot since our date, and I admitted that he had been on my mind a lot, as well. He looked deeply into my eyes and told me that he thought he had fallen in love with me, and my heart fluttered with excitement. I confessed that I had completely fallen for him, also, and thought I wanted to spend the rest of my life with him.

Then he said something unexpected, something to the effect that any woman who was going to be with him had to be a very special and would be willing to do anything and everything he asked her, without question. I was so excited about him being in love with me that I immediately told him that I could do that and I was anxious to prove how good of a woman I could be for him. When I said that he smiled, kissed me and said he was on his way to a party and asked if I would like to come. I agreed to do so without hesitation.

When we arrived at the apartment where the party was, I was a little disappointed. The building was not only old but poorly maintained. The door was opened by a young black man wearing sunglasses and as we entered I was surprised to see only just four or five people, and they were all men. I guessed that we had just arrived early, until the man who opened the door closed it behind us and locked it with an audible click, then took a seat with the others. The room we were in was obviously the living room but it was sparsely furnished with only a ratty couch, a couple of arm chairs that didn't match and a scuffed and scraped coffee table on the threadbare carpet. The only nice feature in the whole was a good-sized fire in the fireplace.

That was when Tony leaned down and whispered in my ear, "Baby, I love you, but this is where you need to prove your love for me; prove you are worthy of me. Remember what you promised?"

I bit my lip and nodded silently then Tony stepped back and stood near the other men seated on the couch and chairs. "Strip for us, baby", he ordered and I didn't want to and looked at him hoping that he would start laughing and tell me it was a joke, but nothing like that happened. I started to take off my clothes and he commanded "Dance, baby, dance like you like it." I wanted to cry, but I did as I was told.

The next few hours were as much of a nightmare as that date night with Tony had been a dream. After I was completely naked, Tony watched while the other men had me service them, sexually, in every way imaginable. They took turns with me in all different ways, and then at the same time. I was naked, covered in sweat, dirt and their filth and I wanted to run, but I remembered my promise and just hoped it wouldn't last much longer.

I kept looking at Tony thinking he might put a stop to it, but he just watched with a look on his face which was a twisted mask of cruel amusement and apathy, the first time I had seen that look, but hardly the last time. Yes, it was a look that I got used to.

The men kept taking me over and over, in every way imaginable and the abuse lasted for hours, but it seemed like days. I think I might have lost consciousness or maybe my mind blocked out the abuse but finally I came back to reality and realized that it was over. There was no one in the room but me, laying in the middle of the floor, filthy and spent and Tony sitting on one of the chairs, legs crossed in his business suit, and smoking a short cigar. When he saw I was awake, he got up, went to the bathroom and brought a warm, wet bath towel, which he used to wash me off and soothe places where the men had gotten too rough.

His touch was gentle and the look on his face and in his big brown eyes conveyed an emotion akin to love or at least that is what I thought it was. After cleaning me off, he rolled me over so I was on my stomach on the floor, and then covered me with another soft, warm towel. I watched him as he strolled over to the fireplace and grabbed the tongs used for moving hot coals and started digging through the embers. He reached inside the fire with them and held up a round piece of metal that looked slightly like a stamp of some sort.

He slowly walked back over to me, and I let out a cry of pain as he stepped hard on the small of my back so I couldn't move, then I felt a searing pain on my right butt cheek. I tried to struggle to get away, but the more I struggled the more weight he put on my back, until I thought my spine was about to break.

He reached down and punched me on the back of my head, and then spat at me, "That is my brand, bitch. You are my property now, got it? From here on out you screw who I say, when I say and for how much I say and the money is mine, understand? You can never leave me and if you try I will hunt you down and kill you. You belong to me and you are nothing without me. From here on out, you don't do anything, even shit, unless I give you permission, understand? I am now your god."

Then he walked back to the bathroom and brought back some kind of salve that he put on the burn and it lessened the burning pain from the brand. He then took off his clothes, lay down beside me and held me in his arms until we fell asleep, together. That night I had violent, horrible dreams, but the fear was mixed with the comforting feeling that I belonged to someone and that he was going to take care of me, although this was never how I had imagined it.

I awoke the next morning in the apartment by myself, completely naked on the floor; even the towels were gone. I walked in to the bathroom and found them folded on the counter, so I took a shower to clean off the mess from the night before. When I was drying off I looked over my shoulder at a burned-in "T" inside a circle. It was red and angry looking, but like my dreams, I also felt – well, like I had a place in the world and that someone cared for me, regardless of how sick it might be, and that was something I had not felt for years.

When I looked around for my clothes where I had kicked them, they were nowhere to be found. In their place was a bag that contained a very skimpy pair of short shorts, a top that revealed too much cleavage and all of my midriff, a pair of extremely high-heeled platform shoes and a note that read 'New clothes for your new life – T.'

I winced in pain as I slid the tight shorts over my damaged bottom, but otherwise the ensemble seemed to fit and I was glad that the brand was high enough up on the cheek that the shorts covered it. I had worn heels before, but these were so high that I twisted my ankle and it took more than a few steps for me to be able to walk halfway decently.

I was embarrassed walking home dressed like that and couldn't wait until I could get home, get a warm, soothing bath, put on some decent clothes and see my little Samantha. I silently thanked God that Kathy wasn't home when I arrived and on the table I found a note saying that she had taken the baby to her mother's and gone to work without me.

She also wrote that she would try to make an excuse to the boss to cover for me. Kathy was such a good friend.

I had barely finished my bath and was about to change into some comfortable clothes when Tony called to tell me to come meet him right away at an unfamiliar address. At that point I hadn't seen my baby in two days, so I told him about Samantha and protested that I had not even had time to see her. He said, "You belong to me and you will do what I say, bitch. If you don't I will kill both you and your brat!" and then hung up.

I was pretty pissed at that point, so I got dressed in a

loose, white t-shirt and some stretch pants in order not to aggravate my new brand and make it hurt worse. I met him where he told me, but when I got there he demanded to know where the clothes were he bought me, and then beat me right there on the street in front of everyone, and sent me home bruised and bloody to clean up and change. After I changed, I went back to the same place and, of course, he had a date for me to work.

From then on, I was at his beck and call – wearing slutty clothes, having sex with strangers for money and completely neglecting my baby girl. Any deviation from his exacting orders, complaining or standing up for myself was met with beatings of varying severity depending on the scope of the infraction - - but there were soft caresses and incredible love making when I pleased him. It was like he was training me like a pet or something.

I wasn't around the house much and when I was around I had bruises and scrapes from the beatings. Kathy was getting pretty concerned about me, and one day she took me to the side and spoke to me about what I was doing, where my life was going and what was happening with Samantha.

I realized that she was right and decided to try to do something about it. But when I spoke to Tony about it, his answer was just another slap down. Then he ordered me to move out of the house with Kathy to a tiny, dirty apartment in a building where he kept the rest of his girls.

Tony paid a woman named Frankie who lived there to babysit for all of his girls. She was a middle-aged black woman with a drinking problem, but she kept the kids fed and clean and pretty much out of trouble.

Sometimes when I would pick up Samantha from her apartment (and she was sober) she would have long heart-to-heart talks with me, and it didn't take long for me to figure out that even though Tony paid her, she didn't have a very high opinion of him and what was said between us stayed between us.

The same couldn't be said about my sisters—the other girls who worked hooked for Tony. He treated us all the same, and so we all knew both his lovemaking skills and his temper. All the girls were in a constant state of jealousy over Tony, and each vied for his attention and favor.

At first I thought they were just jealous because I was the new girl, and they thought Tony was paying too much attention to me. But then he found another new girl to add to his stable, and I found myself getting jealous of her, but it didn't change the level of anger and cattiness I was getting from the other girls.

Then one day I found out I was pregnant. Honestly, I was not sure who the father was, but I assigned it to Tony because if he wasn't, then he got the money for the conception. Tony was excited when he heard the news and during those months life was as good as it got with him.

I didn't have to work as much, I didn't get beaten as much, I got to spend more time with Samantha and he made sure that I got good food to help nourish the baby growing inside of me. However, when Anthony Jr. was born, he looked more Hispanic than black, and what had been good turned very bad.

After he was born, Tony got one look at the kid and had me go back to work almost immediately where the whole cycle abuse and tenderness started again. This time though, the beatings were more severe than ever, and he was crueler to me than before, even when I hadn't done anything wrong.

After two months of this kind of treatment, Tony gave me an assignment. I thought it was going to be like any other day, but when I showed up at the apartment there was Tony and this white guy covered with tattoos. Tony introduced him as Steve, and then told me he had sold me so now I belonged to him.

I felt abandoned, used and heartbroken. I promised myself I would be better to Steve so he wouldn't want to get rid of me.

While Tony beat his girls, he refused to allow us to partake in drugs of any kind – Steve used drugs to control his girls, but didn't beat us as often or as badly. I learned to love Steve and hate Tony, and one night while I was stoned out of my mind, I grabbed Steve's knife from the sheath on the back of his belt and tried to remove Tony's brand. I pretty much succeeded, but did such a bad job mutilating myself that I wound up in the emergency room.

Well, Steve must have thought that I was pretty special, because he paid for a plastic surgeon to fix the damage from both the brand and the knife. He said it was because no one would want to see me naked, otherwise, but I knew better. Then he moved me, Samantha and Anthony Jr. into his apartment with him, and started calling me his 'old lady'. He would brag to his friends about what I had done to make sure everyone knew I was his and not Tony's.

Life with Steve was as good as I had learned to expect, and soon I was pregnant again and gave birth to Steve's son, Mikey. After that, Steve doted on me and the kids, and it really seemed as though I might be able to find the happiness that had eluded me, so far. That was until a cop came by one night with the news that Steve had been killed in a drug deal that went sideways.

As far as pimps go, Steve was pretty small time and had only me and a couple of other girls working for him. The truth was that he made most of his money selling drugs – pot, ecstasy and a little crack and meth. He didn't use himself and that way he was able to provide a decent living and even save some cash.

One day he came home, really excited. Someone had approached him with a couple keys of cocaine to sell for about a quarter of the usual cost. It was obvious that the guy he was dealing with had ripped someone off and was wanting to turn it fast and get out of town, and Steve had the cash to take advantage of the situation. He said it was going to be a big score – big enough to lift him out of the small time, and maybe even buy us a house, but I had a terrible feeling about it and asked him not to go.

Of course he never listened to me, and this time was no exception. I don't know exactly what went down, if the guy he was supposed to meet crossed him, or the one who got ripped off found out, but the police found Steve dead, face down in an alley – no money and no drugs – leaving me broke, alone and with three kids from three different fathers.

I missed Steve a lot, but I couldn't take time to mourn, just had to do what I knew to do to pay the rent and feed the kids – but this time with no man to promote or protect me. I soon learned that working nights were more lucrative, but more dangerous and I had no one to watch the kids, so I pretty much was stuck to the day shift. Not only was it safer that way, but I could also spend nights at home with the kids.

That particular day was pretty much like every other day. I was working under a bridge where I was there was hardly anyone around, but I could see another couple of working girls from where I was standing. After a while I saw two men and a woman – obviously not a working girl – approaching and one of the other girls said something to one of the men. I couldn't believe what I saw next.

The man she had approached walked up to her and at first I thought he was going to hit her, but instead he just held his hand up and she looked like she started to dance…but she wasn't touching the ground, just hanging and dancing in mid-air with her feet a few inches off the pavement. When she stopped dancing she just started to collapse, but I saw the other man catch her, lift her in his arms and then the three of them walked off together.

While there is a lot of competition in the business, there is also a code where we girls kinda look out for one another, and even though this particular girl had a reputation for being uncommonly mean and nasty to the rest of us, I decided that I should follow them in case the police came asking questions, later. They went to an apartment building not far away and knocked on one of the doors until an elderly woman answered. Then they all went in and came out a few minutes later without the girl.

I hid around a corner and watched as the three of them walked away, and then I went to the apartment to see what I could make out. Well, the woman who lived there must have seen me because when I got close she opened the door and asked if she could help me. I lied and told her that I was a friend of the girl they had dropped off, and wanted to make sure she was safe.

The elderly woman then smiled, said that Heather was resting and introduced herself as Helen. Then she asked if I would like to come in for a cup of tea. I accepted the invitation and while she was preparing things, she told me all about one of the men who had been there.

His name was Chris, and she had known him for years since he was from the neighborhood where she used to live. She said that as a kid he used to do odd jobs for other people, just to help out, when he wasn't helping his mother. After she moved away, she didn't think much about him until she was riding a city bus he was on and when he saw her, he sat down beside her.

She said she had been crying because she had just found out that her grandson had an inoperable brain tumor, and the doctors gave him only a few weeks to live. Chris told her that he saw her crying so he went over to find out what was wrong, and she told him the story. She said he sat quietly beside her, holding her hand for a long time, but she was inconsolable and felt such a deep sense of loss that she just couldn't stop crying.

After a few minutes she said that he put his arm around her shoulder, gave her a hug and whispered in her ear that he was going to give her a gift, but she couldn't tell anyone. He then told her that her grandson's tumor was gone and everything was going to be all right.

She said she thought he was high on drugs or something, and scolded him for teasing her. Then, two days later she got a call from her daughter-in-law. She told her that her grandson's headaches had stopped, and when they went to the doctor he told them that the tumor had completely disappeared without a trace and they had no explanation.

She didn't say a word to her, even though she wanted to, but the next time she saw Chris, without thinking she ran to him, hugged him and thanked him. She said he just told her again not to tell anyone, but he might ask her for a favor at some time in the future. She promised she would do anything she could for him but hadn't seen him since, well, until that day, anyway.

After we finished our tea we went in and looked in on Heather. She looked so young, just a few years older than Samantha and her face looked so peaceful. I had never seen her without a scowl on her face, but she was actually quite pretty and the serene look on her face made quite an attractive picture. I thanked her for the tea and left the apartment.

As I was walking back to my stroll, I thought to myself that if he could help her grandson, and he could help Heather, maybe he could help me, too. Then the old doubts and feelings of worthlessness came back.

Why would he help me? I wasn't a nice old lady or a little girl. I was someone who had consciously made bad choices. I had made my bed; shouldn't I have to lay in it now? I tried to put the thoughts of him out of my head, but they just wouldn't go away.

And then I saw him coming back.

He was with the guy who had carried Heather to the apartment, and I started toward him, but then hesitated thinking that I would look like a total fool if he rejected me. Then I thought of my kids, and decided that, regardless of what else might happen, I was going to ask but as I got closer I thought better of it and just thought I would just thank him for what he did for Heather.

He smiled at me when I did, and asked me if I thought I deserved a better life as well. Then he told me to do something that would change my life. He told me to buy a lottery ticket, and that I was supposed to use the money to get my family out of our current situation. He gave me specific rules so I wouldn't waste the money I was given. It was really hard to believe what he told me, but I went immediately to the store across the street and bought the ticket like he instructed.

When I got to the store there was a problem. The ticket cost $2.00 but when I looked in my purse and realized that I only had $3.00 and I needed milk for the kids. I had a hard time deciding what to do, but I bought the ticket anyway. As soon as I did, I kicked myself and questioned what kind of mother I was, using my kids' milk money to buy a lottery ticket. When I walked out of the store I turned right and something fluttered and caught my eye. There, stuck in a crack between the building and the sidewalk, I spotted a ten-dollar bill. I immediately picked it up, turned around and bought both milk and bread for the kids.

The next morning I had completely forgotten about the lottery ticket. I guess I must have blocked it out because I didn't want to set myself up for disappointment in case I didn't win. Later on that day I caught a newscast that said a local convenience store had sold a million dollar winning ticket. I couldn't believe it when I checked my numbers, and they were mine. The payout after taxes was around $560,000.

After putting the money in the bank, the first thing I did was go to the local community college and enroll in a completion course for my high school diploma. I then was able to locate a decent apartment in a good school district.

With school and housing taken care of, the next thing on the agenda was to go shopping. I found a two year old Ford Fusion which would fit our family, and then took the kids to find school clothes for Samantha and some decent things for TJ (Tony Jr.) and Mikey to wear at pre-school and daycare.

We settled in well. Samantha made friends at her new school, right away, and the daycare/preschool was a godsend. For me, it was very different going back to school, but I did really well. I completed my high school requirements in two months, and then registered as a college student, looking at some kind of degree in business.

Some of Samantha's new friends invited us to a nearby church and it wasn't long before we found ourselves really involved. One of the things I got involved with what they called a connect group—helping elderly people in the area. Interestingly enough, even with the kids and school, the time I spent helping these people refreshed me more than other, normal, leisure activities and I found myself looking forward to the few hours I spent there.

In my sophomore year I followed where my heart was leading and changed my major from business to nursing. I took to it like a fish to water. My professors said I was a natural at it, and even the more difficult courses I passed with no problem.

In my junior year I started working part time at the university hospital, and in my senior year I was already handling as many of the duties of a registered nurse that they could legally allow. It was the summer between my junior and senior years that I met Brad.

Brad came to the hospital for a routine appendectomy. He was tall, about 6'4", handsome and soft-spoken, with gentle eyes and the most adorable smile I have ever seen. I tried hard to remain professional when he started flirting with me, but his boyish charm broke down all my defenses. He really grabbed my heart when, after being discharged, he came by with a bouquet of flowers and an invitation for dinner.

He was everything I never knew I wanted. He was sweet, gentle, patient, a kind and thoughtful lover and an absolute sweetheart with the kids. We took our time, and things progressed slowly but nicely.

I was concerned about how he would take it when I told him about my past, but I could not have found a man more understanding. He told me that he appreciated what that I told him, but suggested we never mention it again. I moved the kids out of our apartment and into his house after we had been dating about a year, and then we moved to a bigger place after we married and I graduated.

Oh, and the money? The day I graduated I still had a little over $316,000 in the bank, which I donated to St. Mary's orphanage and home for unwed mothers. I have to admit that it was a little hard writing that check, but I acted in faith and did what Chris told me. These days, my annual salary is over double what I donated.

Starting off as a nurse I specialized in geriatric services, continued going to school and eventually worked my way into management. I am now the President and CEO for one of the largest assisted living providers in the country with over a hundred separate facilities.

Brad and I are still happily married, and he adopted the kids, who have all graduated from college and have good careers of their own. All in all, life has turned out wonderfully for me, since I have a spouse who loves me, a job where I am well compensated and a life about which I could have only dreamed.

Some days I still think about Chris; that young man with the lottery numbers and the day I had the faith to spend two of my last three dollars on an impossible promise made by a complete stranger.

Chapter 12 - The Gospel According to Will

It was a cool, crisp October afternoon, without a cloud in the sky, and the leaves were turning red, gold and brown. I was sitting in a production meeting at the station and things were pretty hectic, with a lot of stories going on about the election coming up in just a couple weeks.

Jenna and I were pretty disappointed when we were assigned to interview some kind of new cult leader who had emerged in the city. Normally, this would be the kind of story that would be a step back for an up and coming reporter, like Jenna, career wise. You could see the disappointment on her face when the news manager gave her the assignment.

Regardless, we are both pros, and didn't say much as we headed to the van to cover the event at the place where we were to meet the guy. I suspected something different when it wasn't an address to an office or a house, but rather we were to meet him in the park. Like I said before though, it was a beautiful day, and if I was going to watch Jenna's career swirl down the porcelain drain I couldn't have picked a better venue.

When we arrived we didn't see him at first. Instead, I noticed a growing crowd of people around a park bench where a young man with a curly mop of brown hair sat on the backrest, his feet on the seat.

The group around him was not what I expected. There were the usual derelicts and the casually dressed onlookers, but many in the crowd were dressed professionally – slacks, khakis, shirts with ties, dress suits and even a skirt accessorized with high heels in the crowd.

As we approached the crowd I heard him speak.

"It is written that you should love the Lord your God with all your heart, all your soul and all your mind, and to love your neighbor as yourself. Now, even though this is true, I tell you that love without action is worthless and it is better thing to serve God and to serve all others with your heart and soul and mind than just to love.

"Most of you work thirty, forty, fifty, sixty or more hours per week for money or worldly goods, but what will it gain you in the end? Everyone knows that you cannot take worldly possessions with you, and if you leave them for your children they will be unappreciative, selfish and may very well squander it on things which may cause them to lose their most precious asset – their souls. Wouldn't it be better to use that time to serve others, and for them to serve you in kind?

"It is written that the love of money is the root of all kinds of evil, and yet you spend so much time and energy in pursuit of it. Are you children of evil? Don't you realize that all good things come from your Father who is in heaven, and that as such they are all freely given to you? Air, water, food, love – all of these in nature are free, but are corrupted by men when profits become involved.

"Is it worth your mental, physical and emotional health to have more than you need? Don't you realize that some of the most miserable people on the planet are the richest?

"Why do you risk your lives, your health, your family and your relationship with God to make a few more dollars for material things which both don't bring true happiness or last for more than a very short time? Why not, instead, invest in relationships with God and other people, because those will last throughout eternity and are more valuable than gold.

"We have all heard that the best things in life are free, but I tell you that the things of real value are those things which take no money but instead take time, patience and love. It is the spirit of man – your spirit and the spirit of others around you – where you will find true riches on earth, because your soul is in the image of God. In the same way it is the spirit of God where you will find true value in eternity.

"Look at the most valuable works of art and antiquity on this planet – they neither took a lot of money to create nor was it an investment which made them possible, instead it was the spirit of the artist which made it special, which makes it valuable, because only value and worthiness can create more value and more worthiness."

I was surprised at his teachings, and even more amazed at the reaction his teachings created. I was expecting a less than enthusiastic response considering the percentage of young urban professionals in the group, but instead I saw openness and an acceptance, which I never would have expected. I didn't even see an eye roll in the crowd.

About that time, a sandy-haired gentleman walked up and introduced himself as Scott, told us that he was part of Chris's organization, apologized for him not being ready when we arrived, and said that he would be with us shortly. Despite the apology and explanation from Scott, Chris didn't seem as though he was in a great hurry to talk to us after his lesson was done, but instead spent a lot of time talking to people in the crowd, touching this one, embracing that one, wiping a tear from another.

When he approached us, Jenna sprang into action in her 21st century reporter's uniform of a white, silk blouse which showed just a little too much cleavage and a business suit where the skirt was just a little too short, and both it and the jacket just a little too tight. Her stiletto heels finished the outfit and guaranteed that every male in the audience would pay attention.

Every hair on Jenna's perfectly coiffed head was in

place, and her smile revealed what must have cost her parents thousands of dollars in cosmetic dental work. She held her right arm straight out with her slender wrist extending beyond the jacket sleeve and her hand held at a fifteen degree downward angle.

"Jenna Burns, Channel Seven News," she said, then waved in my general direction. "And this is my cameraman, Will."

Chris took her hand and said, "Chris Pawlinsky, nice to meet you." After releasing her hand he offered his hand to me and looked me deeply in the eyes with an expression I found simultaneously fascinating and a bit disconcerting. It felt a bit as if he looked through my eyes and into my soul, reading my very essence like a book, and when he finished he didn't judge at all.

After I came back to reality it was time to go to work. While I hoisted the camera to my shoulder, Jenna stood straighter, touched her beautiful, auburn hair, straightened non-existent wrinkles in her outfit and then flashed her dazzling smile. In one much practiced motion, she moved the microphone from her side to its usual place, just below her chin.

I pressed the switch, causing the red light to come on in the viewfinder, to let me know that the camera was recording. I said to her, "You're on"

She was on, too…like she was every day. Beautiful, talented, well spoken; with beautiful ice blue eyes to contrast her dark auburn hair, flawless skin, high cheekbones and a million dollar smile. After having framed her face so many times since we started working together I had developed a secret crush on her, and my job sometimes made me feel like we were making love on a daily basis. In reality it was more of me being the voyeur while she made love to her audience, paying me little mind.

"Hi, I'm Jenna Burns," she began, "and today we

are at Washington Park with the popular new street preacher, Christopher Pawlinsky." She turned to Chris and continued. "So, how do I address you, Chris? As Pastor, Reverend, Rabbi? I have heard people have started addressing you as teacher, so would you prefer that?"

Chris didn't miss a beat. "You can call me just about anything, but I will answer to Chris – I think that is the best."

"Okay, Chris. Word has it that you are supposedly healing people, some with incurable diseases. Is that true?"

Chris looked at her and smiled, "We all do what we can with what we have been given, you know. To make the world a better place for others as well as ourselves."

Jenna wasn't about to let go. "Some say that you are curing AIDS and stage-four cancer. Is that true?"

"Not really," he said. "God heals, I just ask."

"So, then," she continued. "Are you saying that you have some sort of special connection to God, where he answers your prayers and not those of others?"

"That is what you are saying, Jenna, not me," he chuckled. "God answers the prayers of many millions of people every single day."

If Jenna was anything, she was persistent. "Others pray for miracles, too, but yours are the ones that seem to get answered."

"That isn't entirely true, Jenna," he said. "Every day, God works miracles in response to prayer millions of times. Some you hear about, some you don't and some of them are done even before anyone even knows what He has done. Many times, people who are infected with HIV or exposed to rogue cancer cells are healed before there is a symptom, diagnosis or even a realization of the problem.

"God works miracles not accomplished just in the classic sense, as well. Every day, doctors use the skills and the knowledge God has imparted to them to heal people and often bring them back from death's door. Why, every day in hospitals around the world, hearts are stopped, removed from the body cavity, repaired, then put back in place and restarted, routinely. So, I ask you: are those not miraculous actions as well?

"God reveals new methods and new practices each and every day in laboratories around the world, whether it is a new drug to alleviate pain, or a new vaccine to prevent disease, or even new ways to repair the human body. God is in every type of healing whether you recognize Him or not. The mother treating the scraped knee; the doctor prescribing medicine; the surgeon in his operating room – even the shamans and faith healers whose methods most don't understand."

Jenna was trying to come up with another question, but you could tell that she was struggling. Chris took the impetus and continued.

"Look, it is not a matter of faith versus science but rather that the two have a symbiotic relationship. How can one actually separate the laws of nature from the One who established them? In the past people used myths and statements of faith to explain things they couldn't otherwise fathom and when those actions began being expressed in scientific terms it developed into almost a confrontation between the two where people either embraced faith and eschewed science or the other way around.

"But I tell you the truth, God created nature and is revealed through it. Science is a study of that nature and the more we learn, the more man explores the mysteries of nature, the more the nature of God is revealed, and therefore the stronger the faith becomes, if one approaches the question in the right frame of mind."

Jenna was stunned, and paused for what seemed to be hours just looking at Chris. Then she smiled awkwardly and looked at the camera. "And now you know why they call him Teacher," she quipped and then gave her patented sign-off. "I'm Jenna Burns, Channel Seven News."

A bystander suddenly jumped into the camera frame beside her and took the microphone out of her hand. "Hey, everyone," he yelled in the microphone, "when you vote, write in Chris Pawlinsky for Mayor! He has done more for this city in a few weeks than all the rest of these morons have done in years!"

There were two police officers nearby who saw what happened and ran toward the man who, in turn, dropped the microphone and took off running in the opposite direction of the officers. Forgetting the elevation of her hemline, Jenna bent over to retrieve the mic, showing just a little more of her shapely legs and derriere than appropriate for a newscast. She quickly regained her composure, straightened her clothes and looked at the camera.

You could tell by the expression on her face that the whole scene caused her to be a bit off balance, but like a true professional, she used her Teacher tagline again and then reached out and shook Chris's hand as she thanked him for the interview. After loading up the equipment, we climbed back in the van and headed back to the studio.

On the ride back, Jenna was especially quiet and obviously deep in thought. After a while the silence became too much to bear.

"You're being really quiet." I said, softly.

"That Chris guy really got me thinking," she said.

"About?" I said.

"A lot of things, actually," she said. "To tell you the truth, I find it a bit scary."

"Scary?" I said. "Why scary?"

"Because he is either a complete crackpot, or we have something very special on our hands with this guy. The genuine article, if you will, and I am not sure which I think would frighten me more."

She had given me something to think about, so we both stayed deep in our thoughts until we arrived at the station. After we got in the editing studio, the executive producer joined us and we watched the tape together, and then I made a new tape, editing out the intruder and the scene that gave everyone a glimpse of more Jenna than was appropriate. After watching the edited edition, the producer said that he thought he liked the unedited version better.

"More authenticity, and more spontaneous," he said. He also mentioned that it would give us a leg up over the other stations that had interviewed the man known as the Teacher in the past. We decided that we would run the unedited version on the five o'clock newscast, pretending that we didn't have time to edit, and then the edited version would be on subsequent broadcasts.

Well, between the intruder and Jenna's little wardrobe malfunction, the piece was pirated, put on the Internet, and went viral in no time. In a little more than a week it had more than 26 million hits, and is still the most viewed piece in the history of the station.

Chapter 13 - The Second Gospel According to Buzz

It was two days before the election and there was only one word to describe the Mayor's office. Chaos.

He had the usual group all gathered in front of his desk, but the meeting was really for me. "I thought I told you to neutralize this threat – this street preacher – this Chris Pawlinsky!" he fumed. "Now the election is the day after tomorrow, and three different polls have us trailing by two to five points to a write-in candidate who hasn't campaigned for the office and says he won't serve if elected. How could you have let this happen?"

It was true. After that news piece with that reporter showing the world what was up her skirt was broadcast on local news and went viral, Chris's name and face were everywhere. He had even been approached by several late night talk shows on national television networks. Hell. No politician I have ever heard about gets that kind of treatment unless he is a candidate for President, and even then it's rare.

Then, as could have been predicted by anyone in the business, with all this exposure the Teacher's numbers started climbing, not just in the city, but especially here. What was supposed to be an easy sailing campaign for a popular, incumbent mayor—running virtually unopposed—had not only turned into a horse race, but one in which the mayor was trailing and fighting as if for his life.

Now understand, these waves of popularity are not

unheard of, especially with a fresh face. Almost every time it happens though, these meteoric rises in popularity are met with a total 'crash and burn', and by the time the election rolls around, these types are usually nothing more than a punch line on late night TV and not being courted as a guest of honor.

This time it was different. Against all odds, the guy was gaining momentum at just the right time, and even more disconcerting, he appeared to be the genuine article, not just some flash in the pan. The mayor was way passed the point of being concerned about his political future, and in my professional opinion, rightly so.

"We have got to do something, and now!" the Mayor yelled. "Let's hear some suggestions, and nothing—I said nothing—is off the table!"

"We could run a smear campaign," one of the lower level operatives suggested.

"Not enough time, and besides, it would make us look weak, fearful and panicky. The last thing we need right now," I said.

"Maybe, if we got some incriminating photos of him in bed with some hookers or selling drugs to kids outside a school," the Police Chief said.

I just rolled my eyes.

"We could double up on the positive TV and radio ads, we have the money," someone else suggested.

You could see the Mayor physically wince at that one. He was hoping to have enough money left over in his war chest to take a post-election trip with his secretary to somewhere warm and tropical, where clothing was optional but hedonism was mandatory.

The head of the local Teamsters spoke up. "I could get my guys going door-to-door with flyers, in a get out the vote campaign. We could take cigarettes and cheap wine to the homeless – they vote, too."

"Not a bad idea," I said. "But my guess is that the

number of winos and junkies in this town has decreased significantly in recent months, and there is no telling who they would vote for once they got in the booth."

The Mayor glared at me. "Since you are shooting down everyone else's suggestions, what do you recommend, Buzz?" The emphasis he put on my name was akin to spitting out spoiled milk.

"I think that ramping up the ads would help," I said. "And the get out the vote – especially in the working and middle class neighborhoods. Pawlinsky actually polls much lower with those who have been too busy working and making a living to take time off and listen to his teachings or see him in action.

"We might be able to turn this whole late-night thing around on him. Word has it that although they are trying to get him on, he has refused their requests. These comedians turned hosts on late night TV fancy themselves as king makers, at a certain level, and they don't like being refused. It probably wouldn't take much incentive to get these guys to turn him prematurely into a punch line, with or without reason. We might even get one or two to invite you, sir."

The Mayor looked a little sad at the idea of being second choice, and having to beg to get this exposure. I reminded him that at this point, any publicity is better than none.

Then I continued. "Last but not least, this city used to have a reputation for having quite the political machine in place. Now, I know it has been a pretty long time since it was used, but there are still people here who know how, which buttons to push and which cogs to turn to get it working again. We use the ads and the get out the vote campaign to explain the unusually high turn-out, and then we get really creative in turning out the vote."

"From what I understand the mayor polls very well," I chuckled, "almost unanimously—with the recently departed."

Everyone looked around the room at everyone else.

"You heard the man! Now, let's get moving!" the Mayor shouted. Then, almost as an afterthought, he added, "Everyone except you, Buzz."

As the group left the room, I found myself standing in front of the Mayor's desk feeling very much like a schoolboy in the principal's office. The Mayor turned his chair with his back to me to look out the window.

"This has been very upsetting for me, Buzz," he said, "very upsetting. I saw this coming and asked you to take care of it. Now, here we are, two days before the election, having to take drastic measures to hold on to what we worked so hard to attain."

He turned to me. "I saw this coming, but you didn't, Buzz. You are supposed to be looking out for me, heading these kinds of things off. Instead, you let this guy charm you into inaction. This is unacceptable, Buzz – and I blame you. What do you have to say for yourself?"

Scenes and feelings of childhood memories of being dressed down by authority figures started waving over my psyche. I looked at the man speaking and remembered that he was just a caricature - a creature of my own creation. When I started working with him, he would have been lucky to be elected as President of his local garden club, much less the head of a major American city, and now he thought he was going to dress me down like one of his minor underlings?

"Look," I said. "I did as you asked. I checked him out. I met with him. I got assurances from him that he had no political aspirations and so far he has been good to his word. He hasn't campaigned, has not even asked for one single vote and has repeatedly said he wouldn't serve if elected. Your job is not in jeopardy, here, Mayor—only your ego."

The veins on the sides of his head bulged. "You

bought that whole 'If nominated, I will not run, if elected I will not serve' bullshit? You of all people should know that it's political code for 'vote for me.' Somehow every moronic housewife with an IQ of 80 can see it, but you can't? What am I paying you for?"

If anyone with an IQ of 80 can see it, I thought, no wonder it was apparent to you.

When he spoke, it was as if he had read my mind.

"I am a politician," he said. "My ego is my job, Buzz. You have just made too many mistakes, my friend. I think you are losing your grip, and it has almost cost me. Sorry, but I think it is time we parted ways.

"We won't say anything until after the election and you have until next week to clear out your office, so take your time. After the election, we will issue a press release saying that you are leaving to write your memoirs or something."

I was stunned. I made this man. I had taken a nobody, and made him one of the most powerful and important people in the country. I had been with him for years, and had given him everything. I balled my fists, but instead of hitting him, I leaned forward resting my fists on his desk and looked him straight in the eye.

"You will live to regret this, Rick. You will rue this day."

I turned on my heel, walked out of the office, down the hall and took the elevator to the parking garage. Walking as if in a daze, I found my car and drove it to my favorite watering hole, a bar in a four-star hotel. Even though it was only about 10:30, I ordered a Manhattan.

As I sipped the sweetened whisky, I kept reviewing what had happened. Did I really take the threat of this newcomer too lightly? Did I miscalculate the threat and dismiss it too soon? Did I ignore some signs, or is my boy, Ricky, just a complete moron?

I had just decided the whole situation was just a

perfect storm of circumstances that no one could have realistically seen coming when I realized someone was sitting on the bar stool to my right. When I turned to look at him I already knew – it was Chris, just sitting there waiting for me to come out of the cave my thoughts had built.

"Hello" I said.

"Hi," he said. "Are you doing okay?"

"Sure," I said. "Just another banner day at the Mayor's office."

"Yeah, I heard that it was decided that your services are no longer needed, if that is what you mean," he quipped.

I was surprised, but not shocked that he knew. I had suspected that he had a mole in the Mayor's office. But if he really had no political aspirations, why have a spy at City Hall?

"Why am I not surprised you heard?" I asked.

"Because, you are a skeptic who has dealt in secrets and other cloak-and-dagger type of operations your whole life. You automatically assume others operate the same way." He smiled. "I can assure you that I have no spies in City Hall, nor have I bugged the Mayor's office. Sometimes I just know things."

"Do you know that the reason I got fired is because I trusted you when you gave me your word?" I said.

"What have I done that I told you I wouldn't do?" he said.

"You told me that you weren't interested in the Mayor's job, and here you are about to win an election without even campaigning!"

"Do you hear yourself?" he said. "Didn't you just say that I wasn't running?"

"Yeah," I said, realizing that I sounded as ridiculous as the Mayor did. "But there is running, and then there is running."

Chris laughed. "And I did neither. I didn't ask that reporter to interview me, I didn't ask that man to grab her mic and say what he said. I didn't ask that reporter to bend over inappropriately, and I didn't ask them to broadcast it or put it on the Internet. I have been turning down television appearances and interviews left and right. Yeah, I have been running one bang up political campaign, haven't I?"

"You're a good man, Andy. Isn't it time you came over from the dark side, and used your powers for good? I mean, I am always looking for good people. The conditions leave a lot to be desired, but the pay sucks."

I smiled in spite of myself. It was hard not to like the man, and the truth is that anyone and everyone would be able to figure out what really happened regardless of what we pretended or might say in a press release. I couldn't see having many other opportunities any time soon.

"Do I have to live in that apartment complex you turned into a commune?"

Chris laughed out loud, "It really isn't that bad, but no – you can live anywhere you want. Although you might have to trim back your lifestyle significantly."

I held out my hand and said, "Okay, you have a deal. I hope I won't regret this."

Chris smiled, and shook my hand. "Welcome to the team, Andy – I hope you don't mind me calling you that. It is a lot friendlier sounding than Buzz. And for the record, you probably will regret it."

He turned to the bartender. "We will have two more of those, and put it on my tab, Tommy."

The bartender served them with a smile. "On the house, Chris. You know your money is no good here."

"Nor anywhere else, it seems," Chris said, sipping his drink and becoming lost in thought.

James Cory Michaels

Chapter 14 - The Third Gospel According to Scott

The election was over and the Mayor had won, thank God! It had been a madhouse of a media circus around the complex, with all the reporters, cameras and vans. After that little disaster with Channel 7's Jenna Burns, the spotlight had really been shining on Chris and everyone associated with him.

The addition of Buzz to the group had also been a Godsend. His experience in handling the press and juggling the calendar of a prominent man—as Chris had unwittingly become—was absolutely vital, because everyone from network anchors to school newspaper editors wanted to interview him.

The worst, though, was not the news people as much as it was the power groupies, as I had come to think of them. Hardly a day passed without some young woman or man throwing themselves at Chris or anyone around him, to get close enough to the man for some kind of bragging rights.

As a matter of fact, there was this one night in particular, when we had had a busy day and were dead tired, but Chris sensed something was not quite right. He asked me to come with him to check his room and when we turned on the lights there was a strange girl in his bed, her clothes piled on the floor.

We told her she had to leave and turned around to let her get dressed, but when she told us it was okay to turn around she stood there naked as a jaybird, wearing only six inch heels. If that wasn't bad enough, she offered to do both of us if she didn't have to leave.

I was starting to have déjà vu about Samantha and was about to suggest I go get Veronica when she walked in the room. I know that she and Chris were not partners in a physically intimate way, but I don't think I have ever seen a woman so angry. She ordered us out, and on our way I heard her call the girl by name as she verbally tore into her.

After waiting in the common area with Chris for about five minutes or so (it seemed a lot longer) Veronica emerged with the girl in tow, escorted her to the door and told her in no uncertain terms that she should leave and not bother even thinking about coming back. She then came over and apologized to Chris, explaining that the girl was someone she met during her acting days and made the mistake of telling her where she lived. I guess she put two and two together on the address and Ronni's proximity to Chris, and figuring that a sexual encounter with him would be the fast lane to fame, designed a plan and put it in motion.

After that we were all more careful with our surroundings – ensuring we knew who was who and why they were there. Moe was put in charge of security, although I had to smile when I remembered how his last security job had worked out. Chris, himself, didn't seem overly concerned for his own wellbeing, but was having difficulty understanding why people were doing what they did.

As I said before, Buzz came on board, and took over screening requests for Chris' time and handling his calendar. Most of the requests for interviews were rejected; even the ones Buzz thought would be good to increase his exposure and public persona - the major networks, cable news organizations, and the like. There were also some Chris told him to accept that Buzz didn't agree with.

I remember one, specifically, that he and Buzz argued over. It was a young woman who was working as an intern for some run-of-the-mill Internet blogger with a website called, 'Inside Source,' and a following of hundreds. I think she saw it as a way to make her boss and company look good, but Chris somehow guessed that her questions were going to be the ones he wanted to answer – some of them ones even we, his closest friends, were afraid to ask.

Here is part of the interview:

IS: People have witnessed you performing what can only be described as miraculous acts of healing and what can best be described as the exorcism of demons, things which have not been reported since the death of Jesus. Are you on the same level, on par, if you will, with the man known as Jesus of Nazareth?

CP: As I have told others, all healing comes from God, whether through natural means, medical science, or as you say, miraculous acts. He has many channels though which he works many miracles, I just happen to be privileged enough to be one of them, just as Jesus of Nazareth was in his day.

IS: Are you then saying that you are equal to or on par with Jesus?

CP: You said that, not me. Jesus was the only begotten Son of God, being both true God and true man during his time on earth, but only once – in front of the Sanhedrim, did he actually claim to be the Holy One. He usually referred to himself as the Son of Man, which is what we all are. I make no claim to be equal to or on par with Jesus, although I, too, am a son of man.

IS: You don't claim equality, so then, how do you answer those who say that you might be a reincarnation, the second coming of Jesus?

CP: Is that what you think? Would it make any

difference if I were the second coming, or the third, or the fourth, or even the thousandth? I am not the same as Jesus because his mission on this earth was to provide a worthy sacrifice for the redemption of mankind, and that has already been accomplished and need never be done, again.

As it is written: "For by one sacrifice he has made perfect forever those who are being made holy." and, "And where these sins and lawless acts have been forgiven, sacrifice for sin is no longer necessary".

IS: So, then are you denying that you are the Second Coming in the flesh?

CP: Who do you say I am?

IS: I think you are He.

CP: Aren't you supposed to be the one asking questions?

Well, when that interview hit the Internet it didn't take long before there was a loud roar from the religious community, nationwide. We were inundated with requests to roundtable discussions on multiple religious networks around the country – what Chris referred to as roundtable lynchings.

After that interview Buzz was so busy we rarely saw him, and when we did he was inevitably in a bad mood, having been arguing with pushy people who were doing their level best to get Chris on their respective shows in an attempt to discredit him. Chris wasn't buying, though. He just kept doing what he had been doing – healing people, ministering to them, teaching them in the park – but now the crowds were no longer in the hundreds but in the thousands and tens of thousands.

One particular day some people came down from the City Manager's office with some policemen. They spoke very slowly and very quietly and kept using catch phrases like public safety, and crowd control, but their message was ultimately clear. Chris had to find a better way to teach and a better place to teach, because if he didn't, he would face arrest for causing a public disturbance.

We tried to explain that the crowds were really not Chris's fault, that he just walked down the street and people gathered around. The city people didn't dispute that, but crowds that size in the middle of the city, blocking traffic and disrupting commerce, were unacceptable and he was the one who was ultimately responsible.

One of the city officials recommended that we start using a huge, old, amphitheater in the park which had not been used for years and had fallen into disrepair. The shell was still partly there and the city would help restore it and let him use it free of charge, if he could figure out a way to reduce the size and frequency of the impromptu crowds.

Well, Chris, Buzz, me and a couple of other guys from the mission jumped into Moe's car and drove down to look at the place with the city folks. It wasn't much to look at – disrepair would have been a nice way to put it. The shell was falling down on and around the stage, leaving large hunks of plaster and concrete scattered around, and the grass and weeds had grown up in and around the seats until they were virtually invisible. The trees in the area had done their best to retake the space and had grown so large and so close that they choked out a lot of the sunlight and reduced the size of the useable space by half.

I have to give it to Buzz. He immediately started making notes and negotiating with the city manager using political key words, and soon had them agreeing to rebuild the shell if we painted it, and remove the trees, if we mowed and took care of the grass and weeds. He also negotiated some kind of agreement where the city would help pay for Moe's gas if Chris rode more and walked less.

True to their word, the city work crews showed up

the next day to do the heavy lifting while we painted, pulled weeds and destroyed spider nests and ant hills. In no time, the place was acceptable for people to sit without getting too dirty or without the impending danger of something or other dropping on their heads.

After a few more days of work and many more gallons of paint, the place looked pretty darned good. The biggest challenge was trying to get the work done between Chris's lessons, when people weren't present. On the other hand, sometimes when folks who had showed up for the lesson would hang around, they would help out with the work.

However, about the same time the whole amphitheater renovation project was happening, a seemingly well-orchestrated, anti-Chris machine cranked up and started spewing the most ridiculous claims against him. There were claims that he had gotten people addicted to drugs so he could save them; that his healing was mass hysteria, and that he, himself was a drug dealer. It seemed like every magazine and gossip rag on every shelf in every grocery store checkout line had a new illegitimate child of his discovered somewhere.

The requests for interviews doubled in the following week, but now they didn't want to ask him about his healing or helping or even his philosophies, but rather about supposed transgressions and the claims of both men and women that they had been his lovers.

At first Chris tried to ignore them, even though Buzz warned him that these claims could take on a life of their own and that he needed to take them head on – that he needed to defend himself and even formulate a counter attack against those who were spreading the false allegations. Chris refused, though, and kept refusing, even when the attacks gained momentum both in frequency and in viciousness, just as Buzz had predicted.

At the amphitheater, the crowds of people peaked

and then started to drop off. The late night talk shows that had begged to have Chris on now made him a punch line for their crudest jokes. As he rode down the street, some people would cheer while others would shout curses. Profane graffiti appeared on the walls of the complex, and looks of suspicion and disdain could be seen everywhere.

Threats started, with accusations of heresy and blasphemy, and when Chris refused to allow us to respond, then acts of violence against us physically began. Despite police protection they escalated in both frequency and severity until it lead up to this one day when one of the newer team members, Tommie, was beaten to death and his lifeless body deposited on the street outside the complex.

At that point Chris had had enough, and agreed with Buzz that something needed done. We started a vigorous public opinion campaign and, at Buzz's insistence, he agreed to meet with leaders of various religious factions in an informal theological discussion to be broadcast, nationwide.

Chris asked me to accompany Buzz to the meeting to hammer out the details of the broadcast. The building was huge, and we were directed to a lavishly appointed conference room, where the network executives and the representatives of the various celebrity panel members were seated.

The negotiating process was fascinating in itself. Everything was agreed to, from the names of the people on the panel, to how many questions each could ask, to the type and amount of food and drinks which would be available. Even the identities of the sponsors were agreed on, and the amount of money each of the panel members would receive for participating.

Chris had sent explicit instructions to ask for nothing, accept everything offered, and to not negotiate anything. It was obvious, though, that none of the other representatives had such lenient instructions. One representative insisted on fresh pineapple grown in one specific field on one specific Hawaiian island for his employer. Another specified a certain type of sparkling water while another specified the type of coffee. One even demanded bottles of six different 'top shelf' alcoholic beverages be available for the taking.

I could see that Buzz thought Chris was being neglected and that he should be asking or demanding something, if for no other reason than to ensure he get the measure of respect he deserved. However, he just sat there alternating between looking at me and looking forlorn and lost, like he didn't need to be there in the first place if there was nothing for him to do. However, I do have to give him credit because he held his tongue, even when you could see that it went against every fiber of his being to do so.

The date and time were set. It was going to be the following Wednesday night at 8:30 pm on The Jehovah Bible Network, and they were going to meet at a studio right there in town. I thought that since Chris had agreed to meet with the media, that the attacks would stop, but they didn't. If anything they got worse, but at least no one else was physically beaten.

As the time for the show grew near everyone seemed nervous but Chris. He was the ultimate cool character but seemed to be a little sad. He sat with Ronni a lot, and engaged her in private conversation. However, his spirits seemingly lifted on the day of the show and was practically jovial as we climbed into Moe's vehicle for the ride to the studio.

About half way there we encountered a large crowd of people milling around outside the civic center, which was bathed in floodlights and had a fully lit marquee listing the name of one of the hottest female pop star on the charts, today.

She was tall and beautiful, and had legs that seemed to extend all the way to her ears. Adding to her sex appeal was the fact that she was as famous for her skimpy outfits and nearly obscene dance moves, as she was for her singing. Moe said something about being sorry he was missing her show and Chris said rather clandestinely with a smile, a wink and a suggestion, that we might stop back by after the JBN show was over.

Moe dropped us off at the front entrance of the studio and left to find a place to park, and we had barely gotten out of the vehicle when we started getting what can best be described as the red carpet treatment. We were met by a network VP with the requisite Rolex and a suit, which looked like it probably cost what it would take most people months to earn. After shaking Chris's hand, he took him by the elbow and, with his very attractive female assistant, led him off for makeup and sound check. The rest of us were escorted to the green room by some guy in a t-shirt, blue jeans and a headphone around his neck.

Once inside, we were shown where the full buffet of food and drinks was located as well as the location of the overstuffed couches. Everywhere you looked there were television screens, fourteen in total—I counted—all of them showing what the network was sending out over the air. At the moment, it was some historical recount of some stage of a minor prophet's life and was completely boring. I grabbed a magazine to read as I hungrily engaged my plate full of fruit, cheeses, lunchmeats and rolls, with a cocktail to wash it all down.

The three hours between the time we arrived and the program starting seemed like three weeks. The entourages of the other participants joined us, and at one time or another during the wait the principals themselves joined us, each for a minute or two. Since I didn't see any of them eat any of the food laid out for us, I deduced that they probably had their own layouts in their respective dressing rooms.

The cast was set. First was Chris, of course, then some of the biggest names in television evangelism. Damon Hill, the flamboyant, dancing preacher. Dr. William Patterson, the gray haired patriarch of the largest church in the nation—The Diamond Cathedral, located somewhere in Southern California. Then there was Lacy Jean Williams, the Texas Rose, complete with big hair and too much makeup, but not enough to cover the wrinkles which told you her blond hair was not natural – not anymore, anyway.

And last but not least, the Right Reverend Henry K. Jones, 400 pounds of a sweating, pink suited, scripture spouting black man, with a penchant for singing half of his sermons. The moderator for tonight's round table discussion was Billie Rae Henderson, a quiet, serious, brunette evangelical woman, also from Texas, whose clothes and hair style were straight out of a 1980s comedy skit.

Chris was in and out of the green room several times, and each time he was there, the room would get suddenly quiet while he spoke with one or two of us, and then he would leave again. If any of the principals for the show were present they would just watch him and then make quiet comments to each other, which reminded me of the running joke in the movie, Road House, where everyone thought the main character, Dalton, "would be bigger."

At the five-minute mark before the show started, several of the studio people came in and gave us the alert. It was then time to get another plate and find a seat in front of one of the television monitors. The room was perfectly quiet as the show began.

Chapter 15 - The Gospel According to Edna

I timed everything perfectly. I took my chicken potpie out of the oven and while it was cooling, fed the cats, poured myself a glass of milk and set up the TV table. I put the aluminum potpie container on another plate so it wouldn't melt the plastic tray that I had put the milk and a fork on, then picked them all up as one and took them to the living room to watch the big event.

I just love that Damon Hill. He is so handsome, and always clean cut and neatly dressed and he speaks so well. With his sparkling eyes and bright smile, I knew from the first time I saw him that Jesus must have a special place in His heart and in heaven just for him. When he preached, it was like Jesus was speaking through him, and I just loved it when he began to dance. Every Sunday night at 8:00, I make sure that I tune in to the Jehovah Bible Network, just to watch that man preach.

Last Sunday it seemed as though something was bothering him through the entire hour, and near the end he revealed what it was. He told us that he was going to be on some kind of show on Tuesday night where he and some other soldiers in God's Army were going to take on some kind of street preacher who, he said, was spreading false gospel around to try the faith of the saints. He sent out a special request for prayers to keep him and the others safe as they embarked on what he called a perilous mission from God to show the world what a fraud and tool of Satan this man was.

There was no way I was going to miss this show. Not for love or money.

Just as I sat down and got comfortable, the show came on. Miss Billie Rae was moderating it and I smiled as she introduced all the panel members. I knew almost all of them by sight or reputation, and when she introduced the special guest—Mr. Christopher Pawlinsky—I almost felt sorry for him. He looked out of place, with his modest clothes and needing a haircut and all. It was a little sad how his hair kept falling into his face like a teenaged delinquent and everything.

Well, after she introduced them all she turned to Mr. Damon and said that he had the honor of asking the first question. It was just at that moment that I remembered that I had not given my monthly tithe to the Damon Hill Ministry this month, so I got up from my meal and grabbed my checkbook to write the check before it slipped my mind.

You see, I used to go to church on a regular basis, but after George passed away and I got older, I didn't really feel much like getting out, especially early on Sunday mornings. When I discovered Pastor Hill's show, I started watching it instead of attending my usual church.

Then one day he gave a sermon where he told us that it was an act of obedience to tithe on a regular basis and that God would bless His faithful servants. Then he gave out the address to the Damon Hill Ministry and I have been giving, faithfully, ever since – even though I am on a fixed income and sometimes have trouble making ends meet, but I want to show God how much I love Him.

I had just sat back down with my checkbook in hand when Pastor Hill finished his question to Mr. Pawlinsky. Then, the strangest thing happened. Instead of answering the question, the man with the simple clothes and funny looking hair looked straight at me through the TV and said, "Edna Harder, put that pen down and don't write that check to Damon Hill."

My jaw dropped. I couldn't believe what I just heard, but the man continued.

"Edna, listen to me. Damon Hill and his organization don't need your money. They already have sponsors for their TV program who pay for everything they do, and then some. Damon Hill owns six houses, all of which are much nicer than yours. He has a minimum of three cars at each of his houses and he owns more Rolex watches than even he knows.

"Damon Hill is not the man you think he is. He is on his fourth marriage, and currently keeps two mistresses. He has eight children, four of whom he refuses to acknowledge or support. His donations to the poor go to prostitutes and drug dealers from whom he gets his cocaine. Any money you send him just feeds his sexual and drug addictions.

"If you want to do something good with your money, there is a unmarried woman living just a couple houses down from you who just lost her job and found out on Friday that her fiancée was killed in Afghanistan. To make matters worse, she found out yesterday that she is pregnant. If there was ever any person who needs a friend, right now, it is she. She could use some help, some groceries and someone to lend an ear and a shoulder.

"Her name is Rosa Rosales, and she lives at 987 Elm, just three doors down. She is a good girl, Edna, but is just having some trouble. You have what she needs, Edna. Won't you help her?"

I was stunned. I just sat there in shock. The young man turned back to the others at the table and I could hear them ask questions and he answered them in kind, but nothing registered because I couldn't believe what I had just experienced. I couldn't think, I couldn't move, I couldn't do anything. The program ended and I never noticed. I came around sometime after the sun had set and the room was growing dark.

I got up, slowly, cleaned up after myself and turned off the TV. I picked up my checkbook, put it and a pen in my pocketbook and walked out the door and down the street towards 987 Elm.

When I arrived, there was a pretty, young Hispanic woman sitting in a porch swing, lost in thought and not looking at anything in particular. She didn't even notice me as I approached her on the porch until I spoke.

"Are you Rosa Rosales?" I said. "My name is Edna Harder."

"Yes," she said. "I am Rosa. Is there something I can do for you?"

"Actually, no," I said, sitting next to her on the swing. "I was wondering if there might be something I can do for you. Someone told me that you were going through some tough times right now, and that you might need a friend."

She looked at me in disbelief, and it was if the floodgates opened, letting the tears flow like rivers. She hugged me like I was the last thing left floating after a shipwreck and she was about to drown. Her uncontrollable sobs were accompanied by a long string of Spanish, which was completely unintelligible to me, but the pain in her voice was something I guess would be universally understood. I wrapped my arms around her sobbing shoulders and tried to soothe her with gentle pats and softly repeated, "Now, now, dear, everything will be alright." until I was beginning to feel like she might think it was the only thing I could say.

When she was able, she collected herself sufficiently to get a good look at me. "I know you," she said, "you're the lady who lives in the gray house down the street. I heard your husband passed away just after I moved in, but I didn't think I knew you well enough to offer my condolences."

It was now my turn to tear up as I thought about my dear, sweet George. He had passed away suddenly in our bed in the middle of the night without me even realizing what was going on. I woke that morning to find his cold, stiff body lying next to mine and the memories of the shock and sadness were still a deep wound in my soul.

I suggested that we go to my place for tea and cookies. When we got there, Rosa walked around the living room, looking at the pictures of my life with George. We never had had children, but there were a lot of pictures of our vacations around the world to entertain her, while I brewed the tea and got out the special cookies with the powder sugar dusting and the raspberry filling I had been saving for a special occasion.

We sat at the table and talked. She confirmed everything the man on the TV had told me about losing her job at as an office person at a local car dealership, her whirlwind romance with a soldier named Joey, and how she felt when he had to leave her to fight in a foreign land. How he got killed just a few days after arriving in country, and what a shock it was to find out she was carrying his child.

She asked me about George, and called our 46 years of marriage a great love. She laughed at my stories about the two of us together, and cried when I told her about George passing and leaving me all alone.

It was late when Rosa excused herself to go home. I hugged her and thanked her for the wonderful conversation, and told her that I hoped we could get together, again, soon.

The next morning she came over under the premise of thanking me, but she had to go to the employment office for the first time ever, and I could tell she was a little nervous about going there by herself, so I offered some moral support. Now, I had never been there myself because George was a good provider and I didn't need to work, but I don't get out much these days and thought an adventure might be in order, so I told her I would be happy to accompany her.

Rosa came to pick me up in her beat-up, twelve-year-old Toyota compact. When I saw her car, I thought about getting in and out of it and the possibility that I might not be able to do it, so I suggested that we take my Buick, instead.

Now, I don't see well anymore, and I only drive the Buick about twice a month to get groceries, so it is in almost new condition. You should have seen the expression on Rosa's face when I handed her the keys and told that I would be more comfortable if she drove.

I think she was a little nervous about the possibility of damaging the car at first, so I teased her about poking along slower than I do, and that I go slow because I am blind in one eye and can't see out the other—it isn't true, but my eyesight isn't what it used to be. It made her laugh and I think it made her relax a bit.

When we got to the employment office, I sat in the waiting area and entertained myself by watching the people come and go. There is a lot you can tell about people, just by watching them, you know.

When she emerged from the sea of cubicles, Rosa looked much better – a combination of relief and excitement, I should say. She found out that she was eligible for unemployment and that it would start almost immediately. In addition, she had a piece of paper in her hand for a job interview – a position which was similar to what she had been doing and which would pay almost as much.

On the way home, I invited her over for dinner that evening, and we stopped by the store on the way. I bought more groceries than usual, enough for me, and some to give to Rosa, too.

Two days later, on the day of her interview, there

was a frantic knock on the door. I opened it to find a completely frustrated Rosa standing on the front step looking frazzled.

She was getting ready to leave the house to go to her interview, but her car had died in the driveway and wouldn't start again. She hated to ask, she said, but would I please loan her the Buick? Of course I said yes, and she looked relieved and gave me a big hug.

When she brought the car back she had filled the tank and bought a bottle of wine on the way home – then came in and told me about the whole ordeal. The car not starting was just the beginning – she showed up to the interview late, and things went downhill from there. She was certain that she wouldn't get the job and was a little depressed about it. I fixed dinner for the two of us and drank a glass of wine while she finished the rest of the bottle.

While I was fixing myself lunch two days later, I must have spilled some water on the floor, because when I turned from the counter with my sandwich my feet went out from under me and I hit the floor with a big thud, a crack and a sharp pain that shot through my groin and down my leg. When I tried to stand, my leg refused to work at all and the pain was so bad that I didn't even want to move. When I finally crawled to the phone, the only person I could think to call was Rosa.

She came running into the house, completely out of breath, but had already called 9-1-1 to get an ambulance for me, and followed me to the hospital in the Buick. At the hospital the doctors confirmed what I had thought – my hip was broken, and I was going to have to spend the week or so as an inpatient.

I told Rosa to keep the keys to the car and asked her to keep an eye on the house for me. She came and visited me, every day, sneaking some of my favorite snacks past the nurses for me.

When I was released, I came home to a completely clean house, which Rosa had scrubbed from top to bottom. She had also fixed lunch complete with my all-time favorite: freshly baked bread.

That was when I got an idea. You see, George had fixed us up with a long-term care plan, which was already paid by an annuity he had set up and we had never used. I called up the company and found out that I could hire just about anyone I wanted as a caregiver, to help me around the house until I was completely healed. So, since she was still looking for work, I hired Rosa.

The weeks that followed were almost magic. It was so wonderful having another person around the house – someone to talk to, someone to spend time with, just someone around the house making noise.

Rosa was better than efficient. She shopped, cooked, cleaned and helped me in any and every way she could, so when she mentioned that it was time for her to renew her lease, I asked her to just move in with me. Now, my house wasn't a mansion by any stretch, but was a lot bigger than I would ever need by myself.

That was also about the time she was blossoming in her pregnancy, and I suggested that I might be able to help with the baby when he came—we knew the gender by this time. Aren't the advances in medicine just wonderful?

She was crying with joy when she accepted, and told me that she had wanted to ask me to be with her during delivery, but was too shy. Right after she moved in we started pregnancy classes designed for couples – and we surely made a very unlikely couple—a beautiful Hispanic woman and an older lady with a walker. I could only imagine what people thought, but I really could not have cared less.

The coming baby did bring a little stress to our otherwise happy existence. Rosa was torn over whether or not to tell Joey's parents about the baby. She had never met them, and she and Joey had only known each other a few weeks before they got engaged; the engagement expedited by his imminent deployment. She was afraid that they would be suspicious of her and her possible motives for telling them about the pregnancy, especially with regard to the GI life insurance policy Joey had had.

However, she was sure that Joey would want them to know, and probably would have wanted the baby to get the proceeds of his insurance policy. So, with some encouragement from me, she decided to tell them.

I explained that if I had a grandbaby that I would want to know about it, especially if I had lost a dear son and there was a little piece of him left behind. Rosa was a bit afraid to initiate contact so I called them myself and set up a meeting at their house, and then accompanied her to the actual meeting.

As we were getting ready, I could tell that Rosa was both excited and scared, and she barely spoke a word as she drove to the address they gave us. The meeting went very well, although there was some skepticism, and—I detected—a little bit of thinking that it was too good to be true on the part of Joey's parents. However, they agreed to be part of the pregnancy and delivery and then, pending the results of a paternity test after the baby was born, would help with finances using the proceeds of Joey's life insurance.

We met them several times over the next few months until the baby came. When Rosa's water broke, the first call we made was to Joey's parents and there they were, in the waiting room, during the delivery. When the paternity test was completed and the results showed that Joey, Jr. was indeed their grandson, they were good on their word, and did everything they had promised.

During the time Rosa was living with me, helping me and being paid by my insurance company we had no financial troubles, so I started my tithing, again. This time, however, I never did give any more money to Damon Hill Ministries or any other such organization. Instead I wrote monthly checks to local charities on a rotating basis and honestly not only felt better about donating to them, but they seemed to appreciate my contributions more.

Life has been wonderful with Rosa and Joey, and I can say that I have never been happier. At least since George died...

* * *

Edna was never able to finish her story here. She had quit writing for the evening, saying that she was tired, and went to bed early. Then, sometime during the night, she peacefully passed away, hoping upon hope of rejoining George in the great hereafter. Not having any family, she had—unbeknownst to me—made Joey and me her heirs. Everything she had passed to us—the car, the house, everything—but I would trade it all for just another day with this wonderful woman.

Her funeral was lovely and was attended by over 1,600 people. There were so many flowers in the funeral home that they ran out of room in the chapel, and had to put them in adjacent rooms. There were a lot of people there I didn't recognize, but I knew they had come to know her through her generous giving, and were there to pay their respects to a great woman with a heart of gold.

Before reading this, I never knew why she came over to my house that day; she never told me. Now I guess it makes sense, if you believe that the man on the television set actually spoke to her. I thought about it a bit, but decided not to question the story, but just pass on her story and remember my beautiful, loving, faithful and generous friend, Edna. – Rosa Rosales

Chapter 16 - The Third Gospel According to Moe

The atmosphere in the green room after the show was not unlike that of the winning team's locker room after a football game. Me and the rest of the 'Team Members' were practically giddy with Chris's performance, especially Buzz who after every exchanged made a comment like 'Yes,' with a hand sign to show he thought his boy had nailed it.

The truth is that Chris made these other religious figures look silly and unprepared with his understanding of theology and the Bible, especially when adapting those principles to our modern society. There were several times when they would try to trick Chris or make it appear as though he was inconsistent or confused, but they completely underestimated him, and would make them look not only inept, but also unnecessarily mean and cruel.

The other participants' entourages were very quiet when the program ended, and they milled around with each other, shooting looks of hatred and envy at us. Scott went to check on Chris in the dressing room, then came back and asked me to get the car and bring it to the door so we could avoid as much contact as possible. When I walked through the lobby, everybody was talking about what had just happened in the studio, and it seemed that pretty much everybody was saying that Chris had not only just dodged an ambush, but had wiped the floor with the other guys.

I started the car and headed toward the door, but by

the time I got there all those camera guys had already got there and I could tell that Chris was getting closer because there were more and more flashes. As I pulled up, Scott opened both the passenger and rear doors and everyone began piling in, with Chris hiding behind Buzz as he slid into the seat, and then Buzz jumped in the back seat beside Scott. When I took my foot off the brake and stepped on the gas, I almost hit a guy with a camera who was standing in front of the SUV.

When we left the parking lot I turned right instead of left, toward home, to avoid both the press and the downtown traffic. As I started to circle around and get on the freeway, Chris commented "I thought we were going to see the show?"

"The show with Cassandra?" I asked. The singer was so popular that she didn't need to use but one name.

"Yeah, that's the one," Chris said.

"That show has been sold out for months," Scott interjected from the rear seat. "I heard that the Ole! network was broadcasting it nationwide and live, so security is going to be really tight."

Chris just looked over his shoulder, smiled, winked and said, "I know some people."

No one in the car said a word. We knew better than to doubt him. I thought about the woman some referred to as the greatest female artist of our time and her meteoric rise to fame. She was the ultimate performer when on stage, and seemed like a completely different person than the woman responding to interviewer's questions during quieter moments. She explained that she was normally shy and had to completely change her personality in order to sing and dance in the manner she was famous for, and had even gone so far as to give this 'other personality' a name.

When we arrived at the venue, Chris pointed to the sign that said, "VIP Parking Only," and instructed me to follow it. When I drove passed the attendant his head was down and his nose into a book. He paid us no mind. There was an empty spot right by the stage door which had obviously been kept free for someone exceptionally important, maybe the star herself – but it was empty and Chris instructed me to pull in.

We piled out of the car and Chris headed right for the stage door with us following, sheepishly behind. The closer we got, the louder the music grew - a thumping, primal beat of the techno dance number which was racing up the Billboard charts. Again, we walked right past the guards, some armed, who paid us no mind and right up to the door of the venue itself.

When Chris opened it the dark, quiet parking lot was accosted with sound and light and smoke, accompanied by the sickly sweet smell of popular, but illegal drugs. The backstage area was a zoo filled with local dignitaries, movie and pop stars, stage hands and groupies.

Heat and intense light came from the stage area where Cassandra was shaking her stuff and looking good in her spiked high heeled boots, revealing leotard and a black, leather corset. On one side of the stage were backup singers and dancers dancing to the beat, and on the other were the members of the band, completely concentrating on nothing except each other and the music. The carnival like atmosphere provided so many distractions that they were too much for any of us and before we knew it Chris had disappeared with none of us having a clue where he had gone.

Then Buzz spotted him and pointed him out. There was Chris, walking among the dancers and touching each one of them. When he touched them a wisp of something that looked like smoke would come out of them and they would collapse in a heap. All of us had seen Chris cast out demons before, so we knew what he was doing, but he had never done it with so many people looking on.

I looked over at the other two guys and Scott was standing there with his mouth agape, like he couldn't believe what he was seeing and had never seen anything like it, while Buzz had his hands over his face, not wanting to think about damage control effort he was going to have to do as the PR guy for the group. When I looked back at Chris, he had finished with the dancers and had moved to the backup singers who were falling at his touch, just like the dancers had.

It was about that time when Cassandra sensed that something was wrong because the music just wasn't sounding like it should. However, she just kept singing and performing until Chris had moved over to the band, and the instruments began being silenced, one by one, before she turned around to see what was happening.

He had just moved to the last band member when she really caught on to what was going on. That was when she turned and got this look on her face like she was a demon or something. Then she charged him screaming, her mouth open, teeth bared and long nailed fingers twisted so that they looked like an animal's claws. Without stopping what he was doing, he held his hand out, palm facing her and she stopped dead in her tracks. Then he raised his hand, slightly and she began levitating a few inches off the floor.

When he finished with the last band member he turned back to her, suspended in mid-air. He then shouted "Come out of her!" and with a loud scream about twenty wisps of smoke came from her body and disappeared into the darkness above the stage lights. Chris then walked over to her, took her in his arms, then released her from her suspension and softly laid her on the floor.

The whole place was quiet as a morgue, now. No one was dancing and no one was speaking, they were all just staring, wide-eyed, at the stage and at each other. I remember thinking, oh, shit, as I remembered stories about how crowds—reacting over interrupted shows or lost soccer matches—had trampled people as they angrily stormed out into the street. However, no one moved except Chris, who walked to the front center of the stage. He held out his arms and said, in a gentle voice, "Go in peace."

It was almost like a practiced drill, because immediately everyone turned and slowly and quietly filed out of their rows and into the aisles, then out the doors. No one said anything, not even a disgruntled murmur, and Chris just stood there in the floodlights, his arms and hands extended at a slight angle upward, casting a shadow that looked a little like a cross. The performers on stage who had passed out earlier began coming around and when they did, they looked around like they didn't know where they were, stood and silently walked to the dressing rooms – except for Cassandra who was carried off to her dressing room by four stage hands.

Chris stood there in the middle of the stage until everyone left while we stood off to the side, hidden in the curtains. After the only people left were the janitors and security guards, he dropped his arms walked over to us and said, "Let's go." On the way out he turned to a bank of switches and pulled the main lever, leaving the stage in complete darkness.

When we opened the door from the stage area, the parking lot was completely emptied out. Not just the VIP lot, but every parking lot we could see, and there was no one around, anywhere—only the Escalade that was still there where we had parked it. We climbed in and no one said a word on the ride back to the apartments.

When we arrived, Ronni and some others had made a spaghetti dinner, complete with garlic bread and Chianti, and everyone was waiting for us. They had watched the program on JBN, and were all in a mood to celebrate Chris's performance, but when they saw our faces, they didn't say a word, and in silence went to their places around the table and sat down. We all held hands and closed our eyes as Chris prayed:

"Daddy Creator, above all things you are to be honored, cherished and worshiped.

"We come before you as unworthy servants, only given this privilege through Your love and Your Gift to us, the death and resurrection of Jesus the Christ.

"We thank You for all of the gifts You have given us; this day, this food, our health, our families and each other. We recognize You as the Source of all good things, those things we have today, tomorrow and those things we will enjoy after we have passed from this very existence.

"We ask You, Daddy, to be with us now and through upcoming trials and tribulations, and we ask You to forgive our sins and to judge us with more empathy and compassion than we use to judge others. We ask You to send Your Spirit of strength and peace to us today, and in the days to come.

"If it be Your will, let it be so."

As we were eating, the conversation was about everything that had happened that day. Scott and Buzz started telling everybody what happened at the concert and they could barely believe it. Then we talked about the JBN program.

Ronni said that they had all watched at the apartments, and that they all thought Chris had not only held his own during the discussions, but had pretty much taken the others to the woodshed, especially about their attitudes, actions and the way they ran their respective ministries. Everybody pretty much agreed. Buzz said that he had been taking notes and had written down about half a page of zingers which he could turn into soundbites should Chris need to mount a PR campaign.

Chris looked tired and didn't really join in the conversation. When he started eating, though he looked like he was starving and barely looked up from his plate long enough to acknowledge what anyone said.

Somewhere along the line, he stopped eating and turned to Kenneth. "Kenny," he said. "You really haven't said much tonight. Is something bothering you?"

Kenneth looked at him sheepishly and said, "Well, I had to turn my phone off because it was blowing up. There were a bunch of reports that people, all across the country, received strange messages from you during the broadcast—like you were speaking to them, directly, through their televisions or something. All of the reports say that you said personal things to these folks, directly and that no one else heard them.

"At first I thought it was just some crazy talk, but it has been reported by thousands of people and the reports are all the same, just different in what was said in each one."

Chris thought for a moment and asked, "Was anyone injured or hurt in any way by what I supposedly said in these messages?"

Ken scowled. "No, not that anyone has said," he paused for a moment then continued. "But can you do that? Did you do that?"

"What do you believe, Kenny?"

"Chris, I really don't know. Since I came here, I have seen some pretty freakish things, but who would have even considered something like this?"

"I didn't ask what you know, Kenny, I asked what you believe. Do you believe that such a thing happened?"

Kenny sat there for a long time thinking before he spoke. "Yes, Chris," he said, "I do believe it. I don't know how, and just the concept boggles the mind, but I believe it."

Chris then turned to the rest of the group. "What about the rest of you, what do you believe?"

All of us around the table looked at each other.

Some whispered or mumbled to themselves or the person next to them, but then Scott spoke for the group by saying, "Yeah, we believe it, don't we?" The murmuring changed to a general consensus. Then Chris put down his fork and stood.

"You have all seen things with me that before you would have never considered possible. You have seen people healed of disease and addictions. You have seen lives changed for the better by the prediction of lottery numbers or by getting different priorities in their respective lives. Some of you have seen buildings set on fire by the snap of my fingers and demons cast out by my command, and others have even seen angels – heavenly warriors.

"In the Book of Faith it is written that there are those who have seen and because of that believe, but even more blessed are those who believe without seeing. To this point you have seen what I have done, and because of that have faith, but now it is different because you are being asked to believe something you have not seen.

"If this is difficult for you who have witnessed so much, how much more difficult will it be for others you encounter in the future? What will you do and say to grow faith in others after I have gone away?"

At that point the room broke into a din of questions like, "What do you mean?" and "Where are you going?" but Chris just held up his hands for quiet. When the room got quiet, he continued.

"I am going to be here with you for just a little while longer and then you will no longer see me for as long as you are on the earth. However I will always be with you in spirit, and if you continue teaching what I have taught and continue to take actions which will further our beliefs, then you can rest assured that I will always be with you, and with everyone you come into contact with.

"I will live through you, though your actions and

through the actions of those you teach in turn. I will be alive in your stories and in your faith, and in the faith you teach to others."

"But, if you die, you will be raised again, right?" Anna asked

Chris just smiled. "Don't be silly," he answered, and then went back to his spaghetti without another word. Everyone went back to eating and nothing more was said, but from that point on nothing would ever been the same.

Chapter 17 - The Third Gospel According to Veronica

Since the spaghetti dinner, things have been both different and strange. Chris has become sullen and quiet most of the time when he isn't teaching at the amphitheater. The crowds are again getting larger and larger to the point where there just isn't enough space at the amphitheater to seat them all, and the people wind up sitting on the grass or carrying over the picnic tables to sit on in an adjacent space.

The other day, I saw Chris just sitting by himself on the grass outside the front door of the main apartment. Even though I watched him for several minutes, I couldn't tell if he was praying, crying or just thinking. When I walked over and sat beside him, it took him several minutes before even acknowledged my presence. Then when he looked at me, his eyes were as deep and as sorrowful as any I had ever seen.

I asked him what was wrong, and he gave me a weak smile and said "Nothing, nothing's wrong. I'm just thinking."

I decided to try to cheer him up, so I smiled back at him with my best smile and asked, "What are you thinking about?"

"You really wouldn't be interested."

"If I wasn't interested, I wouldn't have asked."

He smiled weakly, took my hand in both of his, looked into my eyes and said, "It's really nothing. Please don't worry yourself."

"Chris," I protested. "I'm really worried about you. You just seem so…strange, lately. You know that I love you and I worry."

He squeezed my hand and said softly, "I love you too Ronni, but this is my burden. There's nothing you can do - but it's nice to know that you care."

I leaned forward. "I DO care, you know I do, and you know I always have. I would do anything for you, anything at all."

He smiled, "Yes, Ronni, I know that - and if there was something you could do, I would ask. But there's nothing right now." Then his smile grew warmer and stronger and he said, "I'll make you a deal. When there is something that you can do for me I will let you know. You'll be the first, I promise!"

Then he reached down and picked a dandelion out of the grass and handed it to me. After that we just sat in silence for a while enjoying the sun and feeling close to each other. He never said anything about it afterward, but I think our little bit of time together raised his spirits just a little, and I know that it did mine.

As I was saying, the crowds around the amphitheater were getting larger and larger and the violence against us seemed to diminish with time, but the distractions seemed to increase, as well. Chris's fame had increased our following, but it also brought us more detractors. It seemed like every day more and more people were coming for his teaching, but also were coming to harass him, and not just him but all of us. There, for a period of about ten days, we had health inspectors and building inspectors nearly every day. They never found anything major, but it was just frustrating that we had to stop what we were doing, and pay attention to them, follow them, answer their questions and try to correct anything they found.

Fortunately, they rarely could find anything, and when they did it was pretty minor. It seemed as though

Chris had them dialed in and before they would show up he would identify several things to be checked and repaired, and we usually had the fixes in place before the inspectors ever got there. As I said, there was no real damage done but it just was not a great deal of fun having them around.

The detractors even showed up at the amphitheater. There was this one day when Chris was teaching in the park, and a group of people simultaneously stood up and began shouting and throwing things. They started with some eggs and vegetables, but one of them had brought some bricks and rocks, and two or three of them started throwing directly at Chris. Fortunately, the police were standing by (as usual), arrested them, and got them hustled out of there, pronto, although we never heard what charges, if any, were pressed against them. They didn't hit anyone, but some of the bricks hit the shell of the amphitheater and caused damage to the freshly painted plaster on the inside of the shell.

Undaunted, Chris continued to teach and day by day the crowds grew even larger and larger. When he wasn't teaching, people were coming to him to be healed. Some wanted healed of physical maladies, others of emotional or mental conditions, some wanted help ridding themselves of addictions of all sorts.

One lady even approached Chris to help her lose twenty pounds even though she wasn't obese by any stretch of the imagination. When she approached him it was all some of us could do to keep from laughing, but Chris just looked at her with those big understanding brown eyes took her hands in his and quietly said, "What I'm going to do for you is something infinitely better. I'm going to give you a gift today, the gift of peace. It comes from the realization of how beautiful and special you really are, and with that realization that you are, and always have been, just perfect."

Then he turned to us and said, "Everyone has pain, and it manifests itself in many ways and for many different reasons, which only the person experiencing will ever understand. Just because it might seem minor to you doesn't mean that it doesn't cause another human being distress of such magnitude that it can be emotionally crippling. You must develop empathy for others who find conditions and circumstances that would seem trivial to you, completely debilitating, just as God has empathy for conditions and circumstances YOU find completely debilitating, but which seem trivial to Him."

He turned back to the woman. "Go in peace. Your sins are forgiven, you are perfect, and God loves you just the way you are."

Haidee leaned toward Tamika and whispered, "He forgave her sins? What has that got to do with wanting to lose twenty pounds?"

Chris glared at her. "You really don't get it do you? Don't you realize that God created you just the way he wants you? The fact that you or anyone else is not happy with her body is a sin because by doing so you think you know more and better than God."

Haidee just looked down at her feet in shame and said nothing.

Chris's demeanor changed immediately upon realizing how he had wounded her. He went to her, took her hand in his, and when she lifted her head he looked her in the eyes and softly said, "It's really not your fault. You grew up in a society which, while denouncing sin, truly embraces it. For example, most people these days don't understand what God means when he says, "You shall not covet."

"Some have taught that coveting means wanting something so much that you would do something immoral for it, but that isn't what it means at all. It means not being happy with what God has provided you, but wanting more or wanting something someone else has. Some might refer to that as ambition, but that kind of ambition often turns to greed. You need to trust God that He knows what is best for you and will provide those things which will uplift and edify you.

"Wanting to be prettier is foolish and futile, because God created you the best way he could for you to be the person you are. It is said that true beauty lies beneath the skin and deep within the soul of the human being. It is also true that those who are the least physically attractive tend to have the most beautiful souls, and conversely, those with the most attractive appearance in many cases have a soul which is dark, and ugly.

"It is better to have a beautiful soul than a beautiful face, because while the face might define human attractiveness, it is the soul with which God finds the most pleasure."

Tears were flowing freely down Haidee's face. Chris embraced her, and Haidee nestled her head on his shoulder and sobbed softly, "I am so sorry...so sorry...so sorry"

Chris just continued to hold her and said, "You were forgiven before you even said it."

Then he said to the rest of us, "Remember that the only sin which is not forgivable is rejecting the Holy Spirit, because by doing so you forfeit your faith and Grace is not available to you. When Jesus of Nazareth died on the cross, his sacrifice was for all of your sins - those you commit today, those you committed yesterday, and those you will commit tomorrow. Because this forgiveness is so all encompassing and so complete, you have true freedom to live your lives to the fullest and to forgive others as you have already been forgiven."

A few days after that he was teaching at the amphitheater and the crowds were the largest yet. He started out, "It is written that blessed are the poor in spirit, blessed are those who mourn, blessed are the meek, blessed are those who hunger and thirst for righteousness, blessed are the merciful, blessed are the pure in heart, blessed are the peacemakers and blessed are those who are persecuted because of righteousness. And while all this is true, I can tell you that you who are alive and standing here today are more blessed than any who have passed before you because of the previous contributions of the poor in spirit, the mourners, the meek, those who thirst for righteousness, the merciful, the pure in heart, the peacemakers and the persecuted.

"Those who have come before have shown you the ways of righteousness, that humility is to be valued over egocentricity; that real happiness is borne of sadness; that meekness defines strength to a greater degree than brashness; that the search for righteousness results in justice; that seeking spiritual purity creates a healthier person than just chasing temporal satisfaction; that peace is preferable to constant war; and that persecution creates empathy. These are the building blocks on which have been laid the foundation of the New Jerusalem with the cornerstone being the freedom you have received from the grip of sin and death through the death and resurrection of Jesus of Nazareth.

"When Jesus was incarnated as man, His job on earth was twofold. The first, and foremost, was to provide the price which must be paid for the sins of all mankind. The second was teaching sinful humanity a new and better way of living. He turned the world upside down with His teachings that the first will be last and the last, first. That empathy for the less fortunate is preferable to exploiting the weak. That kindness is the greatest weapon against your enemies. That physical strength pales in comparison to mental and spiritual strength. To keep your eyes on the heavens instead of on the ground, trusting that if you trip and fall you can get back up and continue on.

"And the cornerstone of the building of this philosophy of peace, purity and truth was the one true and Holy Sacrifice of Jesus, which not only freed you from your own slavery to sin and death, but gave you the example how to grant others their freedom in releasing their sins toward you, and how you become edified, yourself, through that action.

"However, even though Jesus' Sacrifice was sufficient for Grace, it is only a beginning for those things which are to come. We can see that the basis for transforming the world is already in place but just like you have been blessed by those who came before, you need to keep building on this foundation in order to be a blessing for those who come after, as well.

"While we have come far from the days of routine genocide, murdering the less fortunate as spectator sport, public orgies or the social acceptance of vomiting after feasting – we still have far to go. Atrocities and slavery are still prevalent in many areas of the world, but with the efforts of those who came before you, they are better, and it is your job to improve them even more.

"We construct this city, this New Jerusalem, brick by brick – day by day. When you see someone hungry, feed them. When you see someone in pain, comfort them. When you see someone cold, warm them. When you see someone enslaved, by whatever means, free them. Stand up against persecution, exploitation and other wrongdoing. Champion for the weak, heal the sick, help the poor and forgive those who have sinned against you.

"By doing these things, you will bring about the very mystical city many of you look towards. It is the construction of the New Jerusalem which comes from heaven, not the city itself. It's walls of jasper are constructed of justice which comes from God through you, and it's streets are paved with the gold of your good works, sanctified by God. There is no temple necessary in the New Jerusalem, because YOU are God's Church, His Temple, and His Presence is with you always. The light of the city is God's mercy which shines through you for the world to see.

"While we are all constructing this Holy City, we must never forget the first and original job you were sent to do. The world was not made for man, but rather man for the world. Before there was Adam, there was a garden and he was made to be the gardener. He was given dominion over the garden and everything in it, not to exploit it but to care for it, like a parent is given dominion over a child. To those who the greatest has been given, the most is expected.

"In one of the earliest languages spoken by man, the term used for work is literally translated as 'maintenance of the earth'. The earth was given to you to use, yes, but not to misuse. We all know that nature provides for the living in the death of something else, but that doesn't mean that we should revel in death, but in life.

"Just as you wouldn't build a house on a cesspool, you shouldn't build the New Jerusalem on an ash heap. It is time man started using the things God has given you wisely and conserve and protect what you have, rather than lavishly and irresponsibly and destroy the very thing God has given you to preserve you.

"The world is what you will make it. Learn from the wise that have come before, and reject the teachings of those who promote lust, greed and violence."

Chapter 18 - The Third Gospel According to Buzz

I woke with a headache. This was now what, three days in a row? I looked around at the dingy bedroom where I was sleeping in this small apartment and wondered to myself if there were some kind of toxic fumes seeping from the carpet or the walls, slowly poisoning me while I slept. Although the place was clean, it was definitely old and was certainly not what I was accustomed to.

When I pulled my frame from the lumpy mattress, every part of me ached and I swore at it under my breath. On my way to the bathroom, my knees complained every time my foot landed on the floor, and when I reached for the switch the light bulb flashed like it was attached to a camera and left the room in complete darkness.

Fumbling around, I was able to find my toothbrush and toothpaste and while I was able to brush my teeth, I was not about to attempt shaving when I couldn't see what I was doing. Then I found my slippers and shuffled to the kitchen to find a dirty pot with yesterday's cold coffee, and cold, nasty grounds left in the filter.

I tossed the old filter, grounds included, and located a new filter, but when I was opening the can of coffee it slipped from my hand, dumping its contents across the counter and on to the floor of the kitchen. I cleaned them up as best possible, saving what I could and filled the filter with what I had saved, then swept up the rest and put them in the trash with the filter and grounds I had previously taken from the pot.

Grabbing the glass container, I tossed the old coffee, turned on the water and began to rinse it when I noticed that the water was brown and murky and a closer inspection revealed that the bottom was covered with some rust-colored dirt. It was then that I remembered that Scott had said something about working on the plumbing and that we should let the water run for a while to flush out the pipes before using it. Then it occurred to me that I had probably just brushed my teeth with dirty, rusty, brown water with God knows what kind of crud in it.

After a couple of minutes the water began to clear and I made coffee with no further incident, until I got ready to put cream in it, and remembered that I had used the last of it the day before. At that point I decided to go to a coffee place and get something better than the drip-grind swill I had just made. I poured the coffee down the sink and then while putting the pot in the sink succeeded in smashing it against the side of its stainless steel interior, sending shards of glass around the sink and in to the disposal.

At this point I was still being careful not to let out a string of profanities, in consideration of my sleeping roommate Travis. I picked up the pieces of glass as best I could, carefully depositing the broken glass in the trash bag. Afterward, I rinsed the remainder down the drain, turned off the pot and grabbed the hot grounds and filter, burning my finger in the process. I picked up the garbage bag, and started walking out the door when about halfway down the steps one of the pieces of broken glass must have cut a hole in the bag causing it to give way and releasing its contents of dinner scraps, coffee grounds and broken glass onto the open stairway and on to the ground, underneath.

At that point I lost it. I just couldn't do it anymore. I let out a string of profanities in a voice so loud that even the crudest of sailors would have been impressed, and causing several of the residents to open their doors to see who was causing all the ruckus. When Chris came out to help me, he didn't say a word, but I could tell that he was not happy with my behavior.

Instead of saying anything to me, though, he just helped me collect the trash best possible and deposit it in the dumpster. He then reached in his back pocket and handed me a business card from a local coffee store where the manager had written on the back that it could be redeemed for any drink in the establishment.

When he handed me the card he smiled broadly and said, "I was saving this for a special occasion, but you look like you could use it much more than me."

I felt a little ashamed at how I had acted, so I mumbled some kind of thanks and proceeded down the street to the café. The morning air felt a bit cooler than I had anticipated and when I looked down I realized that I was not only still in my slippers, I was hardly dressed for an outing – even one as minor and quick as this one. The result was that I was pretty cold by the time I walked in to the café.

The establishment was pretty much what you would expect, decorated in shades of mocha and chocolate with the scent of espresso wafting through the air. The first person to greet me was a twenty something with visible tattoos and piercings, so I walked up to her and ordered my drink. It came quickly and I was able to find a nice, comfortable chair in the corner to settle in and enjoy the sweet warmth of my coffee confection.

I was on my second or third sip when I heard a familiar voice say hello to me. I looked up to see my former assistant, Phil Kellerman, standing there in front of the chair. He was dressed in a designer suit complete with silk shirt and tie and black Italian loafers. Every hair was in place and the huge links on his French cuffs matched the gold Rolex on his wrist. His teeth gleamed, unnaturally, and it was apparent (but not too) that he had work done on both his mouth and his face.

I put down my cup, stood and offered my hand. "Looking good, baby," I said to him while trying to flash my best political smile. "Life seems to have been very good to you. I heard you had my old job."

"Wish I could say the same about you," he replied as he stepped back and looked me over. "Man, what happened?"

Tact had never been one of Phil's strong suits – which was probably the reason he had been my assistant at the Mayor's office when his time in the political arena was much longer. It was apparent from the look on his face that a sadistic part of him was very much enjoying gloating over my condition – after all, he had always been a bit of a sociopath.

I looked down at my ensemble of dirty sweatshirt, rumpled khakis and beat up slippers, but was determined not to let this boy get under my skin. "Life of leisure, baby," I said as I shrugged my shoulders. "No daily office grind for this kid, anymore." There was no way I was letting this creep get to me.

He sat down beside me. "Man, what a challenge you must be facing working for THAT guy", he said as he jerked his thumb in the direction I had come. "What were you thinking? I mean, going from politics to religion is going from bad to worse, isn't it? Double the headaches for half the money!"

Half the money? I thought. I wish I were getting half the money. None of the money is more like it.

The truth is that I had food to eat and a place to sleep – even coffee in the morning, but I wasn't being paid anything. A long way from the seven figures I had been pulling down from the political campaign funds while working for the Mayor.

"Yeah," I said, "but money isn't everything." I

didn't know if I was trying to convince Phil or myself. Even though I had substituted working for a crooked politician for working for an honest preacher, the job was no easier, and the enemies seemed both more numerous and more adamant in their opposition to the latter.

"Ah, but it helps." he quipped, sunlight glinting off his watch as he raised his cup to take a long pull. He seemed to be deep in thought for a moment, then turned and asked, "So, how does it feel being out of the game?"

"I wouldn't say that I am out of the game, just playing in a different venue is all."

"Still, you must miss the excitement, the glamour and the notoriety of working with the rich, famous and powerful."

"You're saying Chris isn't famous and powerful?" I shot back. "Half of my time is spent fielding calls from national media trying to interview the guy, and powerful? I haven't seen the guy you work for heal a hangnail, much less cure someone of a stage-four cancer. Shit, Rick can't get out of bed in the morning without help."

"I noticed you didn't say anything about rich," Phil chuckled. Even though he was not as good as me, there were still no flies on this one.

"I already told you, money isn't everything."

"…And as I said, it may not be, but it sure does help. To be honest with you, Buzz, it looks like you could use some extra scratch, about now. Planning on using that cup to sell pencils?"

I shrugged and pretended not to be interested, but continued listening to see where this was going.

"Well," Phil continued. "As you are probably aware, your guy has made a lot of enemies. A lot of people who are in the circles you used to run in are pretty concerned about him, and would be highly appreciative of any assistance they could get." He raised his eyebrows in a 'if you know what I mean' kind of way and then added,

"And, in case you have forgotten, the people I am talking about are famous, powerful AND RICH."

I stood up, shook my head, set my empty cup on the table and started to leave. "Look, I might not be pulling down bank, right now, but I am doing fine. I still have quite a bit to show for all those years when I was making seven figures working for Rick, and am hardly anywhere close to destitute."

I turned on my heel and headed out the door, leaving Phil stuttering, "He, he, he….was paying you SEVEN figures?"

The cold wind caught me as I turned left on the sidewalk, away from the apartment complex and toward my old neighborhood. Both my body and my mind were craving a nice, hot shower, a change into some decent clothes and a few moments to relax for a while at my place with a screwdriver for breakfast, and maybe a Manhattan for lunch.

When I turned the corner next on the street where the building in which my condo was located, the first thing I noticed was a moving truck out front, and two guys carrying a very familiar lamp and end table. They were familiar because they were mine.

"Hey!" I yelled. "What the hell do you think you're doing with my things?"

One of the movers looked at the other, then both looked at me, and they started to laugh. "Yeah, right," one of them said, "YOUR things, eh? I guess we got them out of YOUR condo, too, eh?"

I looked down at myself again with painful realization that I didn't look like the owner of high-rise, luxury condo. "Look, just don't move anything more while I get the super, okay?"

"Tell you what, buddy. You get the super, and when HE tells us to stop, we will. But until then, we got a job to do. Understand?"

I went in to the lobby and immediately spotted Bill, one of the doormen. As I headed his direction him he looked as if he were seeing the dead. "Uh…uh…..good morning, Mr. Andrews."

"Bill, what the hell is going on and what are these men doing with my things?" I demanded.

"I was told that they were moving you out, since you haven't lived around here for months, now."

I was indignant. "Who made this decision and why wasn't I even consulted?"

"Let me call Mr. Montague, sir. I am sure he can clear all this up." he said, as he dialed up the building manager's office.

The next time the elevator opened, Alexander Montague III, a neatly dressed man with a slight build; fresh suit (complete with carnation on the lapel) and a pencil thin mustache emerged and walked toward us. The Montagues had been one of the most prominent families in the city, but fell from grace several generations back, when it was rumored, one of the patriarchs fondness of vice trashed the family's good name, and destroyed it's fortune with it.

This particular member had been manager of the building his family used to own for as long as anyone could remember. It was a position given him mostly out of respect for his ancestry and proved to be the only way he could afford to live in the same building to which he was brought home from the hospital as a baby.

"Mr. Andrews," he began, "so good to see you, again. We have been very worried about you."

"Worried about me? Really?"

"Of course, sir," he replied. "You disappeared quite unexpectedly after leaving the Mayor's employ, and no one has seen or heard from you, since. After your maintenance fees had gone unpaid for several months the matter was brought before the board and it was agreed that we should put your belongings in storage and endeavor to find a new resident for your apartment."

"Just a few months absence is justification to move me out and to sell MY apartment out from under me?" I fumed.

"I assure you that it was all done in a manner very above board, legal, and as per the stipulations in the contract you signed when you purchased your apartment," he calmly said.

I knew that this building had more than its share of the most talented legal minds in the city, so I really had no doubt in the actions legality, despite being of questionable morality.

"Fine," I said, resigned. "But I am back now. I will take care of the arrears in my fees, directly, but for now have them move my things back in. I am going to go there, myself, and freshen up a bit."

He looked sick at the realization that he had just lost the substantial override commission he would be receiving if my apartment had been sold to someone else.

"Very good, sir." he said as he motioned the workers to reverse what they were doing and move everything back. "However," he said as he turned back toward me. "There is a matter of payment...."

I cut him off. "I already told you that I would pay the past due fees, directly. At least give me a chance to collect myself."

"I was referring to payment for the movers, sir."

"Direct THAT payment to the person who signed the order," I shot back. It was then that I realized from the look on Montague's face that it was he who had done so and that I might as well have kicked him in the groin. Screw him and his pasty little face and smug demeanor, I thought with some satisfaction as I headed to the apartment.

Although they had started moving me out, by all

appearances they hadn't gotten far – just a few things packed up and moved out of the living room. I left the front door open for the workers and headed into the master bedroom suite where I found everything just as I had left it. Heading straight for the bath, I discarded my clothes on the way and stepped into the shower. The first thing I felt upon entering was the warmth emanating from the heated, imported Italian tile.

Turning the knobs I felt the instantaneously warm water cascading down my body from my overhead, raindrop shower. With the turn of another knob, water was directed from showerheads on the walls, scouring me with clean, hot water and washing all the dirt from the pores of my body. I just stood there enjoying the spray before lathering up with exquisite shower gel and shampoo with a matching scent, then let the water wash everything away.

I dried off on a thick, thirsty, Egyptian cotton bath sheet, then wrapped it around me as I shaved with warm lather from a lanolin infused shaving soap which I had prepared myself with my beaver hair brush. Then I dressed in silk pajamas and covered up with a long satin robe which had been imported from some Asian country.

When I emerged from the bedroom the movers had already completed their task and were gone. I went to the kitchen and prepared myself a cappuccino on the machine with just the touch of a button. Sipping the sweet caffeine laden froth I walked to my overstuffed recliner and let the soft, oxblood colored calf's skin engulf me. Laying back I touched a button on the table beside me and the fireplace lit with a cheery glow, then I closed my eyes and just let the comfort of my home surround and rejuvenate me.

After sleeping several hours in the chair and I awoke to find everything was warm and comfortable. As I stood up there were no aches or pains anywhere in my body as I stretched and yawned, allowing the fresh air to fill my lungs. I looked around and smiled to myself feeling like I was home and realizing how much I had missed it.

Then I walked to the bar, placed several cubes in a short glass and poured in three fingers of a sixteen year-old single malt Scotch. Padding across the living room I headed for my modernly furnished home office, complete with a glass desk, two computer monitors and four televisions, all tuned to different 24-hour news stations. I easily found the headset which was wirelessly connected to a phone that looked like it was from a science fiction movie and slipped it over my ear as I located and dialed the number I wanted.

Tommy Edigar was the political advisor to the Governor, and unlike Phil Kellerman, was someone I respected and thought of not only as a peer, but perhaps even a mentor. He picked up on the third ring.

"Tommy," I said. "It's Buzz. Listen. A little bird told me that some of our friends are getting concerned about a street preacher here in the city, and might not only be appreciative of any help they could get with the situation, but would know how to really show their appreciation. Oh, and do me a favor? Let's keep my former employer and his minions out of the loop, at least for the time being, could we?"

I smiled when the voice on the other end of the line assured me that I could pretty much dictate how everything went from this point, forward.

Chapter 19 – The Gospel According to Arthur

After the dinner dishes were taken away and the mess cleared from the table, Marilyn and Juan went in the kitchen to wash them, while Ronni started the menu plans for the next day. The rest of us excused ourselves and retired to the courtyard to sit on the park benches while we played cards, engaged in conversation and just enjoyed the evening. I had only been with The Team a couple of months, but I never felt more at home in my life.

You see, I grew up in a small, mean, mining town in West Virginia, where men were men, and women were scared to death of them. I don't remember ever thinking that my mother was beautiful, but I am pretty much certain that she was a whole hell of a lot prettier before she married my father. He used to get a load on with the boys after work and then come home and beat the hell out of her.

I asked her once why she didn't leave and after she looked at me like I was stupid, she said that she had been raised here, like her dad and his dad before him, that it was her home and she had nowhere else to go. I wanted to ask her why she put up with the beatings, but I knew she did it to protect her kids. She would rather have him beat her than beat one of us.

This one time I made the mistake of trying to get between the two of them, thinking I might be able to talk him out of it or something, at least one time. The only thing that happened was that he beat both of us, and it was worse than usual. I swear I had never been beaten so badly before or since.

The day I turned eighteen I left home, joined the Marines and never looked back. Even on those long, cold nights in desolate places like Afghanistan I never felt homesick or ever even thought about going back to that hell on earth.

During my four years in the Marines, I did four different combat rotations and saw some of the worst fighting there was to see in the war. If I had wrote down all the places I have been it would look like an atlas of some of the nastiest places on the face of the planet.

I mustered out of the Marines less than a week after I had returned home from the sandbox with no time to decompress and no one to help. I was young, fit, had a wallet full of money and a whole laundry list of urges and desires which had been neglected, but were now coming to the forefront.

Soon after separation the dreams started, waking me from a sound sleep with my heart pounding and my blood racing. I think the worst was when I woke up just before I choked the life out of the girl who had decided that I was an acceptable Mr. Right-Now, and picked me up for a one night stand.

Eventually it got to the point where I didn't want to sleep, afraid of what ghosts might visit or what I might do. One of my buddies suggested that I get some help from the VA, but when I found out it would be months before I could be seen, I thought the next best thing would be self-medication. Soon I not only needed the drugs to sleep, but I needed progressively more and stronger ones.

Then came the voices. They came during the times I was awake, softly at first but building every day with more intensity. The drugs are what brought them and the more and stronger the drugs, the louder and more demanding were the voices. A vicious cycle developed where I needed the drugs to sleep, but the drugs brought the voices and I needed sleep to escape them, and I was such a mess there was no way I would have been able to do anything productive, like hold a job.

Well, it didn't take long before I was out of money, and when the money ran out somehow the friends did, too. My electronics wound up getting stolen or pawned, and soon I found myself living on the street with the clothes on my back and a beat up old duffle bag containing a change of clothes and a few cherished possessions, none of which could be hocked or sold for a nickel.

The grand finale was the day I was standing on the street, naked, cursing everyone and everything and pissing on anyone who came close enough. It took four cops and a taser to subdue me and they didn't even bother booking me at central, but instead took me straight to the nuthouse.

The withdrawals were the worst. I think it took about a week, but it seemed like a lifetime of sweating, shaking, my skin crawling, and puking. I didn't eat the entire time, so I don't know where it came from but I swear I puked my entire body weight in vomit. The heaves and convulsions were so severe that I burst blood vessels in my eyes, and I swear I saw a toenail or two come out. They had me strapped to the bed, but at one point I broke the restraints, and when the ordeal was finally over, I had bent the bedrails and my arms were one big bruise from the shoulders, down.

You would have thought that once the drugs were gone, the voices would have gone, too....but that didn't happen – and didn't they go away, the dreams started, again. My life was hell on earth; no peace at night because of the ghosts visiting me in those violent dreams; no peace during the day because those voices would never leave me alone – whispering their secrets and telling their lies that only I could hear.

In the hospital my physical health improved, but not

my mental health – not at all. After all the drugs were gone the doctors tried everything they could to allow me to stay there, but since there were no funds to help keep me in and I was not deemed sufficient enough of a threat to others (I guess you have to be naked and pissing on people to be considered that), they had to release me and put me back out on the street.

I know that there are some who say that most homeless people are there by choice, but those folks have to be just plain stupid. I mean, who would choose to sleep in the cold on the hard ground, filthy and surrounded by filth? If that isn't bad enough, you eat garbage and learn you can't trust anyone after you have been beaten or ripped off or both enough times.

However, while I was in there was this one guy who got discharged from the crazy hospital and came back, but he didn't come back as a patient, he just came back to visit the rest of us. He looked really good, really healthy and told us that he had met a guy who had healed him. Well, the voices in my head told me that he was full of shit, but it was pretty obvious that something had made the guy better. When the bus left the hospital and dropped me off at the shelter, I remembered what this guy had said and asked around a little bit.

Well, it didn't take long before I got the straight skinny on where this Chris hung out, so I grabbed my duffle and took off. I noticed the crowd long before I got there and the closer I got the denser the crowd became. Soon I found myself in a position where I couldn't move forward, couldn't move back and was completely lost in the crowd.

It was then I heard someone call out to me by name, and when I turned, there was Chris. I will never forget what he said to me.

"I heard you calling, so I came."

I swear I never said a word. I didn't call to him.

Nothing. But, the voices inside my head were now screaming for me to run and hide. At first they told me that he would hurt me. Then they told me that I wasn't worth his time. It was like they were making even less sense than they usually did, except that everything they were saying made it crystal clear that they didn't like him, one bit.

I just stood there, frozen like a statue and when he reached out his hand all of the voices started screaming at once. The noise in my head was worse than anything I had ever experienced, and then when his fingers touched my cheek they stopped. Just like that, they were gone and they never came back. Ever. The dreams have stopped, too.

After touching my cheek, Chris reached down, grabbed my bag and without hesitation said "Come with me, Art. I have a safe place for you." He walked out of that crowd, ignoring everyone and everything else, only paying attention to me. He took me to the apartment complex and that night I slept like a baby and have every night, since joining the team.

Anyway, this particular evening most of the conversation centered around Buzz. It had been over a week since he left after dumping his garbage all over the place and cussing a blue streak. I swear, I didn't know whether to feel sorry for the guy that morning or be embarrassed for him. Well, no one had seen him since that little incident and people were speculating on what had happened to him when he suddenly showed up in the middle of us, like nothing had happened – and for the next couple of hours it seemed like everything was normal, everything was forgotten, I guess.

A little while after Buzz showed up, Ronni stuck her head out the door and called out to Chris, saying that someone was on the phone for him. He left, briefly, and then came out to the table where a bunch of us were sitting.

"Moe," he said, "I need you to fire up the rig, we have a run to make." Then, as Moe started to get up, he looked around and said, "Buzz, Art...why don't you two ride along?"

I thought it was a bit unusual that he was asking me instead of Scott or Travis, but it wasn't an unreasonable request and since I hadn't been out of the complex for a few days I jumped at the chance to go for a ride. Buzz, on the other hand began to protest a bit, but Chris wouldn't hear of it. He even suggested that Buzz ride shotgun (the front passenger's seat) and finally talked him into it. The four of us walked to the SUV and Moe started the vehicle and started backing out.

"Where to, Boss?" he asked Chris, jokingly.

"Helen's place," he replied. "You remember where it is, right?"

"Sure do," Moe said. "My old stomping grounds."

"Exactly," Chris said and then added, "she called saying that she isn't feeling well and wants me to come by."

It made sense to me. After all, Chris was known to heal people – probably tens of thousands by this time. We drove there in silence and when we got to the apartment and stopped, Chris asked us to stay in the car and wait for him, that he wanted to see her, alone. That seemed a little strange, but it was a nice night, Moe had put on some decent tunes, so I was cool with it. Buzz seemed a little nervous, though, and a bit antsy, I would say, but nothing really strange, so I didn't think much about it.

Chris was gone a pretty long time when we saw him come out of Helen's apartment. Nothing in his demeanor seemed amiss and when he got to the car, I asked him, "How is she doing? Is she feeling better?"

"Quite a bit." Chris said, and then we drove back home.

The next morning we were having breakfast when Anna came in with the morning paper and let us know that Helen had passed away the night before. We all looked at Chris who, between bites of bacon said, "Death is just a natural part of this life. Helen wanted me to be there with her when she passed to the other side. Take comfort in the assurance that she made the transition with little pain and that we will all be together, again." Then he went back to eating his breakfast as if nothing happened.

While we understood what Chris told us, Helen had become a special person to everyone on the team, even myself. She was like that grandmother you always wished you had, rather than the one in the house with the hard scrabble floors that smelled of rancid bacon grease, and who made biscuits in a cast-iron skillet over an old stove. A curtain of sadness fell over us and we finished our breakfast with conversation in silence or in hushed tones, if anything was said at all.

Breakfast that morning was the last time I saw Buzz, that day or forever, if you're talking about in person or at the apartment complex. I have seen him on the TV a couple of times, but I suppose that they don't count. Anyway, after we finished eating Chris took him to the side and had a quiet, private conversation. After that Buzz said he needed to run some errands and when Moe offered to give him a ride, he said that it was a nice day and he would rather walk or take a bus. It was after he left that Chris called us together and had a very strange meeting which I will never forget.

I can't recall his exact words, but the gist of it was that we should be careful what we believe, and that we should keep faith in him and in each other, regardless of what happens, what is said about us or what we are told by others. He also added that his time of trial was coming due (I had no idea what he was talking about at the time) and then said something strange - - that we should be especially kind to one another. I remember thinking that if it was HIS time of trial we should be especially kind to HIM, but he definitely said to be kind to each other. That was just like him, never concerned about himself, only about other people.

It was about that time that the doorbell rang. We all sat while Chris got up and answered it. When he did, I looked outside and it looked like we were in a combat zone or something. The whole yard was full of SWAT cops with automatic weapons and riot gear. When Chris opened the door there were three cops, one in the middle and two on the sides with their weapons at their shoulders and trained on Chris. The one who was standing in the middle moved toward the open door said, "Christopher Pawlinsky, you are under arrest for the murder of Helen Emerson."

Chris didn't react but just stood there like he was expecting them. Then he held out his hands in front of himself, with his wrists together for handcuffs, but instead the cop grabbed his arm and spun him around, then threw him on the floor. On his way down he hit his head on the corner of the end table causing a lamp to fall. Ronni cried out a little, but no one moved – it was like we were in shock, or something.

None the less, four cops ran into the room and held us at gunpoint while another one held a shotgun to the back of Chris's bleeding head. The guy who threw him down roughly knelt on the small of his back and used a zip-tie to bind his hands and a second for his arms at the elbow. It was a technique we were taught to use on the most dangerous prisoners we captured, but I thought it was way overboard for someone as kind and gentle as Chris.

Then, just like in the movies, the cop said, "You have the right to remain silent. Anything you say can and will be used against you in a court of law….." as he took Chris away.

Chapter 20 – The Fourth Gospel According to Scott

It was not unexpected, to be honest. Chris had eluded that something both dramatic and nefarious was going to happen to him some time soon, but never really stated what. In the days that led up to his arrest he seemed more sullen, quiet and introspective than usual. Once I was going to ask him if something was the matter but before I could, he mentioned that he had found it difficult, lately, to get any kind of solitude and that prayer, meditation or even just thinking seemed more difficult than usual. Knowing that he did a lot of all three, I accepted that was probably the problem and the best thing I could do for him was to give him some space – so I did.

That was about the same time that Buzz started acting strange. There was that morning he had the melt-down where he went off, screaming and cursing about garbage, of all things. Then he disappeared for a week or so, just to reappear one evening with no explanation and nothing to say for himself, but just joined in as if there was nothing out of the ordinary. Then, just before Chris was arrested the son-of-a-bitch just walked out of the compound and out of our lives forever (at least for the most part). When the arrest took place the pieces of the puzzle fell into place and I have to tell you, I have never been so pissed and felt so betrayed in all my life, not even at my ex-District Manager or ex-wife.

As I watched Chris hauled off that way, the anger welled up inside me. It was so unfair! Helen was one of his oldest and dearest friends, and they were accusing him of what? Of killing her? Really? How could he have done that? Didn't they know anything at all about him? If they did, arresting him would be the last thing they should be doing.

After thinking about it for a minute or so I swear that if Buzz had been within arm's reach I would have throttled the life out of him, regardless of any temporal or eternal consequence – but then I shook off the anger and came back to reality. There were still ten other people who had relied on Chris for guidance, and now they were all looking at me - literally, standing in the living room with the broken table lamp still on the floor and looking at me - and I wasn't sure how, or even if I could handle my new responsibility.

I knew I had to say something, but the only thing I could think of was, "Okay, now is not the time to panic, it is the time to think. Does anyone know a lawyer?"

Everyone on the team was looking at each other and then one, I think it was Travis, who said, "There was that one lawyer that Chris helped kick a drug habit." He turned to Haidee and said, "you were there, do you remember his name?"

It was if a lightbulb had turned on inside Haidee's head. "Yeah, that one guy," she said, biting her lip in thought. "Harry, wasn't it….Harry…"

Marilyn cut in. "You don't mean Harold Etheridge, do you? The big shot defense attorney?"

"Yeah," Haidee said, getting excited. "I think that's the one. Chris called him Harry, but you know how he was….uh, is."

Marilyn rolled her eyes, "Did someone die and leave us a trust fund? There is no way we could never afford him!"

I cut her off. "Never say never. How many times have we seen people do all kinds of things for Chris, just because he needed them?"

Ronni then interjected. "We should contact his family, while we are at it."

Kenny looked puzzled. "He has family? I thought we were his family!"

Ronni looked indignant. "Of course he has family," she said as if she were addressing a preschooler. "His mother, brother and sister live in Florida." She then looked straight at him. "Everyone has family. Everyone has a mother....well, maybe except you...."

"Hey!" Kenny protested and the entire room broke up in laughter. Even Ronni had a smile on her face to let him know it was just a joke.

"Do you know how to get hold of them?" I asked her.

"Of course," she replied. "We talked about them quite often."

To be honest, I felt a little hurt that Ronni knew more about his family than I did, but just put it out of my mind because I knew that it wasn't important. "Okay," I said to her. "Can you take care of that? I will contact Mr. Harold Etheridge, if he will let me in his office." Then I turned to Moe. "Can you drive me?"

"Sure," he said. "When do we leave?"

"As soon as we can," I said, and then thinking out loud to myself, "we need someone to teach the lesson this afternoon."

"But that is Chris's gig," Juan said.

"I have a feeling he is going to be a bit detained today, don't you? We need to keep doing the work he started, remember what he told us?" I thought for a second and then turned to Travis. "Could you teach the lesson this afternoon?"

I think he almost gagged on his tongue. "Me?" he said.

Before I could answer, Anna spoke up. "I can do it today, but someone else can take it tomorrow. What do you think, Trav?"

"What if Chris comes back?" he protested. It was obvious that he was nervous at the prospect of teaching on his own.

"What if he isn't?" she shot back. "Don't you think you should be prepared if you have to teach tomorrow?"

"I guess so."

"Okay, so we all know what we have to do. Everyone has their normal jobs except Anna and Ronni, so let's get to it." Then I turned to Moe. "Ready?"

"Let's roll!" he said, as he walked toward the door.

It was a beautiful day. The sun was shining and the birds were singing, but it seemed strange to me because in my mind it should have been dark and dreary, considering what had happened. There was a huge weight on my heart over Chris being arrested and I was still mad as hell at Buzz, the traitor.

My mind was racing a hundred miles an hour as I kept running over all the things that needed to be done and the new responsibilities I was facing, and I didn't want to miss something or drop the ball. Before I knew it we were pulling into the underground parking garage of a huge, white, commercial building.

After locating a parking space and securing the Escalade, we found the elevators and on the wall beside them was the directory showing the firm of Etheridge, McKinney and Burr on the 41st floor. As we waited for the elevator to arrive I took in the reflection of the two of us in the polished steel door revealing two guys more dressed for yard work than meeting with a high-profile attorney (especially without an appointment) and I have to admit feeling rather out of place. However, what we were doing was important, and I wasn't going to let my pride get in the way of what needed done.

When the elevator arrived on the 41st floor and the doors opened, it revealed a huge and impressive office.

We walked across a deep green carpet to the teak and brass receptionist's desk where there was a very attractive woman who was answering call after call, before even acknowledging our presence.

After what seemed like a small eternity she finally looked up at us and asked, "May I help you?"

"We need to see Harold Etheridge."

"Do you have an appointment?

"No."

"Mr. Etheridge sees no one without an appointment, sorry. Please take one of his cards and call us to set up an appointment." she said, and went back to answering the phones, which were ringing off the hook.

I was getting a little perturbed. "I am sorry, Miss…uh…," then I spotted the name plate with Andrea Baxter emblazoned on it mounted on the counter. "…Baxter, but this is rather an emergency. Is Mr. Etheridge in?"

She looked up from her phones, "And I am sorry, Mr…..uh…" she said.

"Hansen," I interjected. "Scott Hansen." I felt a little foolish and asked myself if this pretty brunette might think I was trying to emulate a notable fictitious British spy, so I grinned and added "Double Oh Four?"

It seemed to work a bit. Stifling a chuckle, she continued. "Mr. Hansen, I am sorry, but Mr. Etheridge has a hard and fast rule about this. You MUST have an appointment."

"Is he in?" I insisted.

At first she looked like she didn't want to answer, but eventually admitted that he was.

"I need you get him a message. I am sure he would want to hear this."

Resigned, she sighed. "Okay, I will send him a message. But I really doubt it will do you much good."

"Would you please let him know that Chris

Pawlinsky was arrested about an hour ago and is facing murder charges? We are here on his behalf." Then I headed for a nice couch and called over my shoulder, "If it is okay, I will wait here until you get an answer. Thanks!"

I sat down pretending to read a magazine while actually watching her out of the corner of my eye. I didn't know if she would be good to her word and get the message to Mr. Etheridge or if she was going to call security. Moe followed and sat right next to me. I watched her answer another couple of phone calls before dialing one out and gave us about 50/50 odds that we were soon going to be escorted out of the building. However, within five minutes another equally attractive woman, whom I assumed was a legal admin or an assistant of some kind, entered the lobby.

"Mr. Hansen?" she called out in our general direction.

"Right here," I said, as I stood and started walking toward her with Moe trailing.

"Mr. Etheridge will see you, please follow me," she said, and turned and walked down the hall carrying a leather portfolio with her short, tight skirt accentuating her curves.

I turned my head toward Andrea and she smiled and gave a small shrug. I smiled back and winked, which caused her to look down a bit and blush, slightly. I considered trying to get her number before we left the office.

We followed the woman in the tight skirt and she led us down the hall to a large glass room which contained a mahogany conference table surrounded by a number of large, black leather chairs, complete with arms. She held the door open while she introduced herself as Shelia and asked us to take a seat at the two chairs already pulled out on the left side of the table.

She then positioned herself at the head of the table

and pointed out a tray with a pot of fresh coffee and several bottles of water in the center. I poured myself a cup of coffee and Moe grabbed a bottle of water while she explained that she was an associate of Mr. Etheridge and was going to get some preliminary information from us.

She took notes as I explained what happened and answered her questions best I could. She only seemed a little annoyed that I couldn't identify the precinct of the officers who had arrested Chris, but otherwise the interview seemed to go well, and I was greatly relieved that at least an associate of Harold Etheridge's firm was going to represent us.

After she heard the story and was satisfied that she had enough information, she excused herself, asked us to wait, and left the room. I looked at Moe while he took a long pull from his water bottle. Putting the cap back on he grinned and said, "Man, did you get a look at that fine female lawyer? Dude, and look at these digs!"

He got up and walked around the room. "Get a load of these chairs! Did you ever feel leather this soft? They have got to cost over a grand a piece….and check out this table!" He knocked on it with his knuckles. "This is solid, man. This ain't no cheap shit. And heavy? I bet this thing weighs…" he paused as he sized it up, "….at least eight hundred pounds."

Then he walked to the end of the room where a matching mahogany cabinet complete with brass handles and hinges was hanging on the wall. When he opened it, he let out a low whistle while sizing up a large high-end, flat screen TV inside. "Scott….get a load of this. It's got to be at least seventy inches! Who says that crime doesn't pay? We all know that lawyers are the biggest crooks ever!" He was putting on such a show I couldn't help but laugh out loud.

I was still laughing when Shelia returned. "Mr. Hansen? Mr. Etheridge will see you now."

I was taken aback for a second, but then my shock turned to elation as I realized that the famous lawyer was going to take the case, after all. "You're not going to represent us?" Moe said, looking a little dejected.

"I will be the associate who helps work the case, but Mr. Etheridge will take the lead."

Moe brightened up. "Nice!" he said under his breath. I shot him a stern look but all he did was start laughing at me. "I saw you checking out the receptionist, so don't try it, *'Mister Hansen,'*" and then he laughed, again.

Shelia directed us to a huge mahogany door which opened automatically when we approached. We walked through it and into one of the most impressive offices I have ever been in, like one you would see on TV or something. The back wall, from floor to ceiling, was nothing but shelves, holding literally thousands of books in expensive leather bindings while on the opposite wall was a roaring fire in the fireplace to add ambiance. Another wall was nothing but windows which gave a gorgeous view of the city skyline and the coast, beyond. In the middle of the room was a massive desk, meticulously organized and in the center of it was an open file.

Shelia directed us to the two chars in front and facing the desk and just as we seated ourselves Mr. Harold Etheridge, a sharply dressed man with a powerful gait and dark hair, graying slightly at the temples, entered though a door on the fourth wall which was built to blend in with the wainscoting and rendered it nearly invisible to the naked eye.

We stood as he walked toward us with his hand outstretched. "Harry," he introduced himself, "I understand that a mutual friend has found himself in some kind of trouble?"

I shook his hand and introduced myself, but my thoughts told me that this guy was a typical lawyer used to dealing with all kinds of scumbags who broke the law. He didn't use terms like 'is in trouble', or 'got in trouble', but 'found himself in trouble' – as if the suspect was just standing on the street corner minding his own business when he was caught up in some sort of draconian dragnet. Then thought a second time that maybe, in this case, it was the appropriate expression.

After we made introductions all the way around and sat down, Harry started the conversation. "So, I have reviewed the case here and Shelia has made some phone calls on Chris's behalf. It appears as though it is probably a case of mistaken identity or based on some kind of shoddy information from somewhere, so we should have him out of custody fairly quickly."

"Any idea when?" Moe asked.

"Well, that is hard to say," the lawyer said. "They are playing some kind of cat-and-mouse game with him, currently – moving him from precinct to precinct without booking him." He leaned back in his chair. "He must have really pissed some people off in some pretty high places. This is the kind of thing they do to mobsters and the like to keep them off the streets and mess with their defense teams."

"Pissed off?" I said. "Probably, more like scared the crap out of them. Things have been really strained with authorities since the election when he almost beat the incumbent without even running."

"Not just political figures," the lawyer continued. "It seems like he has made enemies in a lot of places. He has shown up the law enforcement in this town by reducing crime in ways they never could, ground the drug trade to a slow trickle of what it used to be, and rescued hookers to the point that the act of prostitution in this town is almost non-existent as well. If you don't think that endeared him to powerful people on both sides of the law, think again."

"Yeah, we already had that figured out," Moe said.

Harry continued. "Then he pulled that classic "two-fer" when he made a bunch of TV evangelists and evangelical Christian theologians look stupid on national television. Then, for act two, he not only broke up a concert featuring one of the biggest singing acts in the country, but ruined her career by supposedly casting out the demons who were giving her the ability to sing and shake her ass while wearing next to nothing on stage."

I had been there every step of the way but had never really realized what kind of impact Chris had actually made on our society at large. Not, that is, until I was sitting in this lawyer's office listening to him recap all the events I had witnessed in one quick summary.

"Yeah," Harry went on. "So I figure we will be taking on the influence of the political machine, the legal system, crime organizations, organized religion and the entertainment industry in addition to whatever facts the DA has for building this case against him."

Moe interjected. "You forgot the medical system and the pharmaceutical industry. Chris has been healing a lot of 'incurable' diseases and eliminating the need for a lot of expensive drug treatments and medications."

Harry nodded in agreement, and the weight of what we were facing suddenly became clear to me. There were going to be a lot of people interested in this case and what might or might not become of Chris. It also made me wonder if it were even plausible to hope for a good outcome of the situation.

I looked at Harry. "So, does this mean you won't take the case?"

"You're kidding me, right?" the lawyer shot back. "There is no way I would pass on this case – a case of both local and national interest? We will be in the headlines of every paper in the country! In my business any publicity is good publicity. Besides, it will be nice to actually represent someone who is innocent for once."

"Now, as far as your fee is concerned…" I said, but the lawyer shook his head.

"Even if I didn't owe him," he said. "I would probably take this case pro-bono. However, when you consider the amount of money Chris has saved me that I don't spend putting white powder up my nose just to function, I don't think I could repay him enough."

"Alright," I said, greatly relieved that we were not only going to get the best defense attorney in the city, but for free, to boot. "Where do we go from here?"

"Well," he said. "We have to wait for them to book him which, if they continue to play these silly games, may take as long as twenty four hours. After they finally decide to book him, I will be able to meet with him for arraignment and we will know more about our options at that time."

"Then I guess we're pretty much done for now?" I asked.

"Pretty much. We will be in touch as soon as we know anything," he said, handing me his card. "Sylvia will be your main point of contact, but feel free to call me, personally, whenever you feel necessary."

I shook his hand and said, "Thank you so very much, Mr. Etheridge. You have no idea how much this means to us."

He took my hand with a firm grip, looked me straight in the eye and said, "You are most certainly welcome, Scott."

As we left the office Shelia handed us each one of her cards and asked if we could find our way out. We assured her that we could and proceeded back the way we came. As we walked through the lobby, I heard someone call out to me. I turned and saw Andrea headed our direction.

"Mr. Hansen, I have a message for you." she stated as she handed me a folded piece of paper. I opened it and it read: Call me sometime, 212-555-3969 – Andrea. I looked up, and just as I did, she looked over her shoulder and smiled at me.

Moe, who had taken it upon himself to read the note over my shoulder started to laugh. "Scotty, you dog! You still got it, player."

Chapter 21 – The Fourth Gospel According to Veronica

The day a leader of an organization or a team left would not normally be considered a banner day, but the day Chris was arrested our little team grew in synergy, power, performance and production. The mission continued on with team members not only continuing in the roles they previously had, but also stepping up to take on additional ones, including covering those which were normally assigned to Chris.

Some of the team members took over teaching duties while others sought out the roles of comfort and healing, while others started new projects like learning based child care and providing food, clothing and shelter for the less fortunate. The most amazing thing to me was the ability of those who took on the healing roles and how quickly they became as proficient and successful as Chris himself, and the most surprising of all was that Moe took over that part of our mission.

When I now look at Moe and how he has grown and changed, it is hard to believe he is the same thug I met in that warehouse back when this whole thing started. Even though it has been a matter of months and not years, he is now completely changed; kind, caring and sensitive to everyone he comes in contact with. When I look at the changes he has made, it gives me a new confidence in the human race, and makes me wonder how much I have changed, myself.

Scott has really blossomed, as well. It is hard to believe that the burned out shell of a man in a filthy hoodie is the same man I now know and admire. In Chris's absence he has really stepped up and taken over the team leadership role, and it has suited him, well. He also has a new girlfriend in his life, Andrea, and the whole relationship seems to have rejuvenated him and given him the confidence he has lacked for so long.

As for me, I still pretty much play den mother and take care of everyone, logistically speaking. Planning and preparing, or overseeing the preparation of meals as well as doing the shopping. I guess I have taken on other duties as well, picking up some of the teaching duties, myself – starting off with our evening devotions, and now I will be giving my first public teaching session next Wednesday.

We are also immensely grateful to Harry Etheridge; he has been so helpful to Chris. After Chris was arrested he told us that the police shuffled him to at least six or seven different precincts before they actually booked him, and then it still took several hours before Harry could get in to see him. I guess between the guards and the inmates, they didn't treat him with anything like kid gloves and the first time Harry saw him, he was pretty bruised, battered and beaten.

Harry was going to get him put in a separate holding area but Chris wouldn't hear of it. He said that he couldn't do what was required of him if he was not around people. Harry said he tried to convince him otherwise, but there was no changing his mind.

At the arraignment the DA got the judge to hold Chris without bail. He argued that Chris had some supernatural abilities, the extent of which are unknown, and paraded a whole bevy of witnesses to testify that in some cases he just showed up from seemingly nowhere and at unusual times, and that in other cases (like the one on TV) he could apparently be multiple places doing multiple things simultaneously, so it could only go to reason that he could be a flight risk and possibly even disappear before his court date.

Harry argued that if the basis for his being deemed a flight risk, despite the fact he has no passport, has insufficient cash to buy a ticket and no personal mode of transportation, is because of some unknown supernatural power, then what would prevent him from doing so while incarcerated? The judge, however, who was probably part of the political machine and who therefore had an agenda against Chris, didn't want to hear it and had him held without bail until his trial.

I try to visit Chris at least three times a week, sometimes even more. I think that some of the team members think that he and I are sweet on each other, and although sometimes I wish it were more, it really is nothing like that. Maybe we are closer than the others because of the length of time we have known each other, or maybe we are comfortable with each of us knowing so much about the other that it is just natural for us to be closer. Regardless, I can just imagine how lonely he is in that jail by himself, although he has started another project there behind bars. I have heard him say that we should all be like seeds and grow wherever we find ourselves planted, and as always he is leading by example.

On my first visit I was taken aback at his appearance. He had not yet healed from the beatings he took on the day he was arrested, and it was rather painful to look at. Both of his eyes were black, his nose was bent out of shape and looked broken, one ear was torn and he had a cut lip. Otherwise he was just various shades of red and purple where the bruising was in full bloom.

Since then his healing has come along nicely and the bruises first started turning lighter, then yellow, are now almost completely gone. Scott accompanied me on my last visit and when they saw each other the two men embraced like long, lost brothers. After the initial greetings all the way around Chris asked how the mission was coming and Scott broke everything down for him as to who was doing what and how the mission had expanded. When telling him about the teaching schedule, he included that I was going to be teaching, soon, too and Chris beamed widely at the news and told me he was proud of me.

After Scott was done, Chris said, "Scott, I am very proud of you. It sounds like the mission is in good hands – like I ever had a doubt." Then he changed the subject. "Has anyone seen or heard from Buzz, lately?"

"No," Scott replied, "and as far as I am concerned if I never see him it will be too soon. " Then he added, "And to be honest, I am not sure what I would do if I do see him again."

Chris scowled. "If you do, you will do nothing – and pass that on to everyone else, okay? Having to live with what he has done is sufficient punishment, trust me. It may not seem like it on the outside, but he is dealing with things the depth and breadth of which I hope you never understand. Sometimes having to face your own actions is the harshest punishment one can have and living with yourself and knowing what you have done is the worst possible punishment."

Scott shrugged in resignation. "Okay. If you say so."

"I do," Chris said. "Now, tell me about this young woman you have been seeing."

"I would ask how you knew that, but I learned a long time ago not even to bother…" and he went on relaying about his budding romance with Andrea. As the conversation continued eventually we got around to his case and the upcoming trial.

"Excuse me?" Scott exclaimed after Chris filled us in on what Harry had told him. "They are basing the case against you on the speculation that you could have caused Helen's death in some kind of supernatural manner, because you are able to heal people the same way?

Really?"

"Well, that is what Harry is telling me that he got in discovery with the DA," Chris said. "Helen's autopsy showed that she died of pulmonary embolus, or a blood clot going to the lungs. She told me that she hadn't been feeling well, and I offered to heal her, but she didn't want me to. She was ready to go, to meet her husband and parents on the other side, so I held her hand and comforted her as she passed. Then I called 9-1-1 and left because there was nothing else left to do."

Scott sat forward. "So, they are basing the case against you, primarily, on the fact that you left before the responders arrived, and nothing else – at least nothing else concrete?"

"What else would they have?" Chris asked.

Scott went on. "But, if they have no evidence, then what chance do they have of a conviction?"

"The same chance they had of remanding me in custody instead of bail, I suppose," Chris said.

Scott and I looked at each other and I took Chris's hand as he continued. "The thing Harry is concerned about is that the trial will be held in the press and the court of public opinion, where opinions can be swayed and judgments made based on opinions and misinformation instead of law and facts."

Scott looked down and nodded his head. "That is a big concern. Politicians and pundits alike are taking cheap shots at you, using terms like public menace, agitator, socialist, and even terrorist. And the press is covering it like a cheap suit."

"Yeah," Chris said. "I have been hearing those, too, although I am not certain how they came up with the whole terrorist thing."

"Probably the same way they came up with the whole murder thing. Through a very active imagination," I said.

"…and some spite, mixed in with jealousy and hatred," Scott added.

The conversation then turned to every day, mundane things, for the most part. We spent a few minutes discussing prison food, how Chris was continuing teaching behind bars, etc. Eventually the conversation returned back to the team, the mission and how everything was working with Chris being incarcerated, and naturally Buzz became the topic of conversation, once again.

"I am serious. I don't want any one from the team doing anything to harm him," Chris reiterated.

"I understand," Scott said. "I will respect your wishes, even though it goes against the very core of my being – and will pass your wishes on to the team members."

"Thank you," Chris said. "Now, as part of putting this whole situation behind you, you need to find a replacement for him. You may have noticed a new guy hanging around the mission by the name of Thomas. He is a good man, and you will find that adding him to the team will be a blessing for us as well as for him. I think he could do a lot to help contribute to the continuation of the mission."

I thought for a minute, trying to picture who he was speaking about, and then it came to me. "You're talking about a large guy, nice face and pretty eyes, right? Wears luau shirts and shorts a lot?"

"That's the one," Chris replied.

I thought about it for a second and realized that Thomas (I had no doubt that Chris had his name right, he is never wrong about such things) hadn't started coming around until after he was arrested, and would really have no regular human way of knowing it. But again, I knew that this was not unusual, and knew better than to ask how it worked out that way.

After we left the prison, Scott was a little moody and

introspective, and suggested that we stop and have a drink at a hotel watering hole known for attracting the city's A-list people. It had been a while since I had done anything remotely like that, so I readily agreed.

We walked in and grabbed a seat by the windows, where the afternoon sunlight streamed in and made the polished wood grain in the tables sparkle as if they had tiny veins of gold. We had just started our drinks and light conversation when a fairly large group of well dressed men walked in, laughing and carrying on, paying us no mind at all. Included in that group was none other than our old friend, Buzz Andrews.

I noticed that Scott had seen him, too, so I reached over and gently put my hand on his forearm. "Remember what you promised Chris," I reminded him.

"I know," he said. "But just look at that smug son-of-a-bitch, in his thousand dollar suit, and with his band of Rolex buddies."

I wasn't going to correct him, but the suit Buzz was wearing probably cost several of those thousand dollars Scott was fuming about. Scott looked out the window, probably to keep from making eye contact with him, losing his self-control and breaking his promise, but I continued watching the group of men and especially Buzz.

He was doing his best to fit in, with the hilarity and storytelling. It looked to me though, that when he thought no one was paying attention, he would get this look on his face for a few seconds which could best be described as forlorn, before he caught himself and changed, to keep his melancholy from spreading to the rest of the group.

We finished our drinks without speaking and then left the bar. As we were walking out, I caught Buzz looking at us. Scott refused to even look in that direction, but when I saw his eyes I shot him my best smile. In response, Buzz just looked down, as if in shame.

When we got back to the apartment complex, the

team was sitting around the picnic tables, visiting and Thomas was among them. I took a good, long look at the newcomer.

He was about the same age as most of the group, mid-to-late twenties, and was dressed in a gaudy Hawaiian shirt and cargo shorts with some kind of camouflage pattern. Scott and I joined them, and they all wanted to know the latest on Chris and to hear about our outing. Scott filled them in on just about everything, but left out the part about the bar and the encounter with Buzz.

As he had promised, he relayed Chris's instruction about Buzz and how he was not to be harmed. For the most part the team members accepted what was said, with little grumbling, but Moe couldn't help but let out some profanity when he heard. There had always been tension between the two men and I think he was looking forward to getting a little street justice on the man, to settle an unwritten score.

Then, Scott looked at Thomas and said, "Chris also wanted me to extend to you an invitation to join the team. He said you would be the perfect replacement for Buzz."

Thomas looked surprised. "Really?" he said. "Chris said to ask me? But I never…"

Scott cut him short. "Don't ask. You won't understand it and never will. None of us do. Just accept that is how things work around here."

"Okay," Thomas said. "it's just that I have never been invited to join anything like this, before, and don't know what to do."

We all laughed and Travis said, "Don't worry. Just be open to just about everything and when the opportunity arises, you will know what to do. That is how the rest of us operate."

Scott looked at Thomas. "So, tell us about yourself. What kind of skill set do you bring? Where do you come from, what's your background and what experiences have you had?"

"Not a lot," he said. "After graduation I took some time off and did some traveling, and then took my time deciding what I wanted to do."

"Nice. Where did you matriculate?" Scott asked, trying to show off his vocabulary.

"A couple of places. I attended both Harvard and Yale for a while, but I got my degree from Princeton."

A murmur went through the group, and Scott pressed on. "What did you study?"

"I didn't decide for a while, so I majored in English literature for a while, then Philosophy for a while, but my diploma says Business Law."

"You have a degree in Business Law from Princeton, but you're not working?"

"Not yet," Thomas said.

"Why is that? I would guess that most people who graduate with a degree in Business Law from Princeton would be working in a big high-rise for some kind of prestigious law firm."

"I have had some offers," Thomas said "But I wanted to take my time and make sure that I got the right fit."

"What about your student loans?" Haidee asked.

"My schooling was paid for," he said and then added, "my father is the majority stockholder in the large pharmaceutical company that my great grandfather founded."

Chapter 22 – The Second Gospel According to Will

Jenna was sitting on a bench, sipping on a latte and looking down at the sidewalk. Her shapely legs were crossed and her short gray skirt rode well up on her thigh, making a wonderful vision all the way to her stiletto heels, a view noticed and appreciated by men of all ages as they passed by.

It had been a few weeks ago when the topic of covering the Pawlinsky trial came up in the scheduling meeting, and Jenna not only jumped on the chance, but even fought for it. However, now that we were in the middle of it she was not only having second thoughts, she was downright unhappy that she got the assignment. The issue was that it seems as though Chris's fifteen minutes of fame had come and gone, and Jenna never realized that the train had left the station.

Of course, since she felt that she was partly responsible for that fleeting fifteen minutes, and had parlayed her role in it to more money and more prestige, her perception of the situation was skewed in ways that others didn't have. Instead of the big-trial media circus she expected, it had turned out to be more of a fizzle than a sizzle. We were the only news team on the scene, except for a few junior reporters, who were more interested in playing video games and texting on their smart phones than in the trial or the outcome.

In the months between Chris's arrest and the beginning of the trial, his name had gone from headline to punch line to what could be best described as bread line, with almost the entire world paying little or no attention, at all. Of course the arrest was met with protests about what seemed to most as an abuse of power, and then there were counter attacks from the other side of the aisle, and the vitriol flew back and forth in some kind of media frenzy.

But, as quickly as it started, it ended. People seemed to lose interest and go on with their lives and the media found new and sexier things to discuss. Eventually even the usual groups of young people, naïve in the ways of the world and outraged at social injustices both real and merely perceived lost interest and the momentum started by their youthful exuberance waned as they, too, found other subjects more interesting.

Even though interest died in the whole situation, Jenna thought that the start of the trial would generate new interest and the accompanying hype, but she couldn't have been more wrong. Now, here, in front of the courthouse, there were more pigeons than people, and for all intents and purposes, the birds were paying more attention to what was going on inside.

Our team had been here every day. Jenna was so certain of the success of this coverage, that she had insisted we have the full remote crew – cameras, sound, stringers and the accompanying technicians and assistants – so every day for the past two weeks we have been here, and the most exciting thing we have seen was the mean game of spades being played in the back of the van. There wasn't a lot of room back there, so we formed two person teams and took turns with the winners staying and playing the next team in the rotation. One of the stringers, Billy, and I were a team and we had become pretty adept, winning more games than we lost.

At the beginning of the trial we shot some footage, but somehow it all wound up on the cutting floor. On the same day the trial began, there had been a subway glitch where thousands of commuters had been stranded underground for hours, and that coverage took up so much time that all the other stories were either rescheduled or just cut. Since the timeliness of our story was the key ingredient, it wound up in that second category.

I actually had felt sorry for Jenna that day. She had come to the studios early and was all excited, practicing her opening line over and over until it became second nature and I had tired of hearing, "Today the long-awaited Chris Pawlinsky murder trial started under heavy media coverage and a cloud of speculation with jury selection." The problem was that when we arrived, there were no other media, and jury selection was pretty much routine and boring.

Associates on both sides of the case easily selected a group of six men and seven women with three alternates. There were few challenges, and selection was done in a little less than two hours with most folks wanting to finish up and find out more about the people being stranded in pitch black subway tunnels.

On the next day the trial began with opening statements from both sides. The District Attorney realized his case was weak and was based more on speculation and conjecture than actual physical evidence and facts, so he started off by trying to downplay the importance of those essential case elements. The defense countered by pointing out the lack of the same and actually requested a dismissal during the opening statements, based on those points.

The judge, a political animal, denied the request, as was expected. After the opening statements, the trial was recessed until the next day.

This kind of scene was played over and over, day after day, dragging on to the point where even Jenna was getting disinterested and discouraged. It seemed as though there were more recesses and procedural discussion than actual evidence and testimony introduced and disputed.

Because of the lack of crowds and extraneous activity outside the courthouse, there was literally nothing to shoot, and nothing to report. I was not allowed to take my camera inside the courtroom so I left it in the van with the folks playing spades and spent a lot of time sitting beside Jenna on a hard, wooden bench, hoping that something, anything, would happen. The most scandalous and salacious happening was the occasional waking of jury members, because they could no longer pay attention to the drudgery and keep their eyes open.

By the time the cases were presented and the jury sent to find their verdict, two weeks had passed in a case where the evidence could have been fully covered in twenty minutes. After the judge gave his instructions and dismissed the jury, we all cleared out of the courtroom, checked our equipment and waited – patiently, for the most part, for the verdict to be announced. Since Billy, my spades partner, was sent in to wait for the jury to return and bring us the verdict, I was left with nothing else to do but lean against the van sipping a sports drink and admire Jenna's shapely legs.

After a bit, she looked up and caught me looking at her. Instead of being offended or upset, she just smiled and gave me a little wave. I waved back to her and then she motioned for me to come over and sit beside her. I complied, not knowing what I had in store.

"I guess I really messed up on this one," she said, as I sat on the bench beside her. "I really expected a lot more coverage and a lot more interest. You have been doing this a long time, have you ever seen anything like it?"

I was going to protest that I really wasn't that much older than she, but instead decided that it would give me a chance to play the old, experienced sage – a role I didn't mind at all and one I had seen attract young women like Jenna. The truth was that I was only about three years older and had landed the job at the station only a few months before she was hired, but I decided it would probably behoove me to not correct her and just play along with her assumptions at this juncture.

"Don't beat yourself up about it," I said. "Even Nostradamus didn't get them all right. Besides, remember the first time you were given the assignment to cover this guy? You were so against it you were close to quitting. And look how that turned out."

She just sat there in silent reflection, so I held out my arms to accentuate the lack of crowds and continued in an attempt to be jovial. "Look at it this way, kiddo. You have an exclusive!" I then put this silly grin on my face that I had practiced and perfected to the point where it was almost guaranteed to break up even the most hardened people in extremely somber circumstances.

Jenna first looked at me with an expression of unbelief, then the corners of her mouth began to turn up and before long she was smiling, hugely, and then began to laugh. The more she laughed, the louder and more out of control she got, until eventually some of the crew stopped playing cards and looked out of the van to see what was going on.

When she finally regained her composure she leaned forward and placing her hand on my forearm said, "Thank you. I really needed that."

"No problem, I was happy to do it. You looked like you could use a good laugh."

Without moving her hand she leaned in even more towards me and asked, "May I ask you a personal question?"

Knowing that this was my cue to be smart and funny I said, "Would you mind me answering in a personal way?"

She continued to smile but leaned back and still without moving her hand asked, "Did you know you're the only guy in the station who hasn't asked me out? Even the married guys have tried to hit on me."

I really wasn't expecting this line of conversation and wasn't prepared at all to respond, so I just said, "Okay…and?"

"I was wondering why? Don't you like me?"

The truth was that I was a little intimidated by her. You see, I had seen some of those guys trying to complete a pass (for lack of a better term) and had seen each and every one go down in flames, some quite publically, and had no intention of letting such a thing happen to me. However, I was not about to admit this to her so I knew I had to come up with something, quick.

"I guess I never thought that office romances were very smart," I lied. The truth was that the reason I had left my previous job was because of a relationship with a coworker that ended badly. On second thought, I guess that wasn't much of a lie after all. "Besides," I continued, "I am kind of allergic to rejection."

She smiled, warmly, slid her hand down my arm and took mine in hers, then put her other hand over the top and said, "I really don't think that would be a problem."

My heart started to race and a lump grew in my throat and I was probably about to say something profoundly stupid when I caught Billy out of the corner of my eye running out of the courthouse. As he approached he was out of breath but managed to say, "Verdict's in. He's not guilty! They should be out in a minute!"

Almost relieved that I was rescued from a situation in which I was rapidly losing control, I stood, dropped Jenna's hand then began clapping and shouted to no one in particular. "It's show time, folks. Let's get this story!"

I looked around and was taken aback by the complete lack of response – mostly because there was no one around to respond. Here was this man, very popular by all accounts, being exonerated by a criminal justice system which was more criminal than justice and which had finally got one right and there were no witnesses except our little band.

There was no one there to cheer, no one to celebrate. Even the other reporters seemed to have been swallowed by the concrete of the sidewalk. I shook my head in disbelief and then took off at a sprint for the van and the rest of the crew.

As I arrived at the van the rest of the crew was climbing out and making way for me to grab my camera. It wasn't until I pulled it out of the bag that I began to notice that the sky had grown darker, the clouds more ominous and it was beginning to sprinkle. However, other than quickly installing the rain hood, there was nothing more to do than wait for the players in the comedy of errors to start exiting the building.

Just like the other days, there were no crowds departing, just like there were no news crews or reporters present. The District Attorney and his entourage were the first to depart the building, but as soon as they saw us they made an immediate right turn and headed back into the building through a side door. A few minutes later Chris, his defense attorney and two of his friends—the sandy haired guy and the tall, attractive woman—walked out and headed down the massive staircase which lead to the street and away from the building.

Upon seeing him, Jenna headed his direction at a trot with the rest of us in tow. I started the recording as I ran, figuring that it would be best to get as much footage as possible and that we could clean things up back at the studio. When she reached him she said into the microphone, "Congratulations on the verdict. Do you have any comment for our audience?"

The lawyer started to protest, but Chris stopped him and took two steps towards Jenna, nearly bumping his nose on the end of the microphone held in her outstretched arm.

"Hello, Miss Burns," he said. "It is so very nice to see you again."

"So, Chris. Do you have any comments for our audience?" she repeated.

He moved his hand as if to physically brush off the question and then answered. "Oh, that is all over, now and there really isn't much to talk about. I was saddened though, when I heard about your mother taking ill. Is she doing okay?"

The shocked look on Jenna's face spoke volumes, and pretty much matched what we were thinking and feeling. Jenna was never one for much small talk or idle chatter, and she had never really shared much about herself or her problems with her co-workers, but it still seemed like she would have said something to someone if her mother was ill.

She swallowed hard, gathered her composure as best she could and said, "Much better, thanks, but really…."

"Cancer surgery is a pretty serious thing and I am certain that it gave everyone quite a scare." Chris said. "As a matter of fact, I am surprised to see you here, today. I thought you would have flown home to Milwaukee to be with her."

Obviously rattled, Jenna couldn't hold it together any longer, and tears started rolling down her cheeks. For the moment, she seemingly had forgotten where she was and what she was doing. "Well, my siblings are there with her as well as my father. There really wasn't much I could have done, and I wanted to cover this story."

The look on Chris's face was nothing I had ever seen. The depths of his compassion were so evident in his deep brown eyes that I swear I felt as if he was touching my soul.

We were already standing near the curb, now, as Chris reached up and touched the side of Jenna's face with his fingers while he wiped her tear with his thumb like a loving parent comforting a child. "Nonsense," he said. "There is plenty you could do. For one thing, you could be there and hold her hand to comfort her when she faces fear and the unknown. She knows you love her, but she can't feel your touch when you are this far away. You should really book a flight and go see her, now."

Jenna dropped her hands to her side and began to sob, just as the SUV with the black driver I had already associated as being with Chris's team pulled up. As the other two climbed in the back, Chris said to her, "Stories come and go and every day brings a new one; but you only have one mother, and she not only needs you, but you also need to be with her and the others you love as much as possible while you can be, because, as we all know, life is short."

As he said that last part he looked toward me, which allowed the camera to catch the full view of his face, and I was able to capture the look on his face and the incredible depths of his soul in his eyes. It is a picture which has been used a great deal when people talk about the man and the events of that day.

Then Chris turned and climbed in to the SUV, and it pulled away, leaving the lawyer and our crew standing in the ever intensifying rain. We stood in silence, each waiting for someone else to speak first, so eventually I took the initiative.

"Let's get the equipment out of the rain!", I said to the crew, and everyone seemed more than happy to respond. Jenna climbed in the car, and Billy and I started putting pieces of equipment away in the van as the crew dropped them off and sprinted to the car themselves. Satisfied that everything was put away and secured, Billy and I closed the doors and got into the front, now dripping wet from the rain. The lawyer had gone somewhere, but no one had seemed to take any notice.

I started the van and pulled away from the curb.

Billy shook some of the water off his face, and then turned to me and said, "Interesting story, but nothing we can put on the broadcast, tonight."

"Interesting, indeed," I said, as I reflected on the events of the last hour. I smiled as I maneuvered the van down the rain drenched street.

Chapter 23 – The Fourth Gospel According to Moe

When the verdict was announced the courtroom was silent. Other than the main players, the prosecution, the defense, the jury and the judge, there were only about half a dozen other people in the gallery and three of them were me, Scott and Ronni.

Now, I have been in lots of courtrooms in my time and had witnessed plenty of trials, seen lots of verdicts, too – but never have I seen one with absolutely no reaction to it. Usually there is cheering or crying or even screaming and making threats, but never have I seen no reaction except in this one.

The prosecution stood up, closed their files, put them in their cases and proceeded out of the room. Chris and Harry were already standing, so they just turned, smiled to each other and shook hands. After they walked out the swinging gate separating the front of the courtroom from the galley where the people sit, we stood up and walked out together. I am not sure where the other two or three people went any more than I recognized who they were.

I guess I was expecting someone—anyone—from the press to be in the hallway, but there was no one. No one asked any stupid questions, made sly accusations or did anything you usually saw outside big cases, but maybe this wasn't so big after all. I guess I was just expecting more. As we got to the elevators, I told the others I would bring the car around, so I went down the back stairs to the parking garage and found the Escalade.

I don't know whether it was a premonition or just habit, but I reached under the seat to the compartment I had installed there and pulled out my nickel plated, .44 revolver. I stuck it in the waistband in the back of my pants, then started the engine and pulled out of the parking slot.

When I turned the corner to the exit, the big metal door was down. For a second, I thought I was going to have trouble getting out, but then remembered that this was a secure structure, and as I approached, the door went up with the accompanying flashing strobes and horns warning pedestrians. Leaving the garage I turned on the wipers and lights because of the rain and pulled out into traffic.

When I turned the corner I saw the news crew, thinking it was about time, but when I pulled close to the curb and stopped, I noticed that the reporter was holding her arms to her sides and it looked like Chris was wiping a tear from her face or something. I couldn't believe it. He was the guy who just spent months in jail for something he didn't do, and he was comforting HER?

He climbed in the car and I eased into traffic, the windshield wipers slapping in time to clear the rain, heading toward the apartment complex. Chris looked at the clock on the dash, and then commented that the afternoon teaching should be going on, and asked me to take him to the amphitheater. The rain was coming down hard, and by the time we arrived, it had created a sheer gray curtain over the earth and the sky, causing everything to look dreary and depressing.

As we approached the shell it was apparent that while the team members had continued to keep up their end of the bargain and keep the surrounding area clean, trimmed and tidy. The city though, obviously thought they had better things to do than uphold their part of the agreement. As a matter of fact, they had never repaired the damage done by those bricks that were thrown and now the damaged areas had grown into two huge dark spots on the back wall. In that eerie gloom of the pounding rain, it created the illusion of the shell being some kind of ominous half-buried skull.

Completely undaunted, Chris almost jumped out of the SUV before I got it stopped and led the way over the small rise and down to the earthen and concrete seats where, while usually seating hundreds or thousands, were holding barely a couple dozen people brave enough to endure the elements to hear today's teaching. There probably would have been many more if they knew that Chris was returning today, but with all things considered, how could they have known?

Travis was doing the teaching, and was doing his best to convey a message of both love and service to the faithful few who were there, which included the entire team, now that we were there. When Travis saw Chris, he let out a shout, ran to the edge of the stage and jumped off to embrace him. Unable to contain themselves, the rest of the team also gathered around him to greet him, including Thomas, who had not ever personally met him, up to that point.

After words of congratulations and fondness on both sides were exchanged, Travis motioned for Chris to take his place as teacher. The team members all sat in the front row, together, but the other visitors, sparsely numbered, were scattered in different areas around the theater, forcing Chris to stand close to the front in order to project his voice sufficiently so all could hear. He started off with a short, silent prayer, but then raised his head and began to speak in a clear voice.

"There has been some speculation as to who I am, who I was and who I may become. It is time that I reveal all that to you.

"I have been asked, on several occasions, if I am the

second coming of Christ, the reincarnation of the one known as Jesus of Nazareth. The alpha and the omega, the one who was with God at the beginning, and who is also one with God, and the one who will be mankind's advocate at the end. To this question, I say Yahweh, which is ancient Hebrew for 'I AM', the name God gave to Moses on Mount Horeb."

This caused quite a stir from those in attendance. The reaction from the team members was much more audible from the others, but it was pretty much a universal reaction.

"My purpose on earth, this time, is different, however," Chris continued. "The mission of Jesus of Nazareth was twofold – the first was to provide a sin offering for all of humanity for all time, and only The Holy One of God was sufficient to pay that price. His second mission was to instruct, to teach and His lesson was that of love.

"As I have told you before, and as it is written, the Sacrifice of Jesus was perfect and complete, and was for all sins of all humanity for all time – those inherited from the first men, and those performed every day by the humans, both by actions committed and by actions left undone. On this foundation is built the entity which comprises all believers - believers who are now free to make mistakes and fall short, because their perfection has already been attributed to them by the gift given by God through the death and resurrection of His Son.

"While Jesus' first mission is complete and perfect, his second – no less important than the first – is neither complete nor perfect. The fault is not in the teaching or the lessons to be learned, but in the hearts and minds of the students - the lack of understanding and acceptance by the them, those disciples if you will, who's sinful nature has hampered their comprehension and stymied attempts to put those lessons into practice.

"This is why I have returned at this time, not to destroy the world as you know it, but to help guide you to building a new world, a new church, a new humanity – a New Jerusalem, the one John wrote about in the Book of Revelation."

At this point one of the other people there, a tall and outdoorsy type of guy (okay, he looked like a redneck), with a red, plaid, flannel shirt, blue denim jeans and work boots stood up and said back to Chris, in a voice with a southern twang and loud enough for everyone to hear, "You are wrong! The Bible teaches us that before the Son of God returns we will have the rapture and destruction of the world. There will be war and pestilence and the anti-Christ and the False Prophet, so you can't be the second coming!"

Travis shot the man a dirty look and said, "Why don't you just shut up?"

Chris admonished him. "Travis, let the man speak. He is correct in his limited understanding, and just wants to learn more." Then he turned to the man and, with his hands folded in front of him, said, "When John was on the Island of Patmos, he had a vision of the type which he was not able to completely comprehend, none the less describe.

"In addition, he was writing to the members of the early Church who were being persecuted on all sides. He wrote what he saw, cryptically, in a code, so that they might have understanding without giving away knowledge to the enemies of the fledgling Church which they could use to damage it.

"So, what you have read which was recorded in the Revelation of John is a man trying to describe something he didn't fully understand to people in a way others, who were not in his inner circle, would not understand either. This has led to much speculation about what today's Christians speak of as end times, and many hours wasted in studies of false teachings taken from obscure passages men have used to promote themselves, mostly for their own benefit.

"In every generation since Jesus' ascension there have been claims that one person or another has been the anti-Christ, from the Pope to the current President of the United States. By the same token, there have been hundreds if not thousands of errant predictions of my coming and none have rung true because, just as the Jews of Jesus day were expecting a great king and got a carpenter, the people of today are expecting something even more spectacular than the Jews were expecting, and as such couldn't they be even more wrong?

"As every theologian will tell you, one of the attributes of God is that He never changes. If that is true then why would you expect Him to do something completely different the second time, the third or any other subsequent time, than He did the first time? Just as Jesus' birth was a simple and unnoticed event, wouldn't it come to reason that His second coming would be the same? For that matter, would it make any difference if it was His second, third or even fifth coming?"

No one said a thing, we were all just taking it in. Then Chris continued.

"You see, as I said before, Jesus' death and resurrection and God's grace were just the beginning – the foundation for what is to come, and what humanity, made free to pursue great things, through that grace, can accomplish. It is the foundation for the New Jerusalem – the city whose walls will be made strong by the righteousness of God, reflected through humans, as beautiful as if made of pure jasper, and whose streets will be paved in the gold of their good works, refined and purified by the Holy Spirit.

"This is where the understanding of Jesus' teachings began to fall short. For centuries many people have viewed God as some great, bearded score keeper tracking

where you have done things right and where you have
done things wrong, never considering that the Scriptures
teach us that only one sin will wipe out every good deed a
person thinks he has done, and condemn him to eternity in
hell – an existence without hope, completely separated
from God and everything good.

"You see, your good works, instead of being
performed in some kind of quid pro quo arrangement,
should be the fruits of God's Grace working inside you.
These good works, sourced and purified by God, will be
the building blocks on which the New Jerusalem will be
built, and you – the recipients of that Grace will be the
builders of this Heaven on earth, but before you can do so,
you must first evolve, with God's help.

"You must evolve into trusting children, knowing
that God is all powerful, can handle anything and
everything, and will take care of you, just as He has saved
you from yourselves. You must evolve away from the
desire for wealth, material things and temporal power
which you can exert over others. You must evolve into
beings who value those things that God loves and values
most – yourselves.

"You must evolve into the keepers of the garden
which was your first assigned job, and quit exploiting the
earth and it's recourses for your own gain. Instead care for
it for the benefit of all people, especially those who have
not yet arrived. Quit the stupid thinking that you can
abuse the earth because you will get a new one, and
instead think that where you stand now is where you build
the New Jerusalem, the city with no temple because it
shines with the glory of God's presence."

The man's face grew red and he spoke again. "But
John wrote that both heaven and earth will be destroyed
and that a New Jerusalem would descend from God's
heaven! You are speaking against the Scriptures!"

Chris said, "John wrote that the first heaven and first

earth would pass away, not necessarily that it would be destroyed. Don't you have to clear land before you can build on it? This is the way of things. The care of the earth is in your hands. The building of the New Jerusalem is in your hands. The ways that you must learn; eschewing money and material things, and valuing the earth and each other more than gold is in the realm of your abilities, with God's help.

"Now I have made this teaching clear to you. Take it and build on it. Be good to one another. Care for your fellow man as if he were yourself, regardless of where he lives, what language he speaks, or the color of his skin. Concentrate on loving each other, not condemning. Concentrate on lifting each other up, not tearing each other down. Promote growth and not destruction. Promote love and not hate.

"This is how you will build the New Jerusalem, this is how you will create the Kingdom of Heaven on earth!" Chris shouted, with his hands held straight out to his sides.

By this time the man in the flannel shirt had grown so angry that the veins in his neck and on his forehead were popping up and his face had turned from red to purple. Raising his hand and pointing his finger, he shouted at the top of his lungs, "This man is a false teacher and a liar!"

The word liar was punctuated by the sound of a gunshot and time seemed to stand still as our attention went from the man in the flannel shirt to our Teacher, whose now limp body was being propelled to the back of the stage as a red plume appeared on the front of his white shirt and started to rapidly grow on the rain soaked cloth.

I pulled my gun from where I had put it in my waistband and Travis and I sprinted toward the man who had confronted Chris. I remember thinking that he had shot Chris, but was completely unafraid that he would do the same to me. Travis got to him before I did and took him down with a tackle to the midsection that would have made any professional football player proud.

As the man hit the seats behind him, I lowered my revolver, aimed it between his eyes and began to squeeze the trigger when I realized that something was wrong. The look of anger on the man's face had changed to that of horror and shock – and a quick scan of his hands and the ground around him showed me that he was not armed.

"Where the fuck is your gun?" I shouted. "Pull it on me, you fucking coward!"

The man stammered, "I don't have a gun. I don't even own one. I don't know what happened."

At that point Travis looked up and noticed that one of the other people there was holding a smart phone and had obviously videotaped the whole incident. "Call 9-1-1," he ordered. "Tell them to get the police and an ambulance here as fast as they can!"

Thinking quickly I added, "…and don't tell them who it is for!" I turned to Travis and said, "If they know, they might not respond for a week."

I then turned back to the man in the flannel shirt and told him not to move until the police got there or I would kill him. Then I jumped up and ran to where the rest of the team was crowded around Chris.

When I got there everyone was crying. Ronni was kneeling on the stage, covered in blood and was holding his head and stroking his hair while rocking back and forth and sobbing something I couldn't make out. It was obvious by the amount of blood in the area and the complete lack of response that Chris was already dead.

Scott was standing there in the rain, hands clenched in fists of rage, and he turned toward the man in the flannel shirt, walking as if he was going to break his neck with his bare hands. The man, afraid to move because of what I had told him, now had a look of stark fear on his face and was probably thinking that his life was about to end.

When Scott arrived, however, he knelt down beside the man and with tears rolling down his face, placed his open palm behind his head to cradle it and then quietly asked, "Are you okay?"

It was then that I saw clearly. Scott had not gone to take revenge, but rather to comfort this man, regardless of how he had treated Chris in his last moments, regardless of his own obvious feelings of personal loss. This was how Chris would have acted in this situation, and we all instinctively knew what to do as well.

Team members broke away from the group and went to the small clumps of people still standing in shock in the amphitheater. Each group was then ministered to and comforted by one team member or another, except for Ronni who just stayed with Chris's lifeless body until the ambulance arrived and took him away.

We all answered the police's questions as best possible, and they took the man in the flannel shirt away to both help their investigation and for his own protection. They were actually pretty cool about the whole thing, not even hassling me about having my piece.

When the questions were all asked and answered, and there was nothing left to do, we all headed back to the apartments. Ronni, I think, took it the hardest and I really felt for her and her sadness. I didn't even say anything about her getting blood on the seat of the Escalade on the ride back. When we arrived, I saw a strange woman and three others, two boys and a girl, in their late teens or early twenties.

When Ronni saw them she jumped out of the car and embraced the woman fully, the two of them sobbing on each other's shoulders. It was then that I remembered that Chris had a mother and siblings whom I had never seen, up to now at least. We all went in the apartment and introduced ourselves and each other while Ronni changed.

I guess the owner of a local chicken place heard

what happened on the news, because by the time that Ronni emerged from her room delivery guys had brought multiple buckets of chicken with all the accompanying sides and deserts and large bottles of soda. There was enough food that the table could hardly hold it all. Miriam and her children joined us and it was a time of sadness, remembrance and even joy as we all told stories about Chris and things he had done.

The following day things started to get back to normal. Scott and Ronni started making Chris's final arrangements, and Travis prepared the afternoon teaching while the rest of us took up our own duties around the place. I guess Chris's time in jail helped us with the transition process, because even though we were sad at the loss each of us felt, we had already acclimated to life without Him in our midst.

The autopsy report listed the cause of death as myocardial rupture, caused by two bullets fired nearly simultaneously from two different high-powered rifles in two different locations at an almost perfect ninety degree angle from each other. The two slugs passed through the center of His chest somehow missing all bone and both lodging in the wall of the amphitheater's shell behind him. There are rumors that neither slug had any trace of heart muscle on them, leading to speculation that His heart actually exploded before the bullets struck Him, but I don't see how that really matters.

What does matter is that the murder weapons were never discovered, and no one has ever been charged with the crime, but I still find that being shot is much easier to believe than that His heart just up and exploded.

By the afternoon of the day following, the woman who had recorded Chris's final message on her cell phone posted it on You Tube and within minutes the recording had gone viral. In just over a month it had over two billion views, easily becoming the most watched video, ever. I was especially thankful that the woman edited out everything after the gunshots rang out so the world couldn't exercise it's morbid curiosity on it, and also that my foul mouth wouldn't have such great exposure.

Two days after the autopsy was completed, Chris's body was turned back over to Miriam for cremation and then His ashes were taken to the tallest building in the city and released into the wind, all according to Chris's instructions. I guess He didn't want anyone building a shine or people making pilgrimages – and especially didn't want other people making money on those impulses of others.

After we scattered his ashes, we went back to the amphitheater for a memorial service. When we first arrived it looked very much like the afternoon he was killed, with about the same number of visitors as team members. However, after we started the service, people started filing in. A trickle of a few people, here and there to begin with, then more until there was a steady stream of mourners, but the numbers increased and soon there was nothing short of a flood of humanity there to pay their last respects to our Teacher.

News reports and park officials reported that over 1.5 million people tried to visit the park that afternoon – so many that most could not even get close enough to hear what was being said on the stage, but it really didn't seem to matter much to them. They broke into small groups and began having their own memorials all across the park, down the streets and wherever they saw each other. At one point it seemed as though the whole city was nothing but one huge memorial service with candles, and singing, and crying.

Despite the huge crowds, there were no reports of crime that afternoon and evening. No robberies, no rapes, no murders, not even a case of shoplifting. It seemed as though everyone was too busy comforting and serving others to think about themselves long enough to commit a crime.

As the sun set silently over the city, a quietness and peacefulness settled with it, and when it arose the next morning, it was a new day with a new mission, a new attitude and a new commitment.

Chapter 24 – The Acts of Jeffrey

I never knew Chris when He was alive but I feel like He is my best friend even though I was born thousands of miles away from where He lived, in a different city, a different country and on a different continent. Oh, I had heard stories of Him and some of His exploits, but I had other priorities in my life, and really none of them concerned what He was doing or what He taught. I didn't even care enough to pay attention to much of it, and really didn't give the news of His death even a second thought.

I was much too busy chasing MY life, the good life. I used to tell people that my two biggest priorities were beautiful women and fast cars, or maybe fast women and beautiful cars, either way. I wanted it all. I made a lot of money, had lots of girlfriends, a fancy house complete with gardener and maid, and a car that caused jealousy in just about every man who saw me drive it.

By the time I turned thirty, I had millions in the bank, multiple houses and fancy cars, but the more I had, the more I wanted. I started throwing lavish parties because I wanted more friends, I started gambling to excess for more excitement, drinking to excess and doing the drug scene for more euphoria and I got involved in the international swinging scene for more physical pleasure. I relished the hedonistic lifestyle and there was never enough sex, drugs, alcohol or gambling for me.

The problem with that kind of lifestyle was eventually I quit using it, and it started using me. By the time I turned thirty-five I was broke, and with the money went my friends, the women, the houses, the cars –

everything except the cravings for more and more of everything. I had gone to a Caribbean island with the last of my money in hopes of an escape but instead found myself with a drug habit I couldn't beat and spent most nights sleeping in the bushes beside a tennis court, hoping I wouldn't get beaten or raped, or both, again.

It was one of those nights that I heard the voices singing. I tried to ignore them and sleep, but it was impossible because the sound kept invading my brain. The rule of life on the streets was that you had to fight for the respect you get, and when I grew angry enough I grabbed an empty bottle and headed toward the sound to either scare them or beat them into silence.

When I approached, they paid me no mind regardless of my shouting, my threats and my profane language, but instead kept right on talking and singing as if I didn't even exist. I was too sick to take any kind of physical action against them and eventually I grew tired of ranting with no result so I started to listen. One of the women, a young and pretty thing, very wholesome looking, noticed me standing there outside the group so she got up, came over and took my hand, and led me back to the circle to sit with the rest.

The leader of the group (later I would learn the term, 'Teacher') was a slender man named Jan. He played the guitar and sang a bit, then he would talk about what the team members (that is what the others called themselves) were going to do the next day and how they were going to serve the inner community (what they called the group) and the community-at-large (what they called everyone else). Jan was using terms with which I was not familiar, like building blocks, and contagious service.

When the meeting was over, they then turned their attention to me. They first asked my name (of course), and I guess I looked pretty terrible because they then asked me questions like if I had eaten that day (I hadn't) or if I had a place to sleep. The young woman who had escorted me into the group was named Ingrid, and when she found out that I was hungry she disappeared for a few moments and then returned with some soup, crackers, fruit and some kind of fish for me to eat.

The truth was that I had not only not eaten that day, but it had been several days prior that I had found a half-eaten sandwich left on a bench, and consumed that. I inhaled the food voraciously, and when my stomach had quit rumbling other hungers started to arise. I remember thinking about what Ingrid would look like naked, how I would like to ravish her lithe, young body and how and where I could score some drugs.

Almost as if she could read my mind, she started looking at me and then alternately looking away and giggling. Then she walked over and stood in front of me, he long tan legs accentuated by the white shorts she was wearing. She leaned down and took my face in her hands and I thought I was having one of those erotic dreams come true when she stopped short, whispered something and then gently kissed me on my forehead.

All at once I felt the old cravings leave my body and instead of these desires, I felt nothing but peace. For the first time in as long as I could remember I didn't want to get drunk or high, I didn't want to have random sex, and my mind became sharp. I saw clearly, for the first time ever, that the focus of my life, the pursuit of money and material things was nothing more than a trap. I felt true love and true joy for the first time, and was enraptured by an overwhelming sense of peace.

Not only did I realize that my previous pursuits were empty and fruitless and that I had been on a path of self destruction, but worse, that I had been squandering my skills by not actively helping those who needed it the most. My eyes were opened to the fact that we are all connected to each other and to something else – God. With every interaction we leave something behind, and it is up to us if that is beneficial to ourselves and others, or detrimental.

The rest of the evening was a blur, but that night I had a place to sleep which was comfortable and safe. The next morning I had a place to wash, a healthy breakfast, clean clothes to wear and, for the first time in a long time, something to do that was not associated with hurting myself or others.

That first day I was assigned to a crew assigned to clean up a house in a rundown neighborhood. When we arrived it became obvious that no one outside the crew had a clue that we were supposed to be there, none the less what we going to do, including the elderly woman who lived there.

We just showed up with tools and paint and began trimming bushes, sweeping walks and painting her porch. At first the woman tried to shoo us away but Crispin, an islander who was running the crew that day, explained that we meant her no harm and were not going to charge her any money or want anything in return. She was skeptical, but when she saw that we were doing what we said we would, she went back in the house but still kept a watchful eye on us.

At noon she came out of the house with a meager lunch for us of sandwiches made with stale bread and questionable lunchmeat, but we accepted her gifts gracefully and Crispin insisted that the old woman eat with us. He explained later that the reason for that was to ensure that she ate, too, rather than giving all of her food to us, which she might be prone to do.

About mid-afternoon a group of local toughs came over and started to harass us. I recognized them as a small, informal gang of thugs who liked their drugs and booze and who would beat up people who were hurting and virtually defenseless, like I had been just the day before. Crispin instructed us to ignore them and just keep working, but that just seemed to make them even more adamant on disrupting what we were trying to accomplish.

The more aggressive they became, the more difficult it was for us, but when the old woman saw one of the thugs start to physically assault one our crew she came out, called him by name and told him that if he didn't quit, immediately, she was going to report his actions to his mother. Later on that evening we all had a good laugh about the fact that he acted all tough and mean but still had a child's fear of his mother.

The longer I stayed with the group the more I learned about the disorganized organization of this sect called The Mission. Some people refer to us as a cult, but cults have a tendency to burn relational bridges, while The Mission is all about building them within the organization and without. Based in Christianity, we concentrate on the betterment of ourselves and our surroundings, whether people, things or both.

Some also refer to us as communists or hippies and refer to our groups as communes, but they are actually more in the order of communities. We have families (including children) and some have jobs outside the communities while others work for the common good within them. We understand that the world uses money for commerce, and we partake just like everyone else, but we also barter and even just give, when that is what God leads us to do for the betterment of the common good. I guess you could say that we use money, but we don't allow money to use us.

Each small group, or 'team' has three people in leadership roles – a teacher, the spiritual leader of the group; a steward, the one who handles all of the physical needs of the group; and a shepherd who assigns duties and directs service activities. These positions are, in most cases, quite fluid with different people assuming different roles at different times, sometimes in a rotating basis. The only position where this doesn't normally happen is the teacher, who prepares the lessons and teaches not only the team members, but formal lessons for visitors from outside the group.

Teams usually consist of ten to twenty team members, and healthy teams grow through recruitment. When a team reaches over twenty, they then usually break into two groups and choose new leaders or keep the old ones – there is no set process.

After several months our little team grew to the point where we split and I wound up in the same group as Ingrid where she was chosen to be our steward. After several more splits (Ingrid and I had stayed together, both as team mates and eventually in ways more intimate) I was chosen to become a teacher, and eventually Ingrid and I moved back to my homeland with another team member named Peter, to start more groups there.

To date, there are more than 200 million people around the globe associated with The Mission and dedicated to building better people, better groups, better opportunities and bringing about the Kingdom of God and a heaven on earth – a New Jerusalem, if you will. We have no formal accounting system and we don't keep many records, because we don't put our trust in our accomplishments but rather in how we serve God.

Ingrid and I have been together as a couple for almost eight years, now. We have three children and a better, more fulfilling life than I ever could have imagined when I was chasing more temporal things. In that previous life I chased all of the things the world offers, but today when I see someone with all the trappings of money and material power I just shake my head, remember, and say a little prayer of gratefulness for where I am today and for what God has given me.

Teacher

James Cory Michaels